THEFT

THEFT

THEFT

A LOVE STORY

Peter Carey

faber and faber

First published in 2006
by Faber and Faber Limited
3 Queen Square London WCIN 3AU

First published in Australia by Random House in 2006
First published in the United States by Alfred A. Knopf, a division
of Random House Inc. in 2006

Printed in England by Mackays of Chatham plc

A CIP record for this book
is available from the British Library

ISBN 978-0-571-23147-8

ISBN 0-571-23147-0

2 4 6 8 10 9 7 5 3 1

For Bel

Am I to be a king, or just a pig?

—Flaubert, *Intimate Notebook*

Joachim had been born before the war, in the years when children still had to learn by heart the thirteen reasons for using a capital letter. To these he had added one more of his own, which was that he would, in all circumstances, do exactly what he wished.

—Macado Fernández, *One Man*

THEFT

I

I don't know if my story is grand enough to be a tragedy, although a lot of shitty stuff did happen. It is certainly a love story but that did not begin until midway through the shitty stuff, by which time I had not only lost my eight-year-old son, but also my house and studio in Sydney where I had once been about as famous as a painter could expect in his own backyard. It was the year I should have got the Order of Australia—why not!—look at who they give them to. Instead my child was stolen from me and I was eviscerated by divorce lawyers and gaoled for attempting to retrieve my own best work which had been declared *Marital Assets*.

Emerging from Long Bay Prison in the bleak spring of 1980, I learned I was to be rushed immediately to northern New South Wales where, although I would have almost no money to spend on myself, it was thought that I might, if I could only cut down on my drinking, afford to paint small works and care for Hugh, my damaged 220-pound brother.

My lawyers, dealers, collectors had all come together to save me. They were so kind, so generous. I could hardly admit that I was fucking sick of caring for Hugh, that I didn't want to leave Sydney or cut down on drinking. Lacking the character to tell the truth I permitted myself to set off on the road they had chosen for me. Two hundred miles north of Sydney, at Taree, I began to cough blood into a motel basin. Thank Christ, I thought, they can't make me do it now.

But it was only pneumonia and I did not die after all.

It was my biggest collector, Jean-Paul Milan, who had designed the plan wherein I would be the unpaid caretaker of a country property he had been trying to sell for eighteen months. Jean-Paul was the proprietor of a chain of nursing homes which were later investigated by the Health Commission, but he also liked to paint and his architect had made him a studio whose riverside wall opened like a lube-bay door. The natural light, as he had so sweetly warned me, even as he made his gift, was perhaps a little green, a 'fault' produced by the ancient casuarinas that lined the river. I might have told him that this issue of natural light was bullshit, but again I held my tongue. That first night out of gaol, at a miserably wine-free dinner with Jean-Paul and his wife, I agreed that we had tragically turned our backs on natural light, candlelight, starlight, and it was true that the Kabuki had been superior in candlelight and that the paintings of Manet were best seen by light of a dusty window, but fuck it—my work would live or die in galleries and I needed 240 reliable volts of alternating current to do my stuff. I was now destined to live in a 'paradise' where I could be sure of no such thing.

Jean-Paul, having so generously given us his house, began immediately to fret that I might somehow hurt it. Or perhaps the true alarmist was his wife who had, long ago, caught me blowing my snotty nose into her dinner napkin. In any case, it was only six mornings after we first arrived in Bellingen that Jean-Paul burst into the house and woke me. This was a nasty shock at almost every level, but I held my tongue and made him coffee. Then for two hours I followed him around the property as if I were his dog and every stupid thing he told me I wrote down in my notebook, an old leather-bound volume that was as precious to me as life itself. Here I had recorded every colour mix I had made from the time of my so-called breakthrough show in 1971. It was a treasure house, a diary, a record of decline and fall, a history. Thistles, said Jean-Paul. I wrote 'thistles' in my lovely book. Mowing. I spelled it out. Fallen trees across the river. Stihl chain saw. Grease nipples on the slasher. Then he was offended by the tractor parked beneath the house. The woodpile was untidy—I set Hugh to stack it neatly in the pattern Jean-Paul preferred. Finally my patron and I arrived at the studio together. He removed his shoes as if he meant to pray. I followed suit. He raised the big lube-bay door to the river and stood for a long moment looking down at the Never Never, talking—this is not made up—about Monet's fucking *Water Lilies*. He had very pretty feet, I had noticed them before, very white and high-arched. He was in his midforties but his toes were straight as a baby's.

Although he owned some twenty nursing homes, Jean-Paul was not personally a great one for touching, but here in the studio, he laid his hand on my forearm.

'You'll be happy here, Butcher.'

'Yes.'

He gazed around the long high room, then began to brush those rich, perfect feet across the soft surface of the floor. If his eyes had not been so moist he would have looked like an athlete preparing for some sci-fi track event.

'Coachwood,' he said, 'isn't it something?'

He meant the floor, and it was truly lovely, a washed pumice grey. It was also a rare rain-forest timber, but who was I, a convicted criminal, to argue ethics?

'How I envy you,' he said.

And so it went, by which I mean that I was as docile as a

big old Labrador quietly farting by the fire. I could have begged him for canvas, and he would have given it to me, but he would have wanted a painting. It was that picture, the one I was not going to give him, that I was thinking of right now. He didn't know it, but I still had about twelve yards of cotton duck, that was two good pictures before I was forced to use Masonite. I quietly sipped the non-alcoholic beer he had brought me as a gift.

'Good isn't it?'

'Like the real thing.'

Then, finally, the last instructions were issued, the promises all given. I stood beneath the studio and watched him bounce his rent-a-car across the cattle grid. He bottomed out as he hit the bitumen, and then he was gone.

Fifteen minutes later I was in the village of Bellingen, introducing myself to the blokes at the Dairyman's Co-op. I bought some plywood, a hammer, a carpenter's saw, two pounds of two-inch Sheetrock screws, twenty 150W incandescent floods, five gallons of Dulux jet black, the same of white, and all this, together with some odds and ends, I charged to Jean-Paul's account. Then I went home to set up the studio.

Later everyone would get in a bloody uproar because I had supposedly *vandalized* the coachwood with the Sheetrock screws, but I can't see how else I could have laid the ply on top of it. Certainly, it could not work the way it was. I was there to paint as everybody knew, and the floor of a painter's studio should be like a site of sacrifice, stabbed by staples, but also tended, swept, scrubbed, washed clean after every encounter. I laid cheap grey linoleum on top of the ply and coated it with linseed oil until it stank like a fresh *pietà*. But still I could not work. Not yet.

Jean-Paul's prizewinning architect had designed a studio with a high-arched roof and this he had tensioned with steel cables like the strings on a bow. It was a bloody wonder of a thing, and I suspended banks of incandescent floodlights from the cables which pretty much eliminated both the elegance of his design and the green light coming through the casuarinas. Even with these improvements it was hard to imagine a worse place to make art. It was as buggy as a jungle and the insects stuck to my Dulux paint, marking their death agonies with concentric circles. And of course that big wide door was an open invitation to the little fucks. I went back to the co-op and signed for three of those blue-light insect zappers but that was like a finger in the dyke. All around me was subtropical rainforest, countless trees and insects as yet unnamed, unless by me—you cunt, you little shit—who sabotaged the scrubbed and sanded flatness of my hard-won work. In defence I tacked up ugly flywire but the sections were not wide enough and in despair I had a silk curtain made on credit—Velcro running down its sides and a great heavy sausage of sand along its base. The curtain was a deep, deep blue, and the sausage a rust brown. Now the little saboteurs fell into its sweaty silky crotch and there they died in their thousands every night. I swept them out when I cleaned my floor each morning, but some I saved as life models, for no other reason than drawing is relaxing and I would often, particularly when I had run out of wine, sit at my dining table and slowly fill my notebook with careful grey renditions of their lovely corpses. Sometimes my neighbour Dozy Boylan would name them for me.

By early December my brother Hugh and I were ensconced as the caretakers and we were still there in high summer when my life began its next interesting chapter. Lightning had struck the transformer up on the Bellingen Road and so, once again, there was no good light to work by, and I was paying for my patron's kindness by prettifying the front paddock, hacking with a mattock at the thistles around the FOR SALE sign.

January is the hottest month in northern New South

Wales, and also the wettest. After three days of soaking rain the paddocks were sodden and when I swung the mattock the mud was warm as shit between my toes. Until this day the creek had been gin-clear, a rocky stream rarely more than two feet deep, but the runoff from the saturated earth had now transformed the peaceful stream into a tumescent beast: yellow, turbulent, territorial, rapidly rising to twenty feet, engulfing the wide floodplain of the back paddock and sucking at the very top of the bank on whose edge the chaste studio was, sensibly but not invulnerably, perched on high wooden poles. From here, ten feet above the earth, one could walk out above the edge of the raging river as on a wharf. Jean-Paul, when explaining the house to me, had named this precarious platform 'the Skink' referring to those little Australian lizards who drop their tails when disaster strikes. I wondered if he had noticed that the entire house was constructed on a floodplain.

We had not been in exile very long, six weeks or so, and I remember the day because it was our first flood, also the day when Hugh had arrived home from our neighbours with a Queensland heeler puppy inside his coat. It was difficult enough to look after Hugh without this added complication, not that he was always troublesome. Sometimes he was so bloody smart, so coherent, at other times a wailing gibbering fool. Sometimes he adored me, loudly, passionately, like a whiskery bad-breathed child. But the next day or next minute I would be the Leader of the Opposition and he would lay in wait amongst the wild lantana, pounce, wrestle me violently into the mud, or the river, or across the en-gorged wet-season zucchini. I did not need a sweet puppy. I had Hugh the Poet and Hugh the Murderer, Hugh the Idiot Savant, and he was heavier and stronger, and once he had me down I could only control him by bending his little finger as if I meant to snap it. We neither of us required a dog.

I severed the roots of perhaps a hundred thistles, split a

little ironbark, fired up the stove which heated the water for the Japanese soaking tub and, having discovered that Hugh was asleep and the puppy missing, I retreated out on to the Skink, watching the colours of the river, listening to the boulders rolling over each other beneath the Never Never's bruised and swollen skin. Most particularly, I observed my neighbour's duck ride up and down the yellow flood whilst I felt the platform quiver like a yacht mast tensing under thirty knots of wind.

Somewhere the puppy was barking. It must have been overstimulated by the duck, perhaps imagined it was itself a duck—that seems quite likely now I think of it. The rain had never once relented and my shorts and T-shirt were soaked and I suddenly understood that if I removed them I would feel a good deal more comfortable. So there I was, uncharacteristically deaf to the puppy, squatting naked as a hippy above the surging flood, a butcher, a butcher's son, surprised to find myself three hundred miles from Sydney and so unexpectedly happy in the rain, and if I looked like a broad and hairy wombat, well so be it. It was not that I was in a state of bliss, but I was, for a moment anyway, free from my habitual agitation, the melancholy memory of my son, the anger that I had to paint with fucking Dulux. I was very nearly, almost, for sixty seconds, at peace, but then two things happened at once and I have often thought that the first of them was a kind of omen that I might well have paid attention to. It only took a moment: it was the puppy, speeding past borne on the yellow tide.

Later, in New York, I would see a man jump in front of the Broadway Local. There he was. Then he wasn't. It was impossible to believe what I had seen. In the case of the dog, I don't know what I felt, nothing as simple as pity. Incredulity, of course. Relief—no dog to care for. Anger—that I would have to deal with Hugh's ill-proportioned grief.

With what plan in mind I do not know, I began struggling

with my wet clothes, and thus, accidentally, had a clear view, beneath the studio, of my front gate where, some twenty yards beyond the cattle grid, I saw the second thing: a black car, its headlights blazing, sunk up to its axles in the mud.

There was no justifiable reason for me to be angry about potential buyers except that the timing was bad and, fuck it, I did not like them sticking their nose in my business or presuming to judge my painting or my housekeeping. But I, the previously famous artist, was now the caretaker so, having forced myself back into my cold and unpleasantly resistant clothes, I slopped slowly through the mud to the shed where I fired up the tractor. It was a Fiat and although its noisy differential had rapidly damaged my hearing, I retained a ridiculous affection for the yellow beast. Perched high upon its back, as ridiculous in my own way as Don Quixote, I headed out towards my stranded visitor.

On a better day I might have seen the Dorrigo escarpment towering three thousand feet above the car, mist rising out of the ancient unlogged bush, newborn clouds riding high in powerful thermals which any glider pilot would feel in the pit of his stomach, but now the mountains were hidden, and I could see no more than my fence line and the invading headlights. The windows of the Ford were fogged so even at the distance of ten yards I could make out no more of the interior than the outlines of the AVIS tag on the rear-view mirror. This was confirmation enough that the person was a buyer and I prepared myself to be polite in the face of arrogance. I do, however, have a tendency to bristle and when no one emerged from the car to greet me, I began to wonder what Sydney fuck thought he could block my distinguished driveway and then wait for me to serve him. I dismounted and thumped my fist on the roof.

Nothing happened for almost a minute. Then the engine

fired and the foggy window descended to unveil a woman in her early thirties with straw-coloured hair.

'Are you Mr Boylan?' She had a strange accent.

'No,' I said. She had almond eyes, lips almost too large for her slender face. She appeared unusual, but very attractive, so it is strange, you might think—given my miserable existence and almost continual horniness—how powerfully and deeply she irritated me.

She looked out the window, surveying the front and back wheels which she had spun deep into my land.

'I'm not dressed for this,' she said.

If she had apologized perhaps I would have reacted differently, but she actually rolled the windows up and shouted instructions at me from the other side.

Well, I had been famous once but now I was just a dogsbody, so what did I expect? I wrapped the free end of the Fiat's cable around the Ford's back axle, an exercise which covered me with mud and perhaps a little cowshit too. Then, returning to my tractor, I dropped it into low ratio and hit the gas. Of course she had left the car in gear so this manoeuvre created two long streaks across the grass and out on to the road.

I saw no reason to say goodbye. I retrieved the cable from the Ford and drove back to the shed without looking over my shoulder.

As I returned to my studio I saw she had not gone at all but was walking across the paddock, high heels in her hand, towards my house.

This was the hour at which I normally drew and as my visitor approached I sharpened up my pencils. The river was roaring like blood in my ears but I could feel her feet as she came up the hardwood stairs, a kind of fluttering across the floor joists.

I heard her call but when neither Hugh nor I responded

she set off along the covered walkway suspended between house and studio, a whippy ticklish little structure some ten feet above the ground. She might have chosen to knock on the studio door, but there was also a very narrow walkway, a kind of gangplank which snaked around the outer wall of the studio and so she appeared in front of the open lube-bay door, standing outside the silk, the river at her back.

'Sorry, it's me again.'

I affected great concentration on my pencils.

'Can I use your phone?'

At that moment the electricity returned, flooding the studio with bright light. There stood a slender blonde woman behind a veil of stocking silk. She had mud up to her pretty calves.

'Strong work,' she said.

'You can't come in.'

'Don't worry. I wouldn't track mud into a studio.'

Only later did I think how few civilians would have put it quite like that. At the time I was concerned with simpler things: that she had not come to buy the property, that she was exceedingly attractive and in need of help. I led her back across the walkway to Jean-Paul's 'house of few possessions' where the only real room was a central kitchen with a square table made from Tasmanian blackwood which I was required—his final instruction—to scrub each morning. The table had more character than when Jean-Paul last saw it— cadmium yellow, crimson rose, curry, wine, beef fat, clay— over a month of domestic life now partially obscured by a huge harvest of pumpkins and zucchinis amongst which I now finally located the telephone.

'No dial tone,' I said. 'I'm sure they're working on it.'

Hugh began stirring in his room. I remembered that his dog had drowned. It had completely slipped my mind.

My visitor had remained on the other side of the flywire door. 'I'm so sorry,' she said. 'I can see you have more important things to worry about.' She was drenched, her short yellow hair all matted, like a little chicken saved from drowning.

I opened the door.

'We are used to mud in this part of the house,' I said. She hesitated, shivering. She looked like she should be put in a little cardboard box before the fire.

'Perhaps you'd like some dry clothes and a warm shower?'

She could not have known what a peculiarly intimate thing I was offering. You see, Jean-Paul's bathroom was on the back porch and here we hairy men were used to showering, almost alfresco, with nothing but flywire separating us from the roaring river, the bending trees. It was easily the best part of our exile. Once we were clean we would climb into that big Japanese wooden tub where the hot water cooked us as red as crayfish while, on a day like today at least, the rain beat across our faces.

On the public side, by the open stairs—really just a fire escape—there were canvas blinds and these I now lowered. I gave her our one clean towel, a dry shirt, a sarong.

'If you use the tub,' I said, 'you can't use soap in it.'

'*Domo arigato*,' she called. 'I know how to behave.'

Domo arigato? It would be six months before I would learn what that might mean. I was thinking I should have told Hugh about the damn puppy, but I did not need his outbursts now. I returned to my table full of pumpkins and sat, quiet as a mouse, on the noisy chair. She was looking for Dozy Boylan—who else? There were no other Boylans, and I knew she would have no hope of driving her rent-a-car across his flooded creek. I began to think about what I could cook for dinner.

Having no desire to set off Hugh, I remained silently at the table while she bathed. I rose only once, to fetch a cloth and some moisturizing cream and with this I began to clean her Manolo Blahniks. Who would have believed me? I must have paid for two dozen pairs in the last year of my marriage, but this was the first time I had actually touched a pair and I was shocked by the indecent softness of the leather. The wood shifted and crackled in the firebox of the Rayburn stove. If I have made myself sound calculating, let me tell you: I had not the least fucking idea what I was doing.

2

Hearing the screen door in the bathroom give a small urgent 'thwack', I hid the shoes beneath the table and hurried around collecting muddy pumpkins, stacking them out on the front porch. Not that I didn't notice her enter, or see my Kmart shirt falling loosely from her slender shoulders, the collar's soft grey shadow across her bath-pink neck.

I handed her the cordless phone. 'Telecom are back in service.' Brusque. It has been remarked of me before—the lack of charm when sober.

'Oh super,' she said.

She threw her towel across a wooden chair and walked briskly out on to the front porch. Above the insistent thrum on the roof I could hear the soft American burr which I understood as old money, East Coast, but all this was Aussie expertise i.e. from the movies and I had not the least idea of who she was, and if she had been Hilda the Poisoner from Spoon Forks, North Dakota, I would have had no clue.

I began to chop up a big pumpkin, a lovely thing, fire orange with a rust-brown speckle, and a moist secret cache of bright slippery seeds which I scooped into the compost tray.

Out on the porch, I heard her: 'Right. Yes. Exactly. Bye.'

She returned, all antsy, rubbing at her hair.

'He says his creek is over the big rock.' (She pronounced it 'crick'.) 'He says you'll understand.'

'It means you wait for the "crick" to go down.'

'I can't wait,' she said. 'I'm sorry.'

It was exactly at that moment—well I'm fucking sorry Miss, but what do you want me to do about the flood?—that Hugh's adenoidal breathing pushed its way between us. Doughy, six foot four, filthy, dangerous-looking, he filled the doorway without explanation. He had his pants on, but his hair looked like cattle had been eating it and he was un-shaven. Our guest was three feet in front of him but it was to me he spoke. 'Where's the bloody pup?'

I was at the far side of the stove, hands slippery with olive oil, laying the pumpkin and potato in a baking tray.

'This is Hugh,' I said. 'My brother.'

Hugh looked her up and down, very Hugh-like, threat-ening if you did not know.

'What's your name?'

'I'm Marlene.'

'Have you', he enquired, sticking out his fat lower lip, and folding his big arms across his chest, 'read the book *The Magic Pudding*?'

Oh Christ, I thought, not this.

She rubbed her hair again. 'As a matter of fact, Hugh, I *have* read *The Magic Pudding*. Twice.'

'Are you American?'

'That's very hard to say.'

'Hard to say.' His self-inflicted haircut was high above his ears suggesting a fierce and rather monkish kind of charac-ter. 'But you have read *The Magic Pudding*?'

Now she offered all of her attention. 'Yes. Yes, I have.'

Hugh gave me a fast look. I understood exactly—he would now be busy for a moment, but he had not forgotten this business with the dog.

'Who', he asked, turning his brown eyes to the foreigner, 'do you like the best in *The Magic Pudding*?'

And she was charmed. 'I like the four of them.'

'Really?' He was dubious. 'Four?'

'Including the pudding.'

'You're counting the pudding!'

'But I like *all* the drawings.' She finally returned the phone to the table and began to properly dry her hair. 'The pudding thieves', she said, 'are priceless.'

'Is that a joke you're telling?' My brother hated the pudding thieves. He was continually, loudly, passionately regretful that it was not possible for him to punch the possum on the snout.

'It's not the characters I like'—she paused—'but the *drawings*—I think they're better than any painting Lindsay ever did.'

'Oh yes,' said Hugh, softening. 'We saw Lindsay's bloody paintings. Bless me.'

Whatever urgent business had been in her mind, she put it briefly to one side. 'Do you want to know my favourite person in *The Magic Pudding*?'

'Yes.'

'Sam Sawnoff.'

'He's not a person.'

'Yes, he's a penguin, but he's very good, I think.'

And there she was—a type—one of those rare, often unlucky people who 'get on with Hugh'.

'Who do you like?' she asked, smiling.

'Barnacle Bill!' he cried exultantly. And next thing he was out of the doorway, shadow-boxing, prancing round the table crying: 'Mitts up, mitts up, you dirty pudding thieves!'

Jean-Paul's little house of few possessions was, as I said, a light and whippy structure, designed with no anticipation of hulking prancing men in muddy work boots. The cups and saucers rattled on their shelves. None of this seemed to put

her out at all. Hugh put his arm around my chest. Misunderstanding, she continued smiling.

'Where's my bloody dog?' my brother hissed.

Up close like this, his breath was really awful.

'Later, Hugh.'

'Shut up.' There was the missing front tooth and all that
tartar but since Dr Hoffman was deported, there was no
dentist brave enough to tackle Hugh.

'Later, please.'

But he was hard against my back, with his whiskery jowls
against my cheek. He was a strong man of thirty-four and
when he moved his huge arm around my throat I could
hardly breathe.

'Your puppy drowned.'

I saw my visitor suck in her breath.

'It drowned, mate,' I said.

He let go his grip but I watched him very closely. Our
Hugh could be a devious chap and I didn't want to cop that
famous roundhouse punch.

He stepped back, stricken, and that really was my prime
concern, to get beyond his reach.

'Careful of the bath heater,' I said, but he had already
stumbled, sat on it, cried with pain, and rushed head down
into his room.

Singed feathers, I thought, recalling the rooster in *The
Magic Pudding*.

Moaning, Hugh slammed his door. He threw himself on
to his bed and as the house shook and rattled the visitor's
clear blue eyes widened. How could I explain? All my
brother's misery was painfully present and nothing could be
said in private.

'Can I walk across the creek?' she asked.

Five minutes later we were out in the storm together.

The tractor headlights were weak and the ride very loud
and rough, no more than 20 Ks, but the wind was off the

escarpment and the rain stung my face and doubtless hers as well. She had borrowed my oilskin coat and a pair of gum boots but her hair would, by now, be wild and curling, her eyes slitted against the rain.

For the first mile and a half, that is, all the way to Dozy Boylan's cattle grid, I was very aware of that slender body, the small breasts against my back. I was half mad, you see that, a dangerous male in rut, in a fury with my brother, roaring around Loop Road, the slasher swaying and rattling, the differential whining in my ears.

As we arrived at the grid, my weak yellow lights fell upon the boiling water of Sweetwater Creek, more usually a narrow stream. Jean-Paul's big slasher—what I would call a mower—was attached to the power takeoff and three-point hydraulics. I raised it as high as it would go, a big square raft of metal about six foot by six foot. I should have removed it, but I was a painter and in matters agricultural my judgement was bad in almost every way imaginable. I had it firmly in my mind that the little creek was nothing serious but entering the flood my boots were immediately filled with cold water and then it was too late, and the Fiat was rising and stumbling across the hidden rocks. Then the current caught the slasher and I felt a sick surge in my gut as we began to drift. I steered upstream, of course, but the tractor was slipping down, lumbering over the boulders, front wheels rearing in the air. I was no farmer, never had been. The mower was a deadly orange barge riding on the surface of the flood. I could feel my passenger's terror as she dug into my shoulders and saw clearly, angrily, what a complete fool I was. I had put my life at risk, for what? I did not even like her.

Bless us, as Hugh would say.

Luck or God being with us, we emerged on the far bank and I lowered the mower for the journey up Dozy's steep drive. Marlene said nothing, but when we arrived at the front door, when Dozy came out to greet her, she shed my raincoat, urgently, desperately, as if she never wished it to touch her again. I had no doubt she was afraid, and in the tangled skin she handed me I imagined I could feel her anger with my recklessness.

'You better take that slasher off,' said Dozy. 'I'll babysit it for a day or two.'

Dozy was a rich and successful manufacturer who had, with all the energy and will that marked his character, turned himself into a broad sixty-year-old man with a grey moustache and a strong farmer's belly. He was also a gifted amateur entomologist, but that was not the point right now, and as his guest took refuge inside his house he fetched a fierce flashlight and held it silently while I disconnected the mower from the hydraulics.

'Hugh alone?'

'I'll be back soon.'

My friend said nothing judgemental, but he caused me to imagine Hugh howling across paddocks, barbed wire in the dark, rabbit holes, the river, his terror that I was dead and he was left alone.

'I would have got her in the Land-Rover,' Dozy said, 'but she was in a great awful rush and I was listening to the BBC news.'

He said nothing about her attractiveness, leading me to conclude that she was one of the nieces or grandchildren he had spread out across the world.

'I'm fine now.' And I was, in a way. I would go home and feed Hugh, tune in his wireless, and make sure he took his bloody tablet. Then we would talk about his dog.

Once, not so long ago, I had been a happy married man tucking in his boy at night.

3

Phthaaa! We are Bones, God help us, raised in sawdust, dry each morning. I am called Hugh and he is called Butcher but the pair of us are meat men, not river men, not beggars hiding in damp shacks with floods and mud and mould, with a hook hanging from the front veranda to skin the eels. We were born and bred in Bacchus Marsh, thirty-three miles west of Melbourne, down Anthony's Cutting. If you are expecting a bog or marsh, there is none, it is just a way of speaking, making no more sense than if the town were named Mount Bacchus. The Marsh was a big old teasing town, four thousand people in those days before the PRODUCT MANAGERS came to live. We had a tease for everyone. On New Year's Eve the BODGIES and the WIDGIES would throw eggs at the barber's windows and write in whitewash on the road. My dad woke up one New Year's Day to discover someone had changed the sign above the shop from BOONE to BO NE$. We were Bones thereafter. BO NE$ BUTCHERS.

All in that town were FULL OF HIGH SPIRITS like Sam Sawnoff in the book *The Magic Pudding*.

Like Barnacle Bill and Sam Sawnoff we always fought and wrestled. Bless us. I wrestled with my dad and my grand-dad as did Brother Butcher Bones, a big man if not the biggest. He could not stand to lose to me. God save us what a bag of tricks he had to use Full Nelson. Half Nelson. Chinese Burn. I did not grudge him, never. Wrestling was the best thing any day. Many the time in the sawdust we did the old charge and grab the knackers, blood is thicker than water as they say. This was long ago but we were all large men, none but Granddad larger than myself. When he was seventy-two he had a disagreement with 35-yr-old Nails Carpenter dropping him on his bum in the public bar of the Royal Hotel. Carpenter played RUCK for Bacchus Marsh but would never return to that WATERING HOLE not even when Granddad was safely dead and buried up at Bacchus Marsh cemetery, butcher's grass around the hole, so clean you could have displayed loin chops along the edge. Not even then would Nails return to the Royal although his old mates would barrack him from the doorway, come in, come in, we will shout you a shandy. Nails dropped dead in 1956 while pedalling up the Stanford Hill.

Carpenter should have known to drink his shandy and start again. When they teased me I TOOK IT IN GOOD PART even if I might have murdered them. Like that. I was a GENTLE GIANT. Our father was Blue Bones on account of he had red hair when young so they called him Blue meaning red. That is a general rule to go by if you come from OVER-SEAS. In Australia everything is the opposite of what it seems to mean. E.G. I was SLOW BONES because I moved so rapid, it was my way of moving they referred to. I was Slow Bones some days, Slow Poke others, this last was SMUTTY. Those blokes were ROUGH DIAMONDS from the milk factory or the Darley Brickworks AGRICULTURAL LABOURERS always referring to the bull putting its pizzle in the cow like it was the strangest thing in life.

Look at that Poke, he is poking her. But I could take a JOKE and get a POKE fast slow anyway you like you might be surprised.

The Bones were butchers. We had our own slaughter yards at the former DRAYBONE INN. In the gold-rush days this was where they would change the coach horses for COBB & CO but now it was where we brought the beasts to end their days. Never did a Bones take life lightly. If it was a fish or an ant, then possibly. But a beast's heart tips the scales at five pounds and no matter how many you slaughter you cannot do it without a thought. There was a sort of prayer YOU POOR OLD BUGGER or other stuff more serious I'm sure, and then they cut its throat and caught the blood in the tin bucket to save for sausage. It is a big responsibility to cut up a beast but when it is done it is done and afterwards you go to the Royal and then you come home THE WORSE FOR WEAR I do admit. After that you rest. It is in the Bible re Sunday: you must not work, nor thy son, nor thy daughter, thy manservant, nor thy maidservant, nor thy cattle, nor thy stranger that is within thy gates. Poor Mum.

I was not to be a butcher, bee-boh bless me. My brother was three inches shorter still he took my true and rightful name. It's a doggie dog world.

Butcher Bones had the opportunity to keep up the family business in Bacchus Marsh but by the time Dad had his stroke Butch had met the GERMAN BACHELOR who gave him postcards to stick on the wall above his bunk. Those cards turned his head. The German Bachelor was permitted to be a teacher at Bacchus Marsh High School where he instructed the children of men who had lost their lives fighting Germans in the war. I don't know why he was not in gaol but my brother came home and said his teacher was a MODERN artist and had attended the so-called BOWER HOUSE. If Dad had known the effect of that Bower House on his oldest son he would have gone up to the school and dropped the German Bachelor like he dropped Mr Cox after he strapped me for answering incorrectly. Blue Bones took Coxy out of the room and across the street behind his van. Coxy's feet lifted six inches off the ground. That is all we saw, but knew much more.

It was my brother who inherited the nickname Butcher and that is a joke that anyone can see for it was he who refused the knife and scabbard. From the German Bachelor he got the habit of shaving his skull the DICKHEAD also the postcards of MARK ROTHKO and the idea that ART IS FOR

BUTCHERS NOW. He learned from the German Bachelor that art had previously been restricted to palaces where it was viewed behind high gates by Kings and Queens, Dukes, Counts, Barons. In any case he refused the apron when our poor mother begged him put it on. His father could not speak nor move but it was obvious he would like to clout Butcher across the ear hole one last time. Auld Lang Sine. After Dad had his stroke there was no more SLAUGHTER.

It is hard work to slaughter a beast but when it is done it is done. If you are MAKING ART the labour never ends, no peace, no Sabbath, just eternal churning and cursing and worrying and fretting and there is nothing else to think of but the idiots who buy it or the insects destroying TWO DIMENSIONAL SPACE.

There is nothing sure or certain it would seem no matter how you shave your skull or boast about your position in AUSTRALIAN ART. One minute you are a NATIONAL TREASURE with a house in Ryde and then you are a has-been buying Dulux with your brother's DISABILITY PENSION. You are a CONVICTED CRIMINAL a servant living on a Tick and Thistle farm.

The puppy was a cattle dog but there were no beasts for him to work with so he never learned his purpose on the Earth. Bless him. I wrestled with him before he passed. Ascended, poor tyke. He was a licky dog. He liked a toss, a good fall over in the grass. By dint of playing he got ticks all lined up, dug into the edges of his floppy ears like cars parked outside a Kmart or a Sydney Leagues Club. The day I met him I removed each tick, one by one, God Bless him. My brother heard him barking at the Duck but he was making art and never spared a thought.

Your dog is DEAD Hugh. Butcher Bones gave not a FLYING FUCK about the puppy. He said your dog is dead and then he went off with the woman on the tractor and left me listening to a river the colour of a yellow cur, fucksuck flood, tugging, pulling stones out of the bank, beneath our feet, everything we stand on will be washed away.

4

The phone call I got that night from Dozy Boylan would make me laugh for days to come. 'Mate,' he said, and I knew that he was hiding in his bathroom because I could hear the echo. 'Mate, she's hitting on me.'

He was full of shit, I told him so, although not without affection.

'Shut up,' he said. 'I'm bringing her back to your place now.'

I expressed loud amusement and that was rude and stupid and I have no excuse except—my overactive friend was a sixty-year-old farmer with soup in his moustache and trousers curling above his cinched-in belt. She was hitting on him? I snorted into the phone, and when he turned on me soon after, I never doubted why.

In an astoundingly short time he came roaring across my cattle grid. I'd had a drink or two already and this was perhaps why it seemed so wildly funny, the audible panic of his off-road lugs rippling across the wooden bridge. By the time I had changed into a clean shirt, the old man had already performed a high-speed U-turn and when I emerged on the front porch the tail lights of his All Terrain Invention were disappearing into the night. I was still smiling as my visitor entered. Her hair was drenched again, flat on her head, dripping down her cheeks, collecting in the lovely well of her clavicle, but she was also smiling and—for a moment any-way—I thought she was about to laugh.

'How was the crossing?' I asked. 'Were you scared?'

'Never by the crossing.' She sat heavily in my chair and exhaled—a different person now, messier, less brisk. She produced from the folds of her borrowed poncho, a magnum of 1972 Virgin Hills which she held like a trophy in the air.

Later she told me that I had cocked my head, looking at the wine like a sulky dog, but that was a misunderstanding. This was a prize bottle from Dozy's cellar. There was nothing to explain it and the mystery was made deeper by her manner—she was suddenly so full of energy, kicking off her gum boots, opening up a drawer—did she wait to ask permission? She located a corkscrew, ripped out the cork, brushed down her skirt, sat cross-legged on the kitchen chair and, while she watched me pour the Virgin Hills, she just plain grinned at me.

'OK,' I said. 'What happened?'

'Nothing,' she said, her eyes sparkling to the point of carbonation. 'Where's your brother? Is he OK?'

'Asleep.'

Whatever dark visions she then conjured—probably the drowning dog—she could not stay with long. 'The good thing', she said, raising her glass, 'is that Mr Boylan knows his Leibovitz is real.'

'Jacques Leibovitz?'

'That's the one.'

'Dozy owns a painting by Jacques Leibovitz?!'

I know now that my astonishment seemed put on to her, but the secretive bugger Dozy had never breathed a word about his treasure. Also, you do not go to northern New South Wales to look at great paintings. And again: Leibovitz was one of the reasons I became an artist. I had first seen *Monsieur et Madame Tourenbois* at Bacchus Marsh High School, or at least a black-and-white reproduction in *Foundation of the Modern*. None of this I was prepared to confess to an American in Manolo Blahniks but I was really offended by Dozy, my so-called mate. 'We never even talk about art,' I said. 'We sit in his miserable kitchen, that's where he lives, amongst all those piles of the *Melbourne Age*. And he showed it to *you*?'

She raised an eyebrow as if to say, Why not? All I could think was that I had given him lovely drawings of the Wombat Fly and Narrow-waisted Mud Wasp and he had stuck them to his fridge with fucking magnets. It was hard to believe he had an eye at all.

'Are you insuring it?'

She laughed through her nose. 'Is that what I look like?'

I shrugged.

She returned a clear appraising gaze. 'Do you mind if I smoke?'

I fetched her a saucer and she blew some dungy-smelling fumes across the table. 'My husband', she said finally, 'is the son of Leibovitz's second wife.'

If I did not like her, I liked the husband way, way less. But I was startled and impressed to understand whose son he was. 'Dominique Broussard is his mother?'

'Yes,' she said. 'You know the photograph?'

Even I knew that—the tawny blonde studio assistant lying on an unmade bed, her new baby at her breast.

'My husband, Olivier, he's the baby. He inherited the Leibovitz *droit moral*,' she said, as though having to explain a story she was weary of.

But I was not weary, not at all. I was from Bacchus Marsh, Victoria. I hadn't seen an original painting before I turned sixteen.

'You understand how that works?'

'What?'

'*Droit moral.*'

'Of course,' I said. 'More or less.'

'Olivier is the one who gets to say if the work is real or fake. He signed the certificate of authentication for Boylan's painting. That is his legal right, but there have been people making mischief, and we have to protect ourselves.'

'You work together, you and your husband?'

But she was not being drawn into that. 'I've known Mr Boylan's painting for a very long time,' she said, 'and it is authentic right down to the zinc tacks on the stretcher but the point has to be proven again and again. It's a little boring.'

'And you know that much about Leibovitz?'

'That much,' she said drily, and I watched as she butted out her cigarette, grinding it fiercely into the saucer. 'But when someone like Boylan is told that his investment is at risk, he is bound to get upset. In this case he showed the canvas to Honoré Le Noël who persuaded him he'd bought, not quite a fake, but close enough. May I have more wine? I'm sorry. It's been a hell of a day.'

I poured the wine without comment, not revealing that I was completely gobsmacked to hear Le Noël's name spoken as if he were the local publican or the owner of a hardware store. I knew who he was. I had two of his books beside my bed. 'Honoré Le Noël has become a joke,' she said. 'He was Dominique Leibovitz's lover, as you probably know.'

This sort of talk upset me in ways I can hardly bring myself to name. At the heart of it was the notion that I was a hick and she was from the centre of the fucking universe. What I knew you could read in *Time* magazine—Dominique had begun as Leibovitz's studio assistant; Le Noël was Leibovitz's chronicler and critic.

Now that my visitor was halfway through her second glass, she was talkative as hell. She revealed that Dominique and Honoré had spent almost eight years, from just after the war until 1954, waiting for Leibovitz to die. (I recalled that the artist's strength was very acutely sketched in Le Noël's monograph—a force of life, short, thick legs, huge square hands.)

It was not until his baby son was five, his daughter-in-law now told me, when Leibovitz himself was eighty-one, that the grim reaper came sneaking up on the old goat, pushing him forward as he stood at the dinner table with a wine glass brimming in his hand. He pitched forward and slammed his broad nose and tortoiseshell spectacles into the Picasso cheese plate. That is how my visitor told it, fluently, a little breathlessly. She finished the second glass without remarking on its character and for this, of course, I judged her quite severely.

The plate cracked in half, she said.

I thought, How would you fucking know? Were you even born? But I was a stranger to the notion that one might know famous people and of course she was married to the witness, the child—an olive-skinned boy with very large watchful eyes and protruding ears which could not even begin to spoil his beauty. When his father had fallen dead he apparently had been about to ask if he might be excused, but now he looked to his mother and waited. Dominique did not embrace him but stroked his cheek with the back of her hand.

'Papa *est mort*.'

'*Oui*, Maman.'

'You understand. No one must know yet.'

'*Oui*, Maman.'

'Maman must move some canvases, do you understand? It is difficult because of the snow.'

I have recently observed French children, how they sit, so neat with their big dark eyes, and their clean fingernails collected in their laps. What miracles they are. I suppose Olivier sat like that, watching his dead father, but holding a dreadful secret of his own—he had been, at the very moment when his father fell, about to go and make pee-pee.

'Don't move, you understand?'

Of course there was no need for him to be tortured in the chair. But his mother was about to commit a major crime, that

is remove paintings from the estate before the police were no-
tified. 'Stay there,' she said. 'Then I'll know where you are.'
Then she was on the telephone, persuading her posh lover to
leave his fireside at Neuilly, explaining that they could not
afford to wait for the snow to melt, that he must go all the way
to Bastille, collect a truck, and drive it to the rue de Rennes.

Somewhere in the confusion and terror of the night the
little boy peed his pants, although this misadventure was not
discovered until much later, when Honoré finally noticed
him sleeping with his forehead on the table, and then
Dominique took a bloody photograph. Imagine! Later, for
whatever reason—perhaps the missing *Le Golem électrique*
was in the shot—she tore half of it away. It might have provided the only forensic evidence of that long night when
Dominique Broussard and Honoré Le Noël stole some fifty
Leibovitzes, many of them abandoned or incomplete, works
that would later, with the signature added and some careful
revision, become very valuable indeed. They removed them
to a garage near the Canal Saint-Martin, the source of that
frequently reported 'watermark' on a whole array of doubt-
ful Leibovitzes from widely different periods. From this day
no one ever saw the painting that Leo Stein and the fiercer
(and therefore more reliable) Picasso both described as a
masterwork. Stein referred to it as *Le Golem électrique*,
Picasso as *Le Monstre*.

It was not until lunch the following day that Dominique
reported her husband's death to the gendarmes, and then, of
course, the studio was—as is the law in France—sealed off
and a full accounting made of the paintings remaining there.
No *Le Golem électrique*. Oh, never mind.

Dominique, the daughter of a tax accountant from Mar-
seilles, now had sufficient Leibovitzes, almost-Leibovitzes
and unborn-Leibovitzes to live very well for the next fifty
years. Also, of course, she inherited the *droit moral*. That
gave her the right to authenticate, which is, incredible as it

may seem, the law, but now she chose to give her rather louche reputation a more reliable character and so she set up Le Comité Leibovitz, and installed the esteemed Honoré Le Noël as chair. It must have seemed perfect from her point of view: they could back up their false assertions with those of greedy dealers and collectors on the Comité. The pair of them could spend the rest of their lives signing unsigned canvases and revising abandoned works.

The storyteller was pretty, filled with talk, thirsty for more wine. I poured her a third glass of Virgin Hills and began to permit myself a few ideas.

'Now,' she said, brushing ash from her lovely ankle, 'Dominique discovered Honoré in bed with Roger Martin.'

'The English poet.'

'Exactly. Him. You know him?'

'No.'

'Thank God for that.' She raised an eyebrow. If I did not know exactly what she meant, I enjoyed the sense of complicity.

'So they divorced, of course. But no one knows exactly how their hoard of paintings was finally divided,' she said.

But Dominique, it seems, knew a lot of 'partisans', tough guys, and she almost certainly got the lion's share. So by the time Honoré had been robbed, circled, outnumbered, and defeated on the Comité, he had become a very dangerous man. Certainly he hated Dominique. Towards her innocent son he displayed an even greater antipathy.

When, in 1969, one of her lovely partisan pals strangled Dominique in a Nice hotel, Olivier was already in London, losing the last of his French accent at St Paul's. Knowing less than nothing about his father's work, he inherited the *droit moral*.

'You meet my husband,' Marlene said, 'you think he is so gentle, and he is, but when Honoré began a legal action to take away the *droit moral*, Olivier fought like a tiger. You have seen the photographs? He was a child, so pretty, with lovely eyelashes, seventeen years old, but he loathed Honoré. I cannot tell you to what degree. When you think about the court case, this was really the only point for Olivier.'

We are the nation of Henry Lawson and the campfire yarn, but just the same we are very bloody wary of people doing what Marlene was doing now. We are inclined to wonder, Is she a name-dropper? Does she have tickets on herself? At the same time, no one in this paddock has ever spoken like this, not ever, and I was literally on the edge of my chair, watching with the most particular attention as she blew on her Marlboro so its tip burnt evenly.

'By the time all this was over, Olivier could not so much as *touch* one of his father's paintings. He hated them. He hates them now. These great works of art make him ill, really, physically ill.'

This was interesting, I didn't say it wasn't. 'But why, for Christ's sake, did Dozy hide the painting from me?'

She shrugged. 'Rich people!'

'He was frightened anyone would know he had something so valuable?'

'It's an asset,' she said derisively. 'That's how it is with them. It's there to own, not to see. But if the market believed Honoré's story—that this precious painting was somehow doctored—my husband would have been ruined. We would have been exposed for the loss, a million US dollars, probably more.'

'You and your husband?'

'Yes.' She almost smiled.

'And of course Honoré is just a malicious little shit,' she said, 'but he must be answered, so I sent up two forensic chemists to do an independent pigment analysis. Indeed, I think one of them met your brother in the pub. He thought he was amazing.'

'Sometimes he is.'

'In any case,' she said quickly, 'my independent chemists also echoed Honoré, fretting about the presence of titanium dioxide in the white. This was not in common use in 1913, so for them this was what they call'—she made a mocking face—'a *red flag*. Fortunately, Dominique lived in a pig sty, hoarding every tram ticket, every restaurant bill, so we had a great archive, thank God. And there at last I found, not only the letter from Leibovitz to his supplier requesting titanium white, but also a receipt, dated January 1913. That's enough. It doesn't matter it was not in common use. Honoré can go fuck himself. Your friend has a real Leibovitz. I brought him the documentation personally so it can be with the painting for ever now. I actually attached it for him, in an envelope on the back of the stretcher.'

She held out her glass and I filled it. 'Hence the celebration.'

'Very good wine too.' And I was now, having waited so long, all set to give her a big lecture on what she had been gulping down—the work of Tom Lazar and his vineyard at Kyneton, about this treasure growing in the shitty dun-coloured landscape of my childhood—but just as I was about to establish my sophistication, she let it slip that Dozy's painting was *Monsieur et Madame Tourenbois*, the same work I had first seen in reproduction at Bacchus Marsh High School. This seemed, that night, such a sweet and magical connection, and what my childhood self would have seen as showing off or name-dropping became transmuted into something you could call noble, and we sat there until the early morning, finishing up Lazar's third vintage, the rain drumming on the roof, and I relaxed, finally, while this strange and lovely woman described the entire canvas for me, speaking in a low soft throaty voice, beginning, not at the top left-hand corner, but with the cadmium yellow stroke which marks the edge of the young wife's blouse, a slice of light.

5

The morning sun produced a layer of grey fog which was just high enough to reveal the black roof of the Avis car as it moved slowly along the road to Bellingen. As I watched this pleasantly dreamlike departure, my mind was almost completely occupied with that puzzling creature, the driver. She was an extraordinarily attractive woman and she had shown me, without a question, that she was blessed with the Eye, but she was alien, American, working for the other team, the market, the rich guys, the ones who decided what was art and what was not. They were in charge of history, and so fuck them all, always, for ever.

It was this—not her marriage—that had me folding and refolding her business card until it fell in half. She was, she must always be, my enemy.

Her late father-in-law's painting was also in my thoughts and I intended to phone Dozy Boylan—indeed my hand was on the instrument—to invite myself to a private viewing. But then Hugh leapt on me and in the struggle we busted through the fly screen, and then—you wouldn't want to know—days went by without me contacting Dozy.

Also, I had my canvas waiting. I know I said I could not afford decent materials, and that is true. I didn't use a penny. Instead I called Fish-oh, my old canvas supplier in Sydney, and finally he confessed, very fucking reluctantly, that he had an unopened crate, just arrived from Holland, and this—it was so bloody hard for him to own up—contained a roll of No. 10 cotton duck fifty bloody yards long. Why Fish-oh would act like a mingy withholding bastard does not matter here only that I persuaded him to ship the whole fifty yards

C.O.D. to Kev at the Bellingen Dairyman's Co-op. This would go straight on Jean-Paul's account. It's no good getting old if you don't get cunning.

The Dutch canvas arrived in Bellingen just before Marlene. All the time I talked to her it was in my mind. I could see it lying quietly in the co-op loading dock, amongst the bags of fertilizer, and as soon as my visitor had gone I rushed—not to Dozy Boylan as you might expect—but to the co-op and then we brought it home and I rolled my canvas out across the studio floor, but not a cut, nowhere a cut, so all this, all this *possibility*, was crowding in on me.

And then—thirty minutes later—the lovely adenoidal little Kevin telephoned again, this time to inform me that my custom-made pigments had just arrived, and then not even a bloody Leibovitz could seem important. This paint was from Raphaelson's, a small Sydney outfit who are amongst the best pigment makers in the world. In the five years I had been really famous I would use nothing else and now they had some new, very serious acrylic greens: permanent green, earth green, Jenkins green, titanium green, Prussian green, a phthalo green so fucking intense that just a teardrop of this stuff could colonize a blob of white. Of course art supplies was not the co-op's normal line of merchandise but Kev and I had already done a lot of business together and gifts had been exchanged—a tiny landscape, a charcoal drawing—so the paint went on Jean-Paul's account.

Minutes after Kevin's call, the Bones boys were back in the Holden ute, creeping along the road, a submarine gliding through the milky sea of fog. My house-paint period was over. No longer would I be reduced to adding sand or sawdust to build impasto or using scratchy short-haired brushes on a Dulux Hi Gloss that dried too fast.

'Bloody hot,' said Hugh.

'Clammy, mate.'

'Bloody scorcher you wait.'

Neither of us liked this wet season, but for Hugh, whose main activity was to every day walk into Bellingen and back, the heat was of never-ending concern and, being a fearsome mouth-breather, he needed vast quantities of water in order not to perish on the journey. Even now he was drinking from the billycan he carried with him everywhere. Later, when he set out to walk, he would dive down into the bush to this creek or that dam—he knew them all.

Back at the co-op, I picked up my beautiful wooden box of one-pound tubes—that was Raphaelson's, everything so perfectly presented—and I was happy as a boy on Christmas morning. Every one of these new greens I ordered straight, but also mixed down with pumice and flakes of stainless steel, this recipe designed to give the green a secret mirrored light that would—I knew this before I opened anything—curl my fucking toes.

It's hard to make a civilian understand what this new palette and an uncut roll of canvas might mean to me but I planned to get into some very serious shit and in this I was not deluded. Later, of course, Jean-Paul claimed I had obtained my materials illegally. But did he have the heart to be a patron, or did he want me to continue to spend Hugh's pension on bloody house paints? What had he expected when he started?

Hugh arm-wrestled Kev and won four bucks for his victories, so he was happy too. I added a couple of bags of fertilizer to the bill. It was eighteen bucks a bag at the co-op and Mrs Dyson, my next-door neighbour, was happy to take it off my hands for fifteen. Later Jean-Paul would decide that this was stealing too, but for God's sake, I was not a Sunday painter. I could reasonably expect to pay back any debts. It was a cash-flow issue only and if I had not been interfered with so unconscionably I would have been able to sell the canvases privately—the court never need have known.

The road back to Jean-Paul's place winds through the bush

until it commences its descent into the long green valley at Gleniffer. At this point you can normally see the Dorrigo escarpment and, three thousand feet below in the valley, the Never Never, which was today lying beneath a blanket of fog so dense it was, from some three hundred feet of elevation, a streaky oyster grey. I was driving very very slowly indeed when I saw another pair of headlights coming towards us.

'Dozy,' said Hugh, 'bloody old Dozy.'

He had an eye, Hugh, although it required no special talent to recognize our neighbour's headlights for he had, perhaps because of the unpredictable nature of his creek, converted a long-wheel-base Land-Rover into a somewhat eccentric monster truck, the lights of which sat close together and high up off the road. Seeing their yellow orc-eyed glow, I slowed, pulling up just below the brow of the hill where, with my window down, I could hear Dozy's horrible old diesel grinding down into first gear. According to the custom in those parts he should have stopped to talk, but he passed by me, very close, and so very slowly that there could be no mistaking his look of implacable hostility.

I had only known Dozy Boylan six weeks but we had quickly become friends, often spending two or three nights a week drinking from his cellar, discussing, not art, not literature, but the plants and insects which were his great passion. It was he, my neighbour, who had discovered both the rare Wombat Fly (*tr. Borboroidini*) and the Stalk-eyed Signal Fly (*Achia sp.*). He was smart, so enthusiastic, so filled with life and information. Nothing in my experience prepared me for his rich man's secretiveness and—even worse—this really rather hateful look which he now bestowed on me.

Well, I liked my neighbour and if I had offended him somehow, then I would apologize. I thought, I'll call him in an hour or two. And then I began to think about those lovely heavy tubes from Raphaelson's and that flat, stapled section of the canvas which I had already prepared. As soon as we were back home I was into it, and Hugh had filled his billy with water and set off back along the road, drinking and spilling as he proceeded.

I should have phoned Dozy that night, and indeed I intended to, for I had still not seen the Leibovitz or talked to him about the general bloody wonder of its existence, but I was filing away the beautiful colour charts from Raphaelson's when I came across some papers he had given me when I first arrived. Dozy had a rich and interesting history and apart from running a very profitable Brahmin stud in Bellingen, he had, years before in Sydney, established a now-famous business in what was then called Scandinavian Design. Amongst the old catalogues he had provided, by way of introduction, was a glossy company report in which was contained, along with black-and-white reproductions of 1950s modern furniture, his portrait. It made me smile at first, for he had clearly modelled himself on the actor Clark Gable, although there was, behind that trim moustache and the movie-star good looks, something not quite right, a little crooked, a little heavy in the chin and although these were not in any usual sense defects, they became so simply through his failure to actually be Clark Gable, and what was left was something rather vain and silly. I would never have dwelled on this if it had not so brilliantly explained the half-wild anger I had seen in his eyes this morning on the road. The old man was vain. It had never occurred to me. But he had claimed Marlene had hit on him and I had mocked his bullshit. So fucking sorry to have caused offence.

So I did not call him. I would do it later. I would get over it. He would get over it, or so I thought. I was wrong, wrong about almost everything, and I would wander on blindly for the next few weeks before I finally discovered the real source of Dozy's upset and in the meantime there developed one of those strange silences between friends that, like a torn shoulder muscle left unattended, grows hard and lumpy and finally locks into a compacted knot of injury that no amount of manipulation can undo.

He spoke to Hugh, I know, and sometimes gave him lifts in his Land-Rover but although I saw Dozy many times upon the road, and although he quietly returned my slasher after dark one night, I never actually spoke to him again. I would see that Leibovitz within the year, but by then Dozy would be dead.

6

The undiluted greens I did not even bother with, but the others I was into like a snouty pig—huge luscious jars, greens so fucking dark, satanic, black holes that could suck your heart out of your chest. Green would not be my only colour, but rather my theorem, my argument, my family tree and soon I had all ten bloody power drills committed in one way or another, mixing my demon dark, with gesso, with saf-flower oil, kerosene, with cadmium yellow, with red madder; the names are pretty but beside the point—there is no name for either God or light, only mathematics, the angstrom scale, red madder = 65,000 AU.

Hugh was up and away, all over the place like a mad-woman's shit, gallumping along the bitumen, swearing at the flies in made-up languages but he, Dozy, Marlene, my little boy—everyone was dead to me. RIP, so very bloody sorry.

I painted.

Years later when he laid his pale bored eyes upon this canvas in the loft on Mercer Street, the dealer Howard Levi was nice enough to explain what I had done that steaming day in Bellingen: 'You are like Kenneth Noland' and 'Your

words are not the point, your words are an armature, something you hang the colour from.'

This was not only dumb, it was not even what he thought.
He said—How refreshing. But he thought—Who is this
cunt who hasn't heard of Clement fucking Greenberg?

Levi is dead so I can name him. The others I intend to
keep quiet about a little longer. These New York dealers had
their own particular type of ignorance, quite different from
Jean-Paul's, although they did share one astonishing assumption, that I needed to accept what was already agreed upon
by Dickberg and others. Jean-Paul would say this almost
outright. Levi, on the other hand, found me refreshing.

But it was all the same everywhere: everyone who *loved*
me was trying to get me up to date. Sometimes it seemed
there was not a place on Earth, no little town with flies crawling inside the baker shop window, where there was not also
some graduate student in a Corbusier bow tie who was now,
this instant, reading the party line in *Studio International* and
ARTnews and all of them were in a great sweat to get me up
to date, to free me not only from the old-fashioned brush-
stroke but from any reference to the world itself.

These were weighty issues, but the first question the
Manhattan dealers asked me was of a different order: 'What
are the names and phone numbers of your collectors?'

And the next question would be: 'When was your most
recent auction sale?'

And then, when they actually looked at the canvas, they
would silently ask themselves, What the fuck is this?

All dark and comfortless. They had no eye, only a nose
for the market and I smelled to them like some demented
Jesus fool living in a cotton town in Bentdick, Mississippi.

But I am Butcher Bones, a thieving cunning man and I
made this beautiful seven-foot-high monster with my greens
and my Dutch canvas and when it was done, and I had
cropped it, the result was twenty-one feet long and its bones,

its ribs, vertebrae, wretched broken fingers, were made from light and mathematics.

'I, THE SPEAKER, RULED AS KING OVER ISRAEL IN JERUSALEM; AND IN WISDOM I APPLIED MY MIND TO STUDY AND EXPLORE ALL THAT IS DONE UNDER HEAVEN. IT IS A SORRY BUSINESS THAT *GOD* HAS GIVEN TO MEN TO BUSY THEM-SELVES WITH. I HAVE SEEN ALL THE DEEDS THAT ARE DONE HERE UNDER THE SUN; THEY ARE ALL EMPTINESS AND CHASING THE WIND. WHAT IS CROOKED CANNOT BECOME STRAIGHT; WHAT IS NOT THERE CANNOT BE COUNTED. SO I APPLIED MY MIND TO UNDERSTAND WISDOM AND KNOWLEDGE, MADNESS AND FOLLY, AND I CAME TO SEE THAT THIS TOO IS CHASING THE WIND. FOR IN SUCH WISDOM IS MUCH VEXA-TION, AND THE MORE A MAN KNOWS THE MORE HE HAS TO SUFFER.'

And a Mars black pushed itself into that first 'I' which stood as tall as my brother in his football socks, and a field of alien gooseturd grey, its surface buffed flat as glass, flowed like an invading army from the 'HEAVEN'. Forget it. This stuff can't be talked, or walked, or *garnered* from the auction record. These are my mother's bones, my father's dick, the boiled-down carcass of Butcher Bones, bubbling like a caul-dron of tripe, and for the ten days and nights I wrenched and slapped and sanded until, with the flood still running through my head, the canvas put the holy fear of God in me, made the bloody hair on my bloody neck stand up on end, and if it scared me, who was its maker, assassin, congregant, it was going to terrify Jean-Paul who was a form of life more generous, but ultimately even lower than Howard Levi and the 57th Street Gang.

He had not told me this when he came to fetch me from my prison cell, but I already knew that he and the dealer and the lawyer were concerned that I was going *out of style*.

Oh dearie me. Gracious, what a disaster. What might I do?

They did not know that I was born *out of style*, and was still out of style when I came down on the train from Bacchus Marsh. My trousers were too short, my socks were white and I will commit similar sins of style when I am in my coffin, my ligaments all gone, bone by bone, my flesh mixed down with dirt.

Anyway, the problem was not style. It was my falling prices at the auctions and the value of Jean-Paul's collection. The market is a nervous easily panicked beast. And so it should be. After all, how can you know how much to pay when you have no bloody idea of what it's worth? If you pay 5 million dollars for a Jeff Koons what do you say when you get it home? What do you *think*?

But what could I do about this, even if I wanted to do something? Nothing more than what I had done already e.g. suck up to Kev and get some materials on tick. Should I have telephoned Jean-Paul first? Asked his opinion? It is absolutely irrelevant what galleries and critics and people who buy paintings think. Of course I knew who Greenberg was. As far as I can see he was a technician, a radio repairman. He only said one thing worth knowing: the problem with art is the people who buy it.

For a period on the banks of the Never Never I made paintings unlike any I had ever seen or painted before. Day after day, night after night I terrified myself, hardly knowing what I thought.

And through all of this there was Hugh, and shopping and cooking, and shitting and chopping the thistles, no woman, no drops of lavender sprinkled on her nameless breasts at night.

For every man shall bear his own burden, as our mum would say, and so through all of this was Hugh, and his deep little elephant eyes, every night and morning, through the end of the steamy mouldy summer, until the grass in the front paddock began to fleck with brown like a Harris tweed, and Hugh would still set off into Bellingen with his billy in his hand.

People were kind to him, never said they weren't. City wisdom says these little Australian towns are intolerant but that was not the case in my experience and I fully expected that a place the size of Bellingen would have its Bachelor Gentleman and its Manly Lady Doctor with steel-tipped boots and serge trousers tough enough to sand your walls. There was room for Slow Bones too, room for everyone in a jostling edgy kind of way.

While I mixed paint, Hugh sat in the Bridge Hotel and made his single beer last from ten in the morning until three in the afternoon. I had this all arranged. His chicken-and-lettuce sandwich was delivered to him in his corner, same place each day, beside the radio.

I had no idea I was living in a perfect time. All I saw were irritations: calls from Jean-Paul, my lawyer, and then this long, long silence from Dozy which really did begin to eat my gut. I wanted to see the Leibovitz. It was my right, but I would not call him.

There would always be some crisis.

I thought these upsets were so bloody terrible. Hugh gone missing, Hugh fighting, Hugh distressed, so you can imagine it is a late-summer morning and I am painting and all I can hear are the cockatoos ripping the shit out of the trees above my head, and the cries of magpies, kookaburras, the bull at Mrs Dyson's, and amongst all this many smaller birds, orioles, honeyeaters, grass wrens, butcher-birds, the sweet rush of the wind in the casuarinas by the river—I can hear a great roaring cry, not a bull calf, but like a bull calf on its way to being a steer, and although I continue painting I know this is my brother coming home—big sloping shoulders, meaty arms, lumbering along the narrow bitumen with his shirt-tails out and the empty billy in his hand and his whiskery face crumpled like a paper bag and that odd, Roman nose, flowing with snot and this is why, even when I lived in Paradise, I had no fucking idea of where I was.

7

Bald shiny shaven Butcher Bones said look at my works etc. but nowhere did he confess Hugh Bones was his helper. He signed each painting MICHAEL BOONE it would have been more truthful if it was CROSSED BONES. Every artist is a pirate as he himself has often said. But forgive me I thought every artist was a bloody king these days I must be wrong as usual.

Crossed Bones obtained his roll of canvas by the use of lies and I carried it on my back and lay it kindly in the ute while he fussed about me the NERVOUS NELLY. At home I was his navvy lumping canvas up the stairs to the studio and rolling it out across the floor. No witnesses to this. All private, him and me.

He goes—Look at that Hugh! How about that Hugh! We will make a bloody big picture here Hugh! It is a beauty! Will you cut it for me, mate? Just here, just here, you are a bloody genius Hugh!

But there is only one Genius in his VERSION OF EVENTS. Everyone is amazed that such a creature as Michael Boone would emerge from Bacchus Marsh which they assume must be a cess pit, misnaming it Buckus Marsh or Bacchus Swamp and thereby demonstrating they don't know what they're talking about although the best lamb chops in the southern hemisphere were produced there. Cleaver, saw, wooden block. I wished them to be mine.

When he asked me to cut his Dutch canvas I was very bloody tired, having walked all the way to town and up by the Guthries' dam where I got a whole family of ticks attached to the underside of my balls. I was weary and itchy but he must MAKE ART. Bless me, I never grudged him no matter what he has said about me. For instance, at night I lie in bed and pull my pillow across my head trying not to hear him talk to the DOZY RICH MAN. Oh what a bloody big burden I appear to be, all whisper and distress God save me.

Can you cut it for me, Hugh?

Did I ever hear him tell the Rich Man that his brother can track a single thread down across the canvas, follow it like a single black ant through the summer grass, lying on my stomach THE HUMAN MICROSCOPE? No, never. Bless me, did I complain? Did I ever point out how strange it was to now be granted control of the LETHAL BLADE because never, not ever, would my so-called family give me a SCABBARD, never would they let me draw the blade across the holy living skin. Hold the basin Jason, but never hold the knife. But now I am the one with the MURDER WEAPON and I can lie on the floor in his studio and follow a single weft thread of his Dutch canvas—not to him was this talent granted, nor my superior strength. It makes him very happy to watch me part one thread from its neighbour for nine feet and not one mistake the whole length of it. My perfect cut is a SECRET MARK OF GRACE that's what he told me don't worry that he doesn't believe in God and writes his HOLY WORDS without relent, long handle, stiff three-inch bristles. He pays $10 per brush and in a rage he writes God's words for ever. WHAT IS YOUR PROBLEM? as they say.

I was Slow Bones. I know its meaning no matter what I

said before. They would not give me the knife or steel or scabbard. Instead I must ride the bloody cart and pony taking orders. Lovely Lamb Chops today Mrs Puncheon. And would that be a pound of cat's meat once again? I never could accept I had been forbade the knife although I would have killed the beasts more kindly bless them their big eyes reflecting back my face at me. Thus does God in his mercy see our countenance.

For a long time I blamed my mother for not speaking up on my behalf. She was just a little thing, a cockney sparrow with great black sunken eyes, always on the lookout for the last day, final hour, our turn will come. She had a terror of knives, dear Mum, poor Mum, and who could blame her when you saw Blue Bones or Grandpa Bones walk in the back door? Big men always in a towering rage. Each night my mother took the knives and hid them in the Chubb safe. She had her left breast taken by amputation. God bless her. Therefore it follows. Hide the knives. But my ordained future was nightly locked away.

But when all was lost and gone, in later years, our shop and home turned into a video store, all hope abandoned, then was I appointed knife man to my brother's canvas. Explain this cruelty if you will. In this and other ways I became his MANSERVANT. For instance, in the studio there is a plastic ice-cream tub with tweezers laying in it, like something at the dentist's before he hurts your gums. These tweezers will not get mentioned when Michael Boone is holding forth with his opinions—Clement Greenberg is a radio mechanic, etc. You might be advised to ask him, Oh what is that bloody big bowl filled with tweezers? The answer is—So Hugh the idiot can kneel before me and remove from the wet paint all the little bits of flick and fleck the bodies of the dead the parts of matter the fluff and bumph and snot of life which interfere with the purity of TWO-DIMENSIONAL SPACE.

I have been informed that there is no one else on Earth who could part those threads for nine feet without an error. But then again I do not care, all is vanity, and many times I think I am nothing but a big swishing gurgling pumping clock, walking backwards and forwards along the road to Bellingen each day, spring, summer, flies, moths, dragonflies, all fluttering flittering tiny clocks, a mist of clocks, each moment closer to oblivion. Impediments to art. Who will remove us with the tweezers?

I never wished to die up here in northern New South Wales with the leeches and ticks and bloody flood sucking at the bank, everything damp, mouldy. I was born beneath the WERRIBEE RAIN SHADOW so give me a grave in a dry place, hard yellow soil where you can see the marks of crowbar like witchetty grub tracks on the rock of ages. I never wished to die here but my true home has been turned into a video store, mother, father all lost to me, so I am poor Hugh, bloody Hugh, the human clock.

Butcher Bones is not liked in Bellingen. It was the same in the Marsh. Who can like a man who shaves his head in order to prevent his father cutting his hair? No one liked him any more than they liked the GERMAN BACHELOR and then he was off to the city only returning briefly when Blue Bones had his stroke and his own mother wept begging him to take up the steel and scabbard, he would not although he returned to Melbourne and secretly worked in the William Angliss meat factory. He said I only have one life which is a lie. Now he has the condition of AMNESIA clearly forgetting what injury he had done to home and family and here in Bellingen he is always saying Oh, I am a COUNTRY BOY or I am from the Marsh but they see him there with his dark fast flicking eyes, cheating and lying and putting things on account of Jean-Paul Milan and he is only saved because they steal from Jean-Paul too.

It was one day or another. He was puddling in his paint, I

was approaching the township, the road rising up above the Bellinger River and the last flood had subsided leaving grass as flat as dead men and something like sad vomit not yet hosed away. By the pylons of the bridge there were still the old sticks piled up FLOTSAM JETSAM, a dreadful bower of bark, lantana, all sorts of vegetable and mineral, including a fence post with wire trailing like fish gut from its top hole. That was when I observed it, saw it from a distance, blue and grey, not much bigger than a breakfast sausage. At that moment a dirty big timber jinker came speeding into the corner, dropping gears, throwing bark, raising dust, tossing flies and thrips all breathing life, into the greatest of confusion. The world has ended, thought the fly. My heart was pumping, sloshing blood from one room to the next. Meat and music, two beats per second, I went ploughing down the hill, off the shoulder of the road down the embankment towards the river. What I had seen was my puppy's dry tail, his unlit byre, God save him. It was a shock, bless me, but there he was, his lip curled back, some evil thing had eaten at him. His bottom was half pulled out. God bless him, I pulled his feathery little body up with my whittled stick and I didn't know what then to do. I came up to the road, my new shirt torn by the fence. I was thinking I would get a wheat bag to put him in and take him home, it would be a muddy resting place, tucked up inside the ANCIENT FLOODPLAIN with the river rocks. I should have gone to the co-op they would have accommodated me, but the pub was closer and I went in there. I have my normal corner by the wireless. I didn't put him on the bar, everything hygienic.

Nothing was usual except Merle brought me my schooner and I set out to drink it, even at that moment wishing to be polite. Normally I would make the drink last hours but now I set to finish it immediately. It was that wet-ashtray-stinking time of day, that is, before Kevin from the co-op farts and lights his pipe. At first I had no company excepting a heroin addict with no bum inside his trousers, but then the Guthries entered. There are two Guthries, the bigger one is Evan but his brother is normally of a very decent disposition. I learned the Guthries had been on a fencing contract for three weeks and having just discovered that their cheque had bounced they were not in the best of moods. Gary Guthrie had announced he would take his D24 out to the fence line and destroy the last three weeks of work. He was very bitter. As there was no one but the heroin addict in the pub, and him completely silent, I could not help but hear the conversation. Likewise they observed my puppy. Evan did not speak to me but he told Merle I should be reported to the Health Inspector. I loudly asked Merle did she have a handy box because anything that would hold a dozen bottles could also hold my dog. She said she had just burnt all the cardboard. The heroin addict took his beer out to the footpath.

Evan then gave the opinion I was a moron for drinking with a dead dog. He was a big bugger, legs like the fence posts he spent his life burying in the earth. I did not answer him, relying on the brother, but the brother was downcast, his mind filled with vengeance such as ripping down three miles of fence and dozing it into the creek. In the hop-sour shadows of the public bar his plans were blooming like PATTERSON'S CURSE. Evan made a remark about the cause of the injury to the puppy's bottom, I turned the other cheek, but when he tried to violently confiscate the body, I was swift as an AZURE KINGFISHER flashing across the mustard yellow skin of the flood. I took his little finger, as crunchy as a dragonfly inside the beak.

Evan was what you call an OLD FAMILY in the district. His photo was on the wall, a ruckman in the Bellingen XVIII but now he was forced to descend to the level of the skirting board, howling, holding his FRACTURED METACARPAL against his chest.

IN THE WINK OF AN EYE he was brought low.

Gary moved towards me. I placed the dog carefully on the bar and Evan's protector understood his danger perfectly.

Listen Num-num, he said, you tell your fucking burglar brother he is no longer welcome in the district.

Thus I mistakenly believed that it was on account of Evan Guthrie's fractured metacarpal my brother and I would be cast out. I could not bear it. Everything I blamed Butcher Bones for I had now done myself. I proceeded homewards in great distress, a fly, a wasp, an ENEMY OF ART.

8

I cannot blame Hugh—that would be ridiculous—nor can I equate myself with Van Gogh. Just the same I am entitled to make the point that it was Vincent's saintly brother Theo who brought an end to sixty days of painting in Auvers-sur-Oise. You can find three thousand art books filled with bad reproductions and as many dull opinions that the sixty paintings from those sixty days were a 'final flowering' and the crows in Vincent's wheatfield were a 'clear sign' he was about to kill himself. But fuck me Jesus, a crow is just a bird and Vincent was alive, and there were crows and wheat in front of him and he was producing a canvas every day. He was as mad as a toilet brush—why not?—and as boring as a painter, and Dr Gachet may not have actually *invited* his patient to come and live with him, but painters do these things, so suck it up.

When the sun went down, when the light was lost, Gachet's house must have reeked of Vincent's need. So sorry, on everyone's behalf. At the same time, he was on the phone to God, and after sixty days he went down to visit Theo on the Paris train, not to plan a fucking *suicide*, but to talk about selling some of these paintings. Why not? There is not the least doubt he knew the value of what he had done.

From Auvers-sur-Oise to Paris is a very short journey. I have made it myself, quite recently, and a less romantic trip is hard to imagine, even in Sydney's western suburbs. In my case it was made even less appealing by my companions, one of whom had nasty lip sores and a mighty desire that we should share the same Pernod bottle. Ninety minutes after walking down Dr Gachet's now-famous garden path I was in Paris. Ditto Vincent. Theo was his dealer, his famous supporter, his brother, the man in whose arms he would soon die, but just the same Theo Van Bloody Gogh did exactly what dealers always do i.e. he told him how shitty the market was, that the fashion had not yet changed in his direction, that the collector who had promised to buy had now died, or gone away, or had lost his money in a divorce, etc. Theo, God help him, was *depressed*. He thought it was time for Vincent to face 'reality' which is what Vincent then did, for he went back to Auvers-sur-Oise and two days later he shot himself in the chest.

When I heard Hugh roaring bawling along the road, I had only had forty-seven days and they could not have made me stop with either rope or bullet. I had eight huge canvases stored in a bloody *manger*, and a ninth one lying flat and naked on the floor.

Hugh's face was beaten to a pulp, already swelling, a film of blood and snot all over the wide canvas of his cheeks, some of it spilling on to the desiccated corpse he carried so tenderly it might have been a newborn child. It took an hour to extract the story but even then I was confused, imagining the blood to be the result of his fight with Evan Guthrie. It would be another week before I learned that he had been seen on the road above the river banging his head against an ironbark and all the abrasions and bruises across his face, all the broken tissue that would soon swell up and leave him yellow, pink, purple as a foie gras terrine, all this he did to himself, for he, like me, misunderstood the situation.

This was not the first little finger he had broken, and the previous one had caused me more pain and loss than I can yet reveal. Hugh and I thought ourselves in a similar predicament again but, as you will see soon enough, whilst we were quite correct in thinking our tenancy in peril, nothing was exactly as it appeared to be. In any case, I did not abuse my brother this second time. I was sick at heart but did not show it. I encouraged him to continue with his immediate plan which was to find a high dry place to bury his dog whose queer light corpse I helped place in my best rucksack. Thus he set off, dog in pack, spade and crowbar in his hands, and I returned to my canvas. For I knew the clock was running, that soon the midgets of officialdom would be swarming around us, like a white-ant hatch threatening to glue itself to the perfect holy surface of the living paint.

Being short of supplies and having met resistance from Kevin at the co-op, I had had no work planned that day, but time is precious, passing with every breath and I decided I would touch the thing I had been frightened of the most, the framed embroidery our mother hung above her dreadful bed: 'IF YOU HAVE EVER SEEN A MAN DIE, REMEMBER THAT YOU, TOO, MUST GO THE SAME WAY. IN THE MORNING CONSIDER THAT YOU MAY NOT LIVE TILL EVENING, AND WHEN EVENING COMES DO NOT DARE TO PROMISE YOURSELF THE DAWN.'

I did not want to touch it, no more than put my hand on a flat iron, hiss of skin, smell of flesh. I spent a good hour cleaning up the studio, scraped the lino, laid down paper and a length of unprimed cotton duck. *If You Have Ever Seen a Man Die* I removed the mixers from the drills and set to clean them. There was no actual need to do this, but I slowly peeled all the accumulated paint that had made its own little planet on the X-shaped armature of blades. 'YOU MAY NOT LIVE TILL EVENING' and all the painted past was layered like liquorice allsorts, sedimentary rocks, green, black, gorgeous yellow, sparkling mica, fool's gold they call it in the Marsh. I did not wish to start. I scoured the blades with wire wool until they were burnished and then I screwed up my eyes and plunged the whirling shaft into the heart of Mars black, carbon black, graphite, 240 volts, 100 rpm, phthalo green with alizarin crimson and I had started. I was in. I shook the drips off that last mix, what a very cold light-sucking black was lying there, a lovely evil thing captive in a can. At its lovely nasty little heart was alizarin crimson. I could already calculate how I would edge those shapes as yet unborn—that alizarin crimson would make a border almost as black as black, but also, on the aft of 'PROMISE' like the burning edge of a leaf in a firestorm. Then I invaded ultramarine blue with a force of sweet burnt umber, thus giving birth to a new black as warm as a winter blanket for a twenty-thousand-dollar horse, and then I stained my cotton duck with a very fucking diluted dioxane purple, so watered down it was a pearly grey, a secret skin you can still see behind the smudges of, say, *Morn*, and on that site, and in other places too where my mother's dreadful fear was bent and twisted, you can today observe the pentimento, the erasures, the smudges, the changes of mind as I pushed, sometimes like Sisyphus, at the resistant letters which now must be made to serve me—not the Roman chisel or the language of the poets—until 'DO NOT DARE TO PROMISE' was as ugly and noble as the milk-factory fire of 1953, ten men dead amongst the twisted tin and smoke. On the last day, very early on a dew-bright morning, I made a series of washes, 9/10 gel, and these I lay, lighter than a river mist across the blacktop. As for the work itself, you can see it, finally, years later, in a serious museum, and I will not treat you like some dick-head day trader in an aeroplane who wants to know 'Should I know your name?'

But let me say only that I rubbed at it and buffed and scraped and sanded until it was an argument both within itself and against itself. Jesus it would put the fear of God in you, to see the skeins of secret black, it could choke you, and fuck you, and put your naked toes on to the fire.

This work continued three days. And it was done. Ominously, there were no visitors. And by that time Hugh had disposed of his dog and his little eyes were deep and hidden and he was very quiet around the property, mostly hacking at the thistles. I stayed away from Bellingen, judging it wiser to avoid the crime scene completely and drive the extra thirty minutes to Coffs Harbour. There were already difficulties—limited supplies, no phthalo green, a change of palette I would rather not have made. On the fourth day after the meta-carpal came the first assailant, an idiot from the Bellingen Council with long white socks, a building inspector with a clipboard in his hand. He went around the property with a surveyor's chain, measuring the distance from the riverbank to the septic tank. That's how a small town gets rid of you. They declare your house in contravention of the regulations. Why would I give a shit? It wasn't mine.

Money very short. I cooked baked vegetables until even I was sick of them, and Hugh—God bless him—did not once complain. But all this time no one actually told us why we were now hated. We were fighting the wrong war, for the wrong reasons, and it was not until eleven days after the broken finger that the police came rattling across the cattle grid, not the locals but two plainclothes fellows with a driver from Coffs Harbour. Seeing the car, Hugh fled arrest, charging headfirst across the floodplain and I did not find him until dark when, having heard the police car finally depart, he emerged, wild-eyed and muddy, from a wombat hole.

9

The Art Police are cops, that's all, and they will come and call on you as unexpectedly as Jehovah's Witnesses and for reasons just as stupid. However, on that soupy day in Bellingen I was ignorant of the breed and I mistakenly assumed my visitors were typical.

There was an older man of fifty or so, tall and heavily built like an old-style walloper but with an odd almost lackadaisical gait and a big square head always turning this way and that as if he were trying to spot the Eiffel bloody Tower. He wore a ratty Fair Isle sweater and smoked a stinky pipe from which he continually blew globs of tar and spit on to my pasture. This Detective Ewbank exuded the sloppy good-naturedness of a packing clerk two weeks from retirement whilst, at the same time, having some weird aerial connection with his brainy-looking partner.

The younger man, Amberstreet, was not much more than twenty-five but he had already carved on his face a deep set of V-shaped creases which pointed like diagram arrows towards his pale grey eyes. Barry, his mate called him; his mouth was thin, and downturned, and perhaps because he was so stooped and spectacularly unmuscled, he made me imagine that the Art Police must be a very fucking unusual caste indeed, and in the same way that Jean-Paul's beautiful wife might suggest hidden qualities in her very plain husband, Amberstreet's weird birdlike looks gave a value to his mate's pipe and Fair Isle sweater that could not have been more inflated, not even by Sotheby's.

These cops caught me flat-footed, why wouldn't they? They didn't say they were from Sydney. I thought they had come from Bellingen, for Hugh. Instead they wished to inspect my work and I took them over to the shed to see it. Yes, I had obtained the paint and canvas by what you might call false pretences, so what would they do? Hang me? Yes, I had sold about a tonne of fertilizer to Mrs Dyson and Jean-Paul, I guessed, had got upset. The rich are like that, overcome by panic attacks at the thought they are possibly being *used*. God, what sort of animal would do that to them?

I walked Ewbank and Amberstreet to the shed as if they were Macquarie Street collectors on a studio visit, and I must say Ewbank was very bloody amiable at that stage, even if he did inform me that I had a record or, as he put it, was 'known to the police'. Otherwise he was full of questions about the veggie garden and the Brahmin cattle Dozy had agisted on my roadside paddock. Amberstreet, meanwhile, was very quiet, but even this was in no way threatening. As Ewbank pointed out to me, his mate seemed mostly concerned about the danger of getting cowshit on his new Doc Martens.

The shed was a shed, the back third a loading ramp filled with Mrs Dyson's hay bales, the front two-thirds earth-floored. Here I parked the tractor, stored the chain saw, the brush cutter and what garden tools I had not left out in the weather. Here too I had rolled my nine canvases around long cardboard tubes. They leaned neatly against the wall, just like the rake, the shovel, the scythe and so on. Of course this was not ideal, but I obviously could not have them in the studio shouting in my ear.

'OK Michael,' said Detective Ewbank, 'it's time for show-and-tell.'

I made some joke—forget it now—about a warrant being required.

'It's in the car,' said Amberstreet. 'We'll show you later.'

This gave me a jolt, but I got over it. What was the worst thing that could happen? I'd be charged with making art on Jean-Paul's credit? Fuck him. The patience of the rich is

easily strained. But I remained an obedient little citizen and I
rolled out the first painting *I, the Speaker, Ruled as King over
Israel*, laying it on a springy three-inch cushion of improved
pasture.

So clock this: eight miles out of Bellingen, NSW, me in
my shorts and bare feet and Amberstreet like some crane or
heron with his short upper body and his long thin legs and
cinched-in belt and the whole of his skeleton throwing all its
force into his eyes as he looked down at my canvas. The
work had a sort of nailed-down fuck-you quality with all the
process showing. I had—I hope I told you—already begun to
glue down rectangles of canvas on to the broader field. Even
in the warm misty sunlight it looked very bloody good indeed.

The police said nothing throughout the first inspection,
not even when we found the nest of baby mice living in the
centre of a roll. To tell the truth, I was almost happy. I could
not go to gaol, and the work looked so good, in no way
diminished by the smell of mice, or the waving light-brown
watermark that now ran, like the *hamon* on a Japanese sword,
along the bottom edge.

Amberstreet wished to view *I, the Speaker* again. And I
was an artist. Why wouldn't I wish to show? I watched the
strange little critic, arms folded, shoulders hunched. Ewbank,
for his part, began to whistle 'Danny Boy'.

'What would this be worth?' Amberstreet asked me. 'On
the market, at auction.'

I assumed he was trying to think how to recoup the cost
of Raphaelson's one-pound tubes, so I told him it was worth
exactly nothing at this moment. I was out of fashion.
Couldn't sell a painting to save my bloody life.

'Yes, I understand that, Michael. Five years ago, you
might have got $35,000 for this.'

'No.'

'There's no point in lying, Michael. I know what you used
to sell for. The thing is now, you're in free fall. Isn't that so?'

I shrugged.

'I'll give you five,' he said suddenly.

'Oh Jesus,' said Ewbank, and walked over to inspect the concrete pigsties, whacking at them with a length of irrigation pipe. 'Jesus,' he cried, 'Joseph and Mary.'

'No tax,' said Amberstreet and I saw his eyes all glistening. 'All cash.'

Ewbank, meanwhile, was pissing himself with laughter, shoving heaps of black shag into his fat pipe. His younger colleague's face, by contrast, was creased like tissue paper protecting the bright stones of his eyes.

I won't say I wasn't seriously tempted.

Ewbank had wandered back, puffing on his pipe. He had an extraordinary way of doing this, making his big black eyebrows shoot up every time he took a puff, the result being that he looked to be in a state of active astonishment.

'I couldn't give it all at once. I'd pay you over a year.'

If it had been a lump sum, I might have said yes, but it was not enough to save me so I turned him down. Even now I don't know if what happened next was connected to my refusal, but I don't think so. It was more as if we'd had a little pleasant break and now we must return to work.

Amberstreet frowned and nodded. 'I understand,' he said. He then turned to his partner: 'You got the tape, Raymond?'

Ewbank withdrew from his pocket a dirty-looking handkerchief and then a very snazzy little tape measure of a type I had never seen before, as if he might be a surgeon with instruments designed in Tokyo for a task so specialized it had no English name. My balls tightened at the sight of it.

'Measure the addition,' Amberstreet said, an ugly word for the rectangle which bore the single word 'GOD' with all its gooseturd grey and phthalo green smudged and shifted in the battle with the resistant 'O'.

I watched Ewbank measure it, like you watch your own car crash happen.

'Thirty by twenty and one-half inches,' he announced.

Amberstreet gave me a cherubic little smirk.

'Oh, Michael!' he said to me, taking in his belt one more notch. I suddenly understood he was a scary little shit.

'What?'

'Thirty by twenty and a half,' he said. 'Oh, Michael!'

'What?'

'Not familiar?'

'No.'

'The same dimensions as Mr Boylan's Leibovitz.'

I thought, What is this? Cabbala? Numerology?

'Michael, I thought you were a clever man. We know the exact dimensions. They're in the catalogue raisonné.'

'What would it matter if it was the same dimensions?'

'It would matter', said Amberstreet, 'because as you know Mr Boylan's home was burgled and a work by Jacques Leibovitz was stolen.'

'Bullshit. When?'

Hearing this Ewbank gave a mighty big suck in of his pipe so his eyebrows disappeared into his hair.

'Oh.' Amberstreet smiled incredulously. 'You didn't know!'

'Don't be so bloody sarcastic. How could I know?'

'Like you know John Lennon's dead,' said Ewbank.

'You could try any newspaper,' suggested Amberstreet. 'You could turn on the radio.'

'John Lennon's not dead you dick.'

'Don't change the subject, Michael. We're here to investigate a burglary.'

It was only then, as we stood staring down at my painting, that I realized something very serious was going on.

'Someone pinched his Leibovitz?'

'Three weeks ago, Michael. You are the only one who knew it was there.'

'He never showed it to me. Ask him,' I said, but I was seeing the hateful look on Dozy's face as he passed me in the fog.

'But you knew he had it. You knew he was going away, down to Sydney for the night.'

'He's always going down to Sydney. You really think I'm stupid enough to glue a 2-million-dollar painting to my canvas and then cover it with paint? Is that your point? It's very easy to see you're not a bloody artist.'

'We're not saying you've got it under there. We're saying we need to remove the work for X-raying and IR spectography.'

'You bugger. You just want to nick my fucking canvas.'

'Calm down, pal,' said Ewbank. 'You'll get a proper receipt. You can write the description yourself.'

'When would I get it back?'

The older man's eyebrows shot up alarmingly.

'That would depend,' said Amberstreet.

'On what?'

'If we have to keep it for the trial.'

I really did not know what was going on. A certain part of me thought the fucks were robbing me. Another part of me was thinking I was in very serious shit. I don't know which was the better or the worse, and in the end, after I had spent three hours making a crate, a time they used to photograph my pry bar and my other tools, and after I had personally helped them load it in their wagon, they showed me the huge press file on the Leibovitz theft. I read the front-page headlines by the light of their headlights, still clueless about John Lennon, but relieved to understand that I, at least, was not being robbed.

10

Of course the pipsqueak Michael Boone was ignorant of anything that did not personally benefit him, and on the subject of the wombat he incorrectly used the expression MUDDLEHEADED which might be the title of a book but is wrong because the wombat is a clever fellow who can, God bless him, do a barrel-roll-with-twist inside his tunnel, scratch his ears, flatten himself like dough under a rolling pin and I knew this because I had SEEN IT WITH MY OWN EYES. Of course I never told my brother and he had no idea what plans I had made in preparation for the visit by police, although the moment I snapped Evan Guthrie's metacarpal I expected BYAR-BYAR-BYAR blue light flashing THE WRATH OF THE LAW and then I would not be able to rely on Butcher Bones to save me. Many a time he had threatened to have me put under MANAGED CARE where they would remove the tartar from my teeth.

The coppers were SLOW AS A WET WEEK and thus provided good opportunity to widen one long branch of wombat tunnel. The first time I entered that maze was the day after I buried the puppy and I took my mattock and torch and the lid of a 4-gallon drum of molasses to act as a shield, but I never had trouble with the wombats, quickly learning to make a friendly grunting noise on approach. The smallest I named FELLOW, bless him. He would sometimes sniff my hair but not on the day the police finally visited when I lay inside the entrance with my boots at the mouth, my nose pointing down into the dark, no bad smells, just earth and roots and when I had to fart I was very sorry. After I had FORTY WINKS I emerged to discover the sky black and mixed with ultramarine and the camphor laurel in silhouette and a great yellow spill of light from the shed where I saw Butcher Bones busy with a saw and trestle, cutting pine planks. Bless me, I thought, they are making me a coffin.

The Butcher was a great one for blame, nothing better to get his eyes flicking left to right. It was his SPECIALITY DE MAISON, to always know exactly who was at fault. When the police at last departed and I revealed my presence, I was staggered that the finger was not pointed at me.

'That bitch, that fucking bitch!' he cried, and I was pleased indeed, not being a female. Soon I understood he was referring to Marlene, an admirer of *The Magic Pudding*. He had been so HOT FOR HER but now he explained to me she was BEHIND ALL THIS and suddenly she was pretty much a MASTER CRIMINAL. I knew from experience there was no better proof of innocence than to be blamed by Butcher Bones and this time, like every other, he would soon, with no apology, change his tune with a DO-SI-DO. In any case I was not the GUILTY PARTY and I was most relieved I would not be singing songs in my lonely cell but I was worried they would take an innocent woman in my place. What could I say? My brother's neat little-girl ears were filled with wax and he roared me up for getting my new shirt dirty and then he telephoned Dozy Boylan to boast that he had solved the CASE.

Dozy replied, If you ever call me again I'll come and put a bullet in your arse.

After this the Butcher sat at the table and was quiet a long while. Then he began to stare up at the rafters and I was concerned he had gone mad so I asked him would he like a cup of tea. No reply, but I made it anyway. Four spoons of sugar, as he liked it. No thank-yous offered—who expected them?—but he cupped his sap-stained hands around the chipped old mug which our poor mother had once held IN THE MORNING CONSIDER THAT YOU MAY NOT LIVE

TILL EVENING, poor old Mum, God bless her. The back of my neck had gone VOLCANIC and I asked him, What will we do now, Butcher? If he had raved and ranted and abused me I would have felt in SAFE HANDS but instead he gave me what is known as a WAN SMILE and it was clear all the puff had gone out of him and he left me alone then, crawling into his bed without undressing. What would I do? I was forbidden to touch the light switches or other electrical appliances so my bedroom was bright all night as if I was a battery hen and I dreamed it was summer in the Marsh, me and the pony somehow lost up on Lerderderg Street then captured by the Catholics—what a bloody nightmare. I woke next morning to hear a great howl and I rushed out in my pyjamas to see what NEW MISADVENTURE had befallen Butcher Bones. I found him still dressed as the night before, and in his hand he had the drill, its shaft dripping with his evil bloody alizarin crimson.

What is it, Butch?

Can't you see? The bastards have turned off the power.

My first thought was that this was a punishment from the STATE ELECTRICITY COMMISSION because we left the lights on all night long but after the power had been off for three weeks, and we had been carrying water from the river and digging holes to do our business in, we learned that the citizens of Bellingen had ordered disconnection as if we were hostage-takers who must be driven from our hole. On top of this came an EVICTION ORDER and a DEMOLITION NOTICE because Jean-Paul's house was built too close to the river. Of course the council had approved the building years before so it must have walked closer to the bank than previously. In any case, it was all a PACK OF LIES and after we were finally driven out, the house must have walked back to its approved position on the site.

As for Jean-Paul himself, as Butcher said, he should be condemned by the Ryde Council on account of his arse being built too close to the public footpath and on our long flight back to Sydney, a full eight-hour drive, he was filled with sarcastic comments of this sort about the BOURGEOIS ART COLLEC-TOR but I enjoyed the drive. He took us up to Dorrigo, God bless him, and then into the high country of Armidale where the summers are dry and the paddocks were gold and the windows of the ute rolled down and the seat belts flapping—slap, slap, slap—against the door frames. The old ute had no air-conditioning just a DUCT opened by a foot-long lever which caused the release of long-trapped dust. Lord what perfumes—honey and gum blossoms and rubber hoses. We were Boones, big men, packed in tight, arse by arse, our heads bumping the ceiling on the potholes. My brother was a tense and fearsome driver but he refused to travel at less than ninety miles an hour, below which speed the bent propeller shaft set up a terrible vibration. He drove like his father did before him, with his elbows wide, his chest pushed forward, his angry eyes glaring straight ahead. So we sped like demons hour after hour through the gold and blue as if we were SIR ARTHUR BLOODY STREETON or FREDERICK McCUBBIN both painters Butcher loved even while he sneered at them.

I farted and cried, Fire's on! If you know the Streeton painting you get the joke.

Entering the outskirts of Sydney, we were skint, the last of the fertilizer money being spent on petrol. At Epping Road we abandoned the Pacific Highway, that long familiar winding road once used by black fellows, and then tooled down to Lane Cove and East Ryde. We were both watching the petrol gauge and very quiet and thoughtful as we re-entered the old familiar country of DIVORCE and PATRON-AGE both of these being situated in the exact same street. God help us. Before the Gladesville Bridge we turned on to Victoria Road and then right into Monash Road and as we entered Orchard Court we were already in contravention of a court order that neither of us were permitted to be within

five miles of THE MARITAL HOME. My balls were shrivelled. What would happen to us now? My brother made that
old familiar right-hand turn, past the marital madness, and
straight on to Jean-Paul's lawn. Then Butcher Bones opened
the glove box and removed a hammer, bless me, what had he
become?

11

Being as familiar with that cul-de-sac as with my own pyjamas, I ploughed into Jean-Paul's perfect lawn with 100 per
cent understanding i.e. I knew I could rely on the neighbours to call my patron before I turned the engine off.

I'd already had a whole life in Orchard Court where I had
been not only a celebrity, but a famous lovesick fool. It was
here I brought my bride. I built a bloody tower where she
could meditate—believe it!—and an amazing tree house of
the type a boy might dream about but never see in waking
life—three platforms, two ladders, all lodged inside the
branches of a lovely old jacaranda whose gorgeous purple
petals, fallen two months before, were now rotting like
heartache across the slate-grey roof. I had been a different
man in those days, so naive that lawyers and police could
later decide my own paintings were marital assets i.e. not my
property. The canvases were there now, a whole life's work,
which the court had 'deemed'—as the saying is—that the
plaintiff could do with as she wished.

There had been no room in the ute for anything but
paint and canvas and it was not by accident that the great
alizarin crimson masterpiece was sitting on the top of the
load. I removed the tonneau cover and attacked its crate with

the claw hammer, and as the stainless-steel screws screeched like murder victims, I could already hear the telephone screaming in Jean-Paul's pool house.

I used Hugh's earlobe to persuade him from the ute and he took several swings at me before the penny dropped— restraining order or no, it was in his interests to roll out this canvas across our patron's lawn.

Jean-Paul was a heartless little fuck but he had the worst case of art lust you ever knew, and if his eye was not in the tiniest bit *educated*, it was easily aroused, and this made him buy a huge amount of shit and, on some occasions, bet against the auction records. I admit that I was fresh from vandalizing his *house of few possessions*, causing ructions in the Promised Land, stealing fertilizer and allegedly cheating him in other ways, but all of that would be forgotten if, on looking down on to his lawn, he understood a fraction of what I'd done. Then he would transform himself from a lump of dogshit to a splendid silver thing.

The evening clouds threw a galah-pink cast across the scene; it didn't matter. This painting could suck up the damage caused by pink, by show-off lawns, by secret swimming pools and all that they entail. It was like a fucking stock car, indestructible. As I waited impatiently for my patron to appear I was so very deeply confident, swaying on my heels beside poor frightful Hugh whose nose was running, whose mouth was twisted in a shit-eating grin, a rictus of hope and terror, and together we anticipated the perfect little blow-dried, swept-back 'do' which, if you wished to suck up badly enough, would suddenly remind you—God, I have been disgusting in my time—that Jean-Paul looked just like JFK.

The plan of battle worked very well at first—car on lawn, phone in pool house, painting laid out right way round and, finally, my patron's head appearing in the study window.

Except the head was not my patron's. God, I hardly recognized her. It was the plaintiff, his neighbour, the woman I had fucked back to front and sideways, held in the night, the most beautiful creature ever born. And there she was, the mother of my son, with her prim little mouth and her sharp enquiring nose and her expensive tan and I could not even see the really costly part of her, the shoes. She was visible for just a second, behind the glass. Hugh whimpered, climbed into the ute, and shut the door.

The bomb was now ticking, never mind. I waited for Jean-Paul. He too appeared and I felt him suck on the bait and in less than two minutes I had a hit—the patron at his door—tiny bathing suit, smooth brown legs, knitted cotton sweater, dark glasses in his hand. Stepping down on to the lawn, he did not waste time acknowledging me but went directly at the painting, circling it, staring down, a bullshit parade of connoisseurship. But I had been around Jean-Paul too long, so I'll tell you what he was really thinking while he flicked the wings of his Ray-Bans: What the fuck is this? and How little can I get it for?

'I'll give you a grand,' he said. 'Cash. Now.'

I knew I had him, sans doubt, *sans souci*, sans fucking question, so I began to roll up the canvas. Suck my dick, I thought. One fucking grand.

'Come on mate,' he said. 'You know what's happening at the auctions.'

He was a fool to bargain with a butcher. Worse, he called me 'mate', the first sign of his need and he was not helped by the arrival of a police car whose blue light was in a spastic fit as it came to the defence of Orchard Court.

While Hugh was hiding on the floor of the ute, the policeman parked his car and then, I noticed, locked the door. Then my little boy, my huge beefy eight-year-old boy, burst out of Jean-Paul's house. With a great dreadful cry like a crow or a donkey, he climbed me, the little snarly scabby fierce bony beautiful thing. He got his arms around my neck and I looked at him and he was bawling and Jean-Paul—in the middle of all this, the little creep—was offering me two thousand, and the copper was coming towards me with a determined look upon his face and then Hugh, oh bless him, was out of the car and running low to the ground, as dense and rapid as a wombat in the night. The copper was neither young nor violent in appearance and he let out a big shriek as Hugh struck him from the side and the pair of them went rolling over and over and down into the street.

'I'll give you five,' said Jean-Paul, 'plus the lawyer.'

My son smelled of chlorine and ketchup. He was a big burly fellow with a deep chest and he got all his heavy limbs wrapped around my head. I kissed his arm, and brushed the sweet soft downy hair across my face.

'Don't go, Daddy,' he said.

'I'll take ten,' I told Jean-Paul. 'In cash. And you fix up the cop. That or forget it.'

Jean-Paul fled into the house. I looked into my son's serious brown eyes and wiped the tears from his freckled Butcher cheeks. 'It's not my fault,' I said, 'you know that.' Dear God why do our children have to carry all this weight?

Then Jean-Paul re-emerged with the familiar envelope. Not the first time he had shared his secret—the piles of hundreds he kept taped beneath his kitchen drawers.

'Count it,' he said.

'Fuck you.'

He was carrying a glass of whisky and I remember thinking that he was very naive to imagine he could buy the coppers with a single drink, and so convinced was I of this unworldliness that although I witnessed what happened next, I did not understand it at the time. Jean-Paul ordered Hugh to his feet and then, as the policeman began to rise, threw the glass of Scotch all over him.

'You're drunk,' he said, 'how dare you!'

There was other stuff occurring so what the policeman said, I do not know, but I remember seeing the poor bugger wash his face at the garden tap. Meanwhile, I was showing my son the correct way to treat an unstretched canvas. What else was I to do? Go hiking? We kneeled together on the lawn, in contravention of the court order, and rolled the best work of my life around a cardboard tube.

That was how, when I was bleeding, wounded, Jean-Paul Milan got possession of *If You Have Ever Seen a Man Die* for ten thousand dollars. I should be grateful for the larceny?

12

Although you will never hear this from the Butcher, our patron was our saviour time and time again. Now he loaned us an entire four-storey DEVELOPMENT POSSIBILITY in Bathurst Street, a site well situated, close to the George Street entertainment district and transportation. Of course my brother was a genius so there was no need to thank Jean-Paul. This was a PATTERN OF BEHAVIOUR previously observed. For instance, our mother had sold her twenty acres at Parwan so the Butcher could further his studies at Footscray Tech but in all his thousands of MEDIA PROFILES my brother never mentioned his family's kindness. He portrayed his departure from the Marsh as an ASCENSION from a cesspit, holy fire blasting from his hairy arse.

At Jean-Paul's property in Bathurst Street he immediately set to the front door with drills and hammers, securing a padlock on the outside and a galvanized bolt inside, all this IRRATIONAL ACTIVITY being solely to prevent the legal owner gaining entry and presumably stealing the POST-COMMENCEMENT MASTERPIECES contained therein. Hav-

ing previously served as an ARTHUR MURRAY DANCING
SCHOOL the building was already well equipped with lights
and mirrors FIFTEEN HUNDRED SQUARE FEET per floor
and therefore a good place for making art. But now my
brother did not wish to paint at all. I must be stupid to have
expected that he would. Instead he decided to retrieve the
work confiscated by Detective Amberstreet for in his CON-
FUSED MIND this huge canvas was now hanging on the wall
in the headquarters of the New South Wales police. Imagine. All the VICE SQUAD with their big fat woodies come to
have a Captain Cook.

The first night he ground his teeth and kicked me in the
balls by accident, Lord save us, he thrashed around, giving
orders in a rage. Night and day my brother was in a fret
about the place in history which had been given to him and
then taken back again. What happiness had he gained by
leaving home?

First thing in the morning, nothing would deter him, but
he must have a chat to the police and have them return his
painting ASAP. Had it slipped his mind that he was a SUS-
PECT in a larceny a party to an ASSAULT and in contravention of a court order to go no closer than 5 miles to the
MARITAL RESIDENCE? Had he forgotten he had been ILL
WITH FEAR only last July when he was sent to Long Bay for
his BREAK AND ENTER? He told me police can do what
they like to you. He would have had to be blind not to notice
swarms of coppers on the streets around the Arthur Murray
Dancing School, deaf not to hear their sirens in the night
as they pursued the so-called ASIAN GANGS. Due to the
muggy March weather we had been forced to sleep with
the windows open and thus could hear PERVERTS down in
the alley and DRUG ADDICTS arguing and the footsteps of
people fleeing from the Asian gangs. During the night I was
pleased to have the protection of the locks. At the same time

I never liked to be shut inside a house, so when he went off to the police I was UP AND OFF like a greyhound after an electric hare.

Always about, all my life, whether on the chair in front of our shop or in the pony cart taking orders. In Bellingen always on the road, the air in summer thick with floating thistle seeds and spiders travelling miles like balloonists on their webs, and in the city too, I would rather be outside during the hours when it was safe to be so, and I took a folding chair down to the footpath and witnessed all the human clocks passing me, pumping, sloshing—there is one, there another, and each one the centre of the world. You can go half mad looking at them, like gazing at the stars at night and thinking of infinity. What a strain it is. Our mother suffered it, always looking at eternity with her watery eyes, poor Mum, God bless her.

I was not sitting on my chair long before a young policeman told me I could not do that without a permit from the City of Sydney. As the SEAT OF GOVERNMENT was just behind St Andrew's Cathedral I went there and MADE ENQUIRIES, but no one could understand me and so I walked around the streets and when I was tired I would open my ILLEGAL CHAIR but not for long.

There were police everywhere in Sydney. What threat this represented Butcher never could decide. One moment he was screaming about the expense of his parking tickets and the next he was tearing them up like confetti and declaring that if you did not pay them they would get lost in the system. Many is the time he overparked and double-parked, even outside police headquarters in Darlinghurst, a location he would return to time and time again. First off he left me in the ute while he went in to locate his painting. Returning, he would not say how the police had responded, but that night his DRINKING PROBLEM surfaced once again.

Shortly thereafter we had a visit from a certain Robert

Colossi, a thin curly-haired POT-SMOKER who was con-
tracted to take photographs of Butcher's paintings for the
galleries. But my brother soon had reason to regret he had
paid one thousand dollars cash for UNUSABLE transparencies and he threw them in the bin and immediately drove to
an address in Redfern and I waited in the ute. When Butcher
came running out I understood this must have been the residence of Robert Colossi because he was carrying a very
heavy HASSELBLAD camera valued in excess of $2000 this
being JUST COMPENSATION for his loss. After this time,
this asset was stored on top of the hot-water service and
Butcher would not unlock the door no matter who rang the
bell. To me he gave a knocking code SOS but he would not
provide a key in case I was robbed by the photographer.
Soon he gave a key to a total stranger, a woman who worked
in the bookstore in the Queen Victoria Building. It is a fair
guess she was short and had big bosoms but as she never
used the key I have no right to say.

As Colossi's transparencies had been a PILE OF SHIT my
brother determined that the pair of us would visit the galleries and display the paintings IN THE FLESH. The following Monday morning he parked the ute on the No Standing
place in Bathurst Street and so we had a BLUE with a parking
cop which resulted in a threat of immediate arrest and a
hundred-dollar fine but Butcher said this did not matter
because the ticket would be lost in the system. As we loaded
the ute my heart was racing like a TWO-BOB WATCH but
soon we were in Paddington outside the PINAKOTHEK and
we parked in sight of the front door and carried the first
crated painting inside, a big room ugly as WATSON MOTORS
with shiny concrete floors and so-called works of art hung
around the walls. These paintings were red and blue and
green, so badly done the colours winked and jumped like
fleas on a blanket thereby creating a feeling of ANXIETY
beyond the range of VALIUM.

The young NANCY BOY behind the desk mistook us for FEDEX or DHL and he could not wait to get us put in our proper place which he judged to be the loading dock.

Where's Jim? says Butcher Bones, and we laid our crate down on the floor.

There's no Jim, said the Nancy Boy. And you can't bring that crate in here.

But the Butcher was wearing our father's wide thin grin. Jim Agnelli, he says.

Mr Agnelli passed away, said the fellow.

If Butcher felt grief, he did not have the time to show it. Well, he said. I am Michael Boone.

This name seemed not to have the effect he had desired. He added: And I came to show Jim what I've been up to.

He did not say, Shame I missed him, but that was his tone.

In that case, said the young fellow, I'd be happy to look at your transparencies. Perhaps you could leave them with me.

You know who I am? the Butcher asked but it was clear the young fellow had not been reading five-year-old issues of *ART & AUSTRALIA*. Well never mind, he said, you'll bloody know me in a moment. Hugh, he ordered, get the drill.

Yes sir, no sir, but just the same I wished my father Blue Bones could see me as I sought the LETHAL drill and screwdriver attachment, displaying the nous to return with a thirty-foot extension cord to reach the 240V outlets. Quick as a wink, I had it all set up. Nobody told me do not touch the switches.

The young fellow was not so pleased to see the drill and soon we were the object of a HISSY FIT but nothing could stop the Butcher where his ART was concerned and soon the drill was screaming and he had the screws out of his crate and we were rolling out his canvas a dreadful blasphemy the WORK OF A MADMAN in my opinion.

I expected the Nancy Boy to have CONNIPTIONS but

instead he folded his arms across his chest and cocked his handsome head and a little smile made its presence known at the corner of his mouth.

Oh Michael BOONE, he said. Of course.

That's right, said the Butcher, but he didn't puff himself. Instead his big chin shivered and his eyes went smaller than before. He was out of style. Even I saw that. I helped him roll up his canvas and he could not wait to make an exit. The Nancy Boy must have felt sorry for him as he stopped and picked up all the screws we had abandoned in our rush.

Transparencies are really so much better, he said as he dropped the screws into my palm.

You would think the Butcher would be destroyed but he bought 12 bottles of wine @ $40 per and in the morning he had got his puff back. What he needed was an ARMANI suit and that night when I came home with my chair he was looking like a bouncer at a strip club. I did not ask him how much money we had remaining but he immediately decided we would go to an OPENING together and he advised me to eat and drink what was on the trays because our funds were running low and we would not be having dinner from then on. It turned out that there was nothing on offer but Kraft cheese and pickled gherkins and I knew I was going to be badly BOUND UP if this continued. Afterwards he must have had an urgent need to NETWORK because he took me back to Bathurst Street and locked me in FOR SAFETY, bless me. I walked up and down the stairs a great deal and for a long time I sat on my chair just inside the door to the street. On one occasion someone attempted to enter and I successfully pretended to be an angry TIE DOG.

Early next morning Butcher was back and we once more loaded up the ute and when he had shaved his head again we set off like ELECTROLUX MEN to present our wares. The Armani suit now smelled like an East Melbourne brewery and I was in no way surprised that my brother required the

HAIR OF THE DOG before he faced the galleries. It was a dreadful business for him, day after day without relent, and there was no SMOKE-OH, no free time to wander off down George Street and set up my chair in the shade beneath the Cahill Expressway. Some of the proprietors were nice to Butcher and once we got taken to a Chinese restaurant but many of the younger generation could not give a FLYING FUCK about Michael Boone and by the third day he was DRUNK AS A SKUNK from brekkie onwards and that was how he came to crash the ute into a Jaguar parked in the lane beside Watters Gallery. As always he could admit no fault and when he had reversed twice and crashed twice more, he sped off down the dead-end lane, bouncing against all sorts of bins and cars leaving behind an entire bumper bar which might easily have been used in evidence against him.

That was a Wednesday night. There were no openings and he bought a flagon of McWILLIAMS CLARET @ $8.95 and then took me to the Hare Krishna Temple in Darling-hurst where even my brother looked a giant of AUSTRALIAN RULES. There was not a steak or chop or even a decent butcher's sausage. Eating their horrible foreign food I thought I would go mad myself to see what we had come to. I resolved to take my chair and set off to the Marsh again, and I might have done it if I could have found the road. Sometimes I am sorry I didn't do it. It would have been a better life by far if I was not afraid.

13

The moment you think you've got the bugger happy, he is in the shit—there's been a brawl, an accident, frottage, larceny, arson, a misunderstanding about removing goldfish from a bowl. Every new town or street or city is a problem which was why, in Bathurst Street, I was very pleased to discover, in the middle of Arthur Murray's former dance floor, a lop-sided, dingy, bronze, battered, twenty-dollar steel chair, no longer much to sit on, but useful for more than hiding dope or changing lightbulbs.

'Bloody chair,' Hugh said. 'Bless me.' And took posses-sion with his big square arse.

My brother had been raised on a chair, had spent his life after third grade on a chair, rocking back and forward in front of the shop. So when he stood and folded up his trea-sure, I didn't have to ask him where he planned to go. He was so fucking happy, I had to smile.

Outside was a decent width of footpath, and although close to the crowds of George Street, it was quiet enough for what Hugh craved, the chance to politely watch the world go by. Soon I set him up, potato chips on one side, Coca-Cola on the other, and as I headed back inside he turned to me, wrinkling his nose up towards squinting eyes, a sign that he was either very happy or about to fart. Beauty, I thought, that's done. But of course it wasn't done at all and half an hour later, coming down to check on him, I found him missing.

I wish I could say this shit gets easier with practice. It does not help that he's ham-armed, slope-shouldered, wildly strong—each time I think he's dead, drowned, run over, picked up by sick-ohs in a van with sliding doors. And there is not a thing that I can do but wait, so all that afternoon while I was unsuccessfully trying to organize a line of credit, I ran up and down the stairs like some hairy reincarnation of our mother waiting for Blue Bones to turn up from the foot-ball in Geelong. Each time she thought him dead, declared us orphans, and each time he came in piss-faced drunk, and we boys helped him down the hall, all sixteen stone of him.

'Come on Butcher, come on young'un, be a good fellow and go down to the Chinaman's for me.' At the Chinaman's they could not see my mother's face, so it was easy for them to love my dad.

In similar fashion I now waited for my brother and when I heard him hammering on the door I became the living fury in my mother's eyes.

'You stupid cunt, where have you been?'

Well, he and his chair had been Waltzing Matilda. This sounds good but it was crap—he liked to wander, but he could not be trusted with a key and he would have gone ape shit if I was not there when he finally returned. That's how I began to take him and his damn chair around the galleries, but never mind, there were problems worse than Hugh. For instance, it was soon made very clear to me that I would never get a show without my two most persuasive pieces; one of these had been stolen by the cops, the other by Jean-Paul. Easy. You would think, Just borrow them. But Jean-Paul would not co-operate because—oh dearie me—he could no longer trust me.

'I will have it photographed,' he said, 'if that would help.'

'I'll need a ten by eight.'

'Relax, my friend.'

You prick, I thought, don't tell me to relax, you fucking thief.

'You shall have your ten by eight.'

When he says 'shall' and 'shan't' he is pretending that he and his old man never came from Antwerp on a ten-pound migrant ticket, that they never built shearing sheds and ate cockatoos for their dinner. So where did all this 'shall' and 'shan't' shit come from? Suddenly he sounded like old Lady Wilson hiring her shearers—Did you shar har last yar? No? Then you shan't shar har this yar.

I asked Jean-Paul: 'When *shall* I have my ten by eight?'

'Tomorrow,' he said, his eyes narrowing.

I waited a day and called his office and of course no one had heard of any ten by eight and as for Jean-Paul he was now in Adelaide addressing a conference on Surgically Removing the Assets of the Elderly and Infirm.

Three times I had visited the police, four times I called the number on Detective Amberstreet's card but he was a Sydney cop and so he never phoned me back. So, fuck that—I threw Hugh's chair in the back of the ute and we headed over to that nasty bunker the police have built in Darlinghurst. It was now late March but still very hot, so I already had the chips and Coca-Cola and I had planned setting up the chair in the shade across the road by the Oxford Gym.

But Hugh was frightened of police and when he saw the bunker he would not leave the vehicle: he locked the door and clamped his hands across his fleshy wattley ears.

'You silly cunt,' I said, 'you'll cook yourself.'

In reply he farted. What a little flower he was.

I entered police headquarters intending only to track down Amberstreet but I quickly understood that if I continued walking no bugger would prevent me and that is how, less than ten minutes later, I emerged from the lift on the third floor and saw the word 'ART' nailed to the wall. Of all of the thousands of people who have seen that horrible building, which one of them could have imagined this particular crucifixion? Beside was a double doorway opening into a large windowless space at the rear of which was an iron cage of the type you might make for monkeys in a zoo. Here were stored crates, canvases, about thirty-two bronze casts of those Rodins which are always the subject of lawsuits and seem to breed like rabbits in the spring. The door of this cage was now ajar but my inevitable next step was interrupted.

'Who are you?' It was a tiny uniformed woman with the most magnificent long straight nose.

I asked for Amberstreet.

'Detective Amberstreet is not here,' she said. She had an awful lot of braid and silver and piercing bright blue eyes.

'Then how about *Detective* Ewbank.'

'He passed away.'

My God, the last time I saw the moron he had my painting.

'Oh no,' I cried. 'No!'

Her eyes moistened and she lay her hand upon my sleeve. 'He was up in Coffs Harbour,' she said.

'What happened?'

'He had a heart attack, I believe.'

But what about my canvas? It could still be in Coffs Harbour District Hospital. If the crate had dropped, it may have split and now it could be—worse than the hospital—in some Coastal Charters office at Coffs Harbour airport, all crunched up and folded, like a take-out menu in the back of an office drawer.

'Detective Amberstreet has gone to the funeral,' she said, her nostrils flaring with sympathy. 'Out at La Perouse.'

If not for the intimacy of the nostrils, I might have asked her for the denomination of the deceased. This would certainly have helped because that cemetery at La Perouse is bloody endless, and when Hugh and I had driven through the Presbyterians and edged along the Jews we got ourselves jammed in by a factory wall which made the northern border, and our only way down was along a narrow road through a nest of Chinese mausoleums. Below us lay the Catholics and, down at the very bottom, where the cemetery is bordered by the Chinese market gardens along the creek, I spotted the remnants of a single funeral party. We had Buckley's chance but I edged the ute out of the grass and parked. Hugh took out his chair. I set off down towards the burial.

I was about halfway down the hill, sticking mainly to the narrow bitumen, when I heard a great holler behind me, and

looking back I saw Hugh pointing excitedly at—I didn't
know at which religious territory—but in the general direction of the airport and Botany Bay Container Terminal.

Had he spotted Barry Amberstreet?

I hesitated, naturally. But then Hugh and his chair were
off down the hill, jumping graves, falling, rolling, up again,
through the Presbyterians and Methodists, charging towards
the shadow of the Bunnerong power station. There was a
solitary figure in a suit down almost to the bottom edge. He
looked thin enough to be our man. I was wearing my leather
slips-ons which were useless for this business, but Hugh was
wearing sandshoes and he ran with great certainty, his head
pushed forward, his left arm pumping as if he were prisoner
at the Oxford Gym.

Behind me, the cars were leaving the Catholic funeral
and what did I think I was doing anyway? Why could I not
wait to see Amberstreet tomorrow? Because I could not
fucking bear to have my painting missing. Because it was my
last hope. Because if this work was in Coffs Harbour I would
be on the next plane. Because I was a child, a driven, anxious
fretful fool, and now I was running parallel with my huge
demented brother, linked and mirrored like a double bloody
helix, and by now, having lost my poofter shoes, I was on the
very lower levels of the cemetery, down with the Anabaptists
and Jehovah's Witnesses, and I might as well have been a dog
running for a stick, for I could no longer see the fellow in the
suit, nothing but the final chain-link fence which I now
watched Hugh climb, wrenching the chair brutally when its
leg got snagged. It was the beach that got me, made my eyes
sting, my throat hurt, the sort of beach, the comparison with
other beaches—the memory of Hugh holding my tiny boy in
the pearly foam of Whale Beach surf. Now he stomped out
on to that polluted sand at La Per-fucking-rouse and there
he removed his Kmart shirt and, with his flesh all a creamy
rosy ruin, sat to watch the rusty containers on the distant

wharf. Behind, as in an amphitheatre, the dead pressed against us in their serried ranks and I jammed my finger through the wire and wept.

14

Baldy was in a rage with the sand from La Perouse and, as always, it was personal i.e. mountains had been born and broken—bloody rock, bloody tides, fish were dead, shells hollow, corals snapped like bones—therefore the grains of sand now lying on the seat of the Holden ute must have travelled through eternity with the SOLE INTENTION of irritating his pimply arse. Our father Blue Bones was much the same and we brothers cowered before his fury when TRACKED-IN SAND was detected on the carpets of the VAUXHALL CRESTA and then there were such threats of whippings with razor strops, electric flex, greenhide belts, God save us, he had that mouth, cruel as a cut across his skin. As a boy I could never understand why nice clean sand would cause such terror in my dad's bloodshot eyes, but I had never seen an hourglass and did not know that I would die. None shall be spared, and when my father's hour was come then the eternal sand-filled wind blew inside his guts and ripped him raw, God forgive him for his sins. He could never know peace in life or even death, never understood what it might be to become a grain of sand, falling whispering with the grace of multitudes, through the fingers of the Lord.

At Bathurst Street my brother claimed I had TRACKED IN SAND to the former Arthur Murray Studio and then he showed SIGNS OF INSTABILITY like our mother, poor

Mum, always sweeping, always tidy in case called. IT IS I
LORD. Oblivion ooh wop bop da. Butcher's eyes were bright
with blame so I plied the broom as he demanded and when
he hurled the pot-smoker's camera crashing to the lane
below, I knew not to question him for I understood he had
been unhinged by his rejections and he could not bear it any
more. Soon he finished his $8.95 McWilliams Cask and
announced we were going out to eat. He was sufficiently
cashed-up so might have shouted me a real mixed grill, kidneys, bacon, chops, steak, pork sausage, but he was saving his
funds for IMMORTALITY and I knew he was about to put us
both through the agony of an OPENING NIGHT and it was
with a heavy heart, bless me, that I observed his little blame-
filled eyes, watched him sponge his suit, smelled the wet-hop
perfume, like a public bar, bless me, it made me think of
Bellingen.

Come on, young'un, said he, and bring your bloody chair.

I wished to refuse but did not have the guts, blumey, God
knows what injury I may still cause to him. We drove to the
Australian Galleries in Paddington with not a word between
us. The cat had my brother's tongue and would not release
it, not even when I farted BETTER OUT THAN IN as our
father liked to say, also—FARTING HORSE NEVER TIRES.
He was in a grim bright state when we entered the VENUE,
all toothpaste and hair oil with a single red capillary showing
on his nose. He was the formerly famous Michael Boone and
he located the FEATURED ARTIST, and drank three glasses
of Tasmanian Pinot noir while he praised him bare-faced.
This painting a bloody ripper! That one a fucking beauty!
Only I could recognize the secret rage, the ROILING SEA
between the Butcher's fangs and fur. The recipient of his
false witness was a PRETTY BOY with long curling blond
hair and he ignorantly bathed in Butcher's scorn, and I could
not bear it, bless me, I was afraid for them both, for myself
as well, because if I lost my brother I was lost myself. On

account of my previous MISUNDERSTANDING no one would have me any more. I attempted to divert my brother but he had gone dangerously sweaty in the pouches beneath his wine-dark eyes so I took my chair from the region of the Pinot noir and I sat in the alcove where not even the waiters would look for me. I was so hungry, but even more afraid, so I sat rocking on my chair, back and forth, the human clock, all the blood sloshing squirting circling and I took deep breaths causing it to OXYGENATE and turn a bright, bright crimson, and if you had cut my throat I would have hit the wall, bless me. What a mess I would have made. Such were my thoughts when a woman's voice spoke. She said: No singing God-save-the-queen to men with colds in the head.

This was a QUOTATION from the great book by the terrible painter Norman Lindsay.

Don't you know me?

The speaker was pretty and very slender, what is called a GAMINE with tiny boobies and a silk dress you could have fitted in your pocket with your hanky.

How is your brother?

Bless me, it was Marlene Leibovitz although she looked very different from the time her rented car was bogged. She was now more of the ARTISTIC TYPE with her hair done in the SLEPT-IN STYLE but just the same she was very friendly and she squatted at my side and let me share her plate of snacks. I suppose I must have seemed HALF-WITTED to be so pleased when I knew Butcher had blamed her for stealing the painting and ruining our lives. I told her we had trouble with the police and had been forced to leave the district with nothing but the paintings and what materials would fit into the ute. She lay her hand upon my strong arm and she said her life had also been destroyed by those exact same events. Her husband could not take the strain of the responsibility and from the time of the theft they were ESTRANGED.

Her hair was very particular, corn yellow, never dyed, so

she had no need to spend a KING'S RANSOM every month to maintain a lie. Her eyes very blue and liquid. I thought she might be Dutch or even German like the bachelor. She soon found herself a chair and together we had a picnic and waiters in ponytails and black suits leaned down to serve us while we talked about *The Magic Pudding* and I told her how Butcher had built his former son a tree house in the jacaranda, almost exactly identical to the PUDDING YARD on page sixty-three, she knew it well.

This led to me confiding in her the loss of both boy and pudding yard and all the other misfortunes that had fallen upon the brothers Bones. I told her very frankly what a LOW EBB we were at, how the police had not returned the master-piece and the galleries would not spare my brother the time of day.

He is a great painter, she said. As no one had expressed this opinion since 1976, I was surprised. She added, He should not suffer that.

Just then I caught sight of Butcher Bones who had borne false witness against her. He was busy sucking up to some-one new and he had an awful glaze to him, nodding his big head and listing at 45 DEGREES, so his victim would think himself the most interesting man alive. Who could guess that the round red stickers on the wall were like hot spikes driven beneath my brother's broken fingernails. I stood to move my chair out of his line of sight but of course my movement caught his eye and he turned, a great gleaming drunk, holding out his arms, bellowing.

My God! he cried. The missing Mrs Leibovitz.

I could have shat myself.

15

I had been an almost decent man the night Marlene and I had talked in Bellingen. But at the disgusting Stewart Masters show I was shickered, three sheets to the wind, and everything I cast my eyes on seemed false, meretricious, nasty as sequins on a dunny door, but then, there she was—narrowed eyes, swollen lips, and those twin honey-coloured wells made by her clavicle. She smiled and her eyes slitted as she offered me her hand and I thought, You stole that fucking Leibovitz.

And Hugh—Goddamn—he bloody *winked* at me.

Oh, I thought, fuck you. You think it is all hubba-hubba?

But he was folding up his chair for travel, sending his glass sliding, slamming, shattering against the gallery wall.

Marlene Leibovitz stood to dodge the flying shards.

'Let's go!' My brother kicked the glass beneath a desk. 'The Buchanan,' he said. 'Bo-bo-lula.' I abbreviate to spare you, don't be sorry, there is no translation except that when he said 'the Buchanan' he meant 'the Balkan', a restaurant on Oxford Street where he intended that I entertain Mrs Leibovitz while he, the great fat carnivore, filled his face with grilled Croatian meats. And you know what? Five minutes later the three of us were in the ute, thundering along Oxford Street, Hugh's chair crashing around the tray behind and the art thief—for that is how I knew her then—light and silky as a wish beside me. My passengers were both talking, Hugh about the need to pound the flesh of unborn calves with a wooden hammer, over which brutality I clearly heard Marlene Leibovitz tell him she was having trouble with the police. This interesting news cut straight through the Pinot noir but then I had to run a red light beside Ormond Street, and by the time we were nosing up to Taylor Square I was beginning to wonder—my fellow drunks will understand—if I had imagined it.

I would have asked her about the police but then I had to park and, as I wound down the windows to permit the junkies easy access, she told me anyway. The Art Police, she claimed, had burgled her apartment. 'But you know all this,' she said.

'I don't think so. No.'

She frowned. 'They put out an Interpol alert for him.'

'For who?'

'For Olivier, my husband. He ran away. Don't you read the papers?'

My brother was now stomping off through the crowds with his chair swinging so dangerously there was no time to answer.

'You do remember,' she insisted, hurrying behind.

I remained distracted by my brother and she insisted, 'We talked about my husband.'

'In a sort of way.'

'No.' She took my sleeve. 'In a very specific way. His father's work makes him ill. You do remember that?'

I did not know what to say or where to look and I certainly did not enquire how someone might be made ill by a great painting.

'The police are persecuting the only man on Earth who can't have done it.'

Why did she want to tell me quite so much?

'He is physically incapable of *touching* a Leibovitz.'

I shrugged.

She folded her arms and surveyed the traffic and we maintained a stiff silence until our table was ready and Hugh had been permitted to unfold his chair. Watching him, Marlene Leibovitz's eyes were surprisingly soft, and when she smiled—not much, a tiny stiffening of the muscle in her upper lip—I thought for a mistaken moment that she was going to cry.

'You think I did it don't you?' she demanded, breaking a bread roll and pushing it, rather indelicately, into her mouth. 'You said to me, "the missing Leibovitz". That was really rude, Michael.'

'Your name is Marlene Leibovitz. You've been missing.'

'Sure,' she said.

A peach-pink dress lay like a silk sheet across her lovely brown body, and I could not hold her watery gaze. 'I'm sorry if I was rude,' I said. 'The whole thing really fucked my work. I lost my studio for one thing.'

'All right,' she said calmly. 'If you want to know the truth, it was Honoré Le Noël who stole Mr Boylan's painting.'

But then the waiter was there and Hugh had particular demands and I saw Marlene quietly blow her nose.

'Now listen,' she said as the wine was poured.

And she told me again about Honoré Le Noël being found in bed with Roger Martin. Dominique had thrown him out of 157 rue de Rennes, which he accepted readily enough, not least because he had a far nicer place in Neuilly. But when she demanded he resign from the Comité, he would not budge. Until that moment Dominique thought the Comité was hers. She had assembled it after all. Yet when she demanded the Comité dismiss him she was told that M. Le Noël was the great Leibovitz expert and it would damage everyone to do so preposterous a thing. In the end she stacked the Comité with her own allies, but that took years of scheming and Honoré had all the time in the world to completely fuck her over.

In 1966 Dominique, being short of cash as usual, brought a late-period masterwork into the light. *Ampère* was its title. She put it up for auction in New York, but Sotheby's, knowing a little of her reputation, wanted the Comité to endorse it and so the painting was crated up and shipped back to Paris. This must have been what Honoré was waiting for—and who knows, maybe he had been whispering to Sotheby's—and he now convinced enough members of the Comité that this was a canvas that Dominique had tampered with. This happened to be completely untrue, but he was the expert, and he was obviously a bad man to have as your enemy for he now managed to make the Comité doubt its own good sense. This didn't happen in a single night, but over weeks or months. At the height of the dispute Dominique walked into La Coupole and threw a jug of water over Honoré, but that weakened her cause still further and the Comité refused to endorse *Ampère*. Once that had happened, *droit moral* or no, Sotheby's would not take it for its show.

'Having declared the work a fake,' Marlene told me, 'the Comité had *Ampère* destroyed.'

'What?'

'They burnt it.'

'You're shitting me.'

'This is France. You've got to believe me. It's the law. That's why you never want to let a painting near these Comités. They did it with police supervision. Later, of course, it all came out. They'd incinerated a masterpiece. And it was a huge *scandale*.'

'They burnt a Leibovitz!'

'I could cry,' she said.

'So why would he steal Dozy's painting?'

She chewed more bread and nodded vigorously. 'It will turn up in France. You watch.'

'How? Why?'

'He is rich and he has nothing else to do. He's like some insane deposed king who imagines he can get his throne back. He's obsessed with "the Leibovitz Case". He sat next to Boylan on an airplane, both in first class, they got to chatting. Boylan has a Leibovitz. Honoré is a leech that has found a vein. Next thing you know he has travelled to Australia. He removed paint samples, and he is not someone famous for his manual skills. He returned to Paris and wrote a condition report on the painting. It's an insane document. He claims it's a middle-period painting dressed up to look like a valuable early period. How does he know? What right does he have? Because he feels he owns Leibovitz. Because he's an expert. He claims to have X-rays to prove his case, but no one has ever seen them. Believe me, Michael, I've got nothing to gain from this. I could never bear to hurt a work of art. Please don't think badly of me. I really cannot bear it.'

At this moment, to my surprise, Hugh placed his greasy hand on Marlene's naked arm and, as I noticed the fat spill of tears caught briefly in the lower lashes of her left eye, I too took her hand. What then are we to do with my emotions? Should they be burnt or nailed up on the wall?

16

Marlene would be my brother's girl, that ripped my sausage casings when I saw it, but it was not new that I should understand this before the man himself. Sometimes I have wanted to smash and bash him smite him for his cruelty and he never knows I was in love with the so-called Alimony Whore even worse than he was. In that way we were twins, the best part of us identical. In the Buchanan, I laid my hand on Marlene's tiny arm and I watched all her sad water seeping from her lovely eyes you never saw such blue—hair threads of ultramarine, the blues of an opal, bless us, arranged in the pattern of a human eye.

Butcher always said there was no God, no miracles, he had sat in judgment and found Marlene guilty as a thief but then I saw that ugly smirking look on his face and it made me sick to picture what he would do, his fat dick being in no way deterred by having condemned her without a trial. The artist is always for himself alone, allegedly a MONK, a PRIEST or KING, in spite of which assertion he was always seeking a woman who would let him lie with his BUG IRISH face between her breasts. Who could not fall asleep with the scent of lavender rising from a woman's skin?

When previously resident in Sydney my brother would drive me to A TOUCH OF CLASS in Surry Hills, although not before he had scared the living Christ out of me with condoms and instructions on where my mouth could go. I knew more than him and always had. The girls were very nice NO BATTERIES NEEDED, YOU'RE MY LOVE TOY BABY at least three of them saving to put their children through Sydney Grammar, but Butcher was always waiting outside for me to finish. He said he didn't mind the time, was just thinking, but there were many thoughts that never crossed his mind and when I touched Marlene's arm my feelings occupied a country closed to him, denied entry, UP SHIT CREEK without a paddle.

In Bacchus Marsh we knew many girls with names we pronounced Mah and Wah and Lah. That was a joke. Doo-Wah! That's another.

MAH-LEEN and not MAH-LANE—they included Marlene Warriner, and Marlene Boatwright and Marlene O'Brien and Marlene Repetti so I was not surprised to learn Marlene Leibovitz was really Marlene Cook and she had been born in Benalla, a very nice town in North Eastern Victoria, not much bigger than Bacchus Marsh.

This surprised my brother greatly as he had her pegged as a NEW YORKER. But she was Marlene Cook, whose mother had the COFFEE PALACE. She was the girl who always WROTE AWAY for information about THE STORY OF SUGAR or the history of AUSTRALIA'S OWN CAR. When I learned this I sadly knew she would be well suited to my brother for he had always caused trouble at our post-office box number 46, causing it to get clogged up with BROCHURES and FREE SAMPLES to the detriment of more important business.

All this writing away was what led them apart from their own people, in her case to become an IMAGINARY AMERI-CAN, an expert on the work of Leibovitz when her only edu-cation had been getting thrown out of Benalla High School for insubordination—she admitted so herself, so who would doubt her? Never did I forget I also was cast out from fourth grade. I hid inside my bed for a whole week drawing on the sheets. They never knew what pictures I saw, how close they came to violent death, God save me. Blood pouring through their eyes and noses.

And here you are too, Hugh, she said, eating pork ćevapi in Taylor Square. Who could have imagined this in Bacchus Marsh?

I did not share her opinions but I did not care because it was very nice to be with her. She made Butcher quiet, sooth-ing that MAD RAGE which had been brought about by the work of the pretty-boy painter and the general problem of being OUT OF STYLE. She went for the plum pancakes and THREE FORKS and when I was completely STONKERED we all drove back to Bathurst Street, although not before the Butcher bought two bottles of D'ARENBERG DEAD ARM SHIRAZ @ $53 per, the unit price being an indication that he planned to make her like him more than me. Such is life. Who knows what he remembers about the night where his

entire life began to change? All he ever mentions is that we
left my chair behind in the restaurant and we had to go back
and explain to the waiter it was legally our property. It is not
my fault that there are so many aggressive drunks and criminals in Darlinghurst at that hour of night.

Finally we came up the stairs at Bathurst Street, not even
pausing on the first floor but heading on up to the second.
The lights of the dancing school were better than we might
have hoped and Butcher had previously banked and aimed
them at the longest wall and now, in spite of the injury suffered when retrieving my chair, he was able to assist me
when tacking the canvases in place. One for the money, two
for the show. He was a bloody bower bird displaying snail
shells and dead spiders to the female, puffing up his feathers
to make himself look larger, running back and forwards,
bless me chook-chook-chook.

Until now Mrs Leibovitz had been VULNERABLE, but
now her eyes lost all sign of feeling and she revealed what is
known as a professional character standing in the EXACT
SAME way as Detective Amberstreet on a later date, supporting her left elbow with her right hand while the left cupped
her chin and covered the evidence of her pretty mouth.
Surely this was not the result my brother wanted?

She did not say a word, preferring to nod when she had
seen enough, and at her bidding we two large men rolled up
one canvas and tacked up the next one. Bless me, I was not
sure what was happening. No one touched the Dead Arm
Shiraz, although it had been offered with the shells and
spiders.

Then she said, I can get you a show in Tokyo.

Bless me.

This was not what I had expected. Had he? I cannot
guess. If I had been him I would have set off hollering and
running around the room, THE BUTCHER'S DANCE by

Arthur Murray. But his Boone-eyes stayed dark and tiny like my father when considering the possibility a well-priced beast might be hiding a NOTIFIABLE DISEASE.

Where?

The male's mouth was just a slit, a contrast to the female's which was parted in surprise. The windows were open to the street and we could hear shouting, perhaps the WESTIES had come to beat up the SOFT FACES as they were called. The woman scratched her bare brown upper arm and asked him did he know Tokyo. He treated her as if she was trying to pick his pocket.

How can I get a show in Tokyo? His face was an egg or river stone, no place to crack it open.

At Mitsukoshi, she said, smiling and frowning to a very large degree, her forehead corrugated like low tide—sand worm in secret panic beneath the feet.

Mitsukoshi?

The department store.

A department store, says he, as if it might be disgusting to buy a pair of socks or that he had never lived fifteen years behind a bloody shop which had been his heritage and obligation.

Marlene could not have known we were in danger of a sermon based on ideas put up his batty by the German Bachelor. Just the same she CUT HIM OFF AT THE PASS, firstly uncorking the fifty-dollar Shiraz and pouring it into a coffee cup, then explaining to my brother, as he walked up and down like a horse on a lunging rope, that all the most important shows in Japan were in department stores. I could not see why she would tolerate him but of course this is the LIBERTY given those of so-called genius that they are permitted to act like TOTAL MORONS. Marlene Leibovitz persisted, finally producing from her purse a notebook inside which she had stuffed papers big and small amongst them a card with silver on its edge. On this card were three important things. The first was the name of the Mitsukoshi department store and the second was the angry Duco-dripper Jackson Pollock but it was not until a CROWN PRINCESS was revealed that my brother finally WHOA UP.

Well fuck me dead, said Butcher.

It is a big bloody mystery to me that a man so dead set against QUEEN ELIZABETH OF ENGLAND could get himself so rigid about the crown princess of Japan, but soon he had a great STIFFY, THROBBING LIKE A SOCK FULL OF GRASSHOPPERS. And who am I to understand his secret squirming brain? All I know is that Butcher saw the silver Japanese characters on the back and was therefore so completely converted to Mitsukoshi that he could never change his mind, not even when he discovered the Jackson Pollock exhibition had been opened by a TELEVISION PERSONALITY.

From that night began his enthusiasm for uncooked fish of every kind and as a result of eating TUNA RIGHT OFF THE BOAT he was infested with a parasite producing bloating, cramping, diarrhoea and unusual bowel movements. This was not the least of the excitements in the months ahead.

17

There is always Hugh, and his chair and his chicken-and-lettuce sandwich, and you cannot take a slash or park the truck without considering him, and it has been like that since—to be extremely fucking precise—his twentieth birthday which he celebrated by trying to drown his father in the bath. Blue Bones was a shocking bastard, as strong and slippery as an old goanna, and he flipped Slow Bones on his back and, aided no doubt by all the dreadful bawling, half filled his lungs with soapy water before Mum broke the door down with the kindling axe. If you relied on Hugh for family history you would never hear this incident, for he loved his daddy to the point of giddiness, and we all four acted a loud and violent melodrama on the day I arrived to take him down to Melbourne. Our poor mother. She had been a pretty girl.

Hugh and I were thenceforth joined at the fucking hip and I will not depress myself by remembering the living arrangements in those years when I was half mad with rage and disappointment to find myself reduced to cutting beef for William Angliss in a factory out at Williamstown, and my brother often suffered badly, being abandoned in cars at night, pubs past closing time, in the care of car thieves, junkies, Monash undergraduates. By the time I met the Plaintiff, as she now prefers to be known, he would not tolerate being left with others and there was no choice but that he continue in my so-called care.

I had bought the house in East Ryde when my auction prices were riding high i.e. in 1973 the Art Gallery of New South Wales had finally condescended to give me a retrospective. I cannot tell you how beautiful the street was then, when there was still light industry, before Jean-Paul, before the pool houses, the BMWs. The land sloped towards the north and the garden was a wild and living thing with secret daffodils and cherry tomatoes tangled in the grass, also twisted geriatric apple trees, Ribston Pippin, Laxton's Fortune, varieties since eliminated by product managers, chainstore buyers, all greater pests than the Codling Moth.

The Plaintiff was tall and as graceful as a cat, and I was as vain and foolish as a twenty-eight-year-old could be, plodding through the popping lights of cameras with a bloody tigress on my arm. Who would not have envied me? She was gorgeous as a movie star, honey-coloured, her genetic history a continual puzzle although people would often say she was a queen. From the first night we met my hop-sour house began spilling such perfumes—cumin, cardamom, basil, leeks softening in my battered frying pan. It was summer and the garden was drunk with fermented fruit and new-cut grass and in a humble corner of my studio she set up a table where she drew very small images of imaginary natural objects, completely original, like no one else, and these she slowly carved into blocks of wood and printed. I loved their scale, their seeming modesty and would get into an awful fury to see them overlooked in favour of the big bragging bullshit of Sydney art. And yes, I was in love with her, and fought for her, perhaps embarrassingly. Certainly I bullied my gallery into showing her and my friends into buying her. Who could not see the hairline fracture in the pedestal? Me, your honour, not to save my bloody life.

Of course we fought. But if you have grown up in a house where your mother hides twenty-seven knives each night, the bruises of these conflicts would seem more like love bites. We fought violently when she wished to relegate my brother to a garden shed, but she also called him Brother Hugh, Frère Hugh, Brother Bones. She kissed his big fat cheek. She made him blush. She cooked ćevapi, just for him, beef, lamb, pork, garlic cayenne pepper, but then again—she found him wandering in his sad immodest underpants and suddenly she was in a dreadful fright, ordering me to lock him in his room at night. I asked her was she mad, without ever once considering that she really was. She claimed to be terrified of kidnappers and I thought, Oh, that's all, and—please don't laugh—installed a dirty big padlock inside our bedroom door.

Now I hear that everyone saw the marriage was a disaster, but at the time I was shtupping her stupid three times a day, and this padlock seemed like a tiny pimple, a human imperfection on the cheek of her perfect goddess arse. I did not foresee the Codling Moth, the maggots soon to come.

When Billy Bones was born, she kept the lovely little bugger in our bedroom and I was very moved by her, until I discovered she feared Hugh would break the door down and eat the baby in the night. She was on guard, behind the padlock, and perhaps we would all be together still, me and the Plaintiff, with Billy Bones between us scratching our shins with his dirty boy toenails, had she been able to stomach the wafting perfumes of his dirty nappies. The smell of shit made her gag. So Billy Bones was soon put out to the nursery guarded by a Fisher-Price Alarm. Who bought the alarm? I did.

The suspected cannibal, for his part, kept a wary sort of distance from the baby, rather like a cat watching the arrival of a puppy in the house—he observed closely, he stayed distant, in his corner. The mother, however, remained on guard, wakeful while I snored complacently into her ear. And guess what. Poor old Hugh was immediately caught red-handed. The cunning old wombat had crawled along the passage and removed the two AA batteries from the door alarm, but there is nothing, it seems, that can escape a mother's ears. I was brought to the crime scene, beneath all the mobiles I had fondly strung up from the nursery ceiling. There in the half-light, under this great shadow flock of eagles, cockatoos, galahs, birds whose wooden wings rose and fell dreamily in the balmy Sydney air, was the great hunched form of the Meat Eater, leaning down above our son.

'Hugh!'

He jerked wildly, holding the baby in his arms, and it was clear, in the glare of the emergency flashlight, that more than the Fisher-Price Alarm had taken his attention. The shitty nappy had been changed and young Bill Bones had been transformed into a clean tight perfect bundle, like a pound of chops and sausages. There you are Missus. Will there be anything else today?

The Plaintiff, to her credit, laughed.

And thus did Frère Bones, immediately, without delay, and for a period of almost seven years, become the beloved Uncle Bones, wrestler, babysitter. And when, later at Bellingen, I saw him with his puppy, all wrapped up inside his coat, it nearly broke my heart because the silly old bugger held that dog, alive and dead, as once he held my son.

My son loved my brother, why wouldn't he? He grew up chasing after him through the grass, eating aniseed-flavoured apples, sailing wooden boats in the little green pond. They loved to wrestle, both of them. Even when Bill was six months old it was the thing that made him happiest, to roll him back and forward almost violently. From the minute he could walk he was a charging bull running at our manly legs and there was not a day when he would not demand a wrestle the moment that he saw me. It is hard to credit now, but Slow Bones was happy. He was like a big dog with puppies always playful permitting all sorts of nips and barks and scraps. So I cannot explain what happened when it finally did. Perhaps it was only that Bill would not let go, or he had grabbed a private part by accident, because Hugh then did to Bill what I had always done to him, the move I made when I could not beat him by other means.

I was in the studio when I heard the howls, Hugh's deep-chested bellow, Billy's shivering metal sheet of pain. I can see them now. I wish I couldn't. My brother holding my son out to me as if he wished to push him away, or thrust him back through a cobweb veil of time. At first I did not know what I was seeing: the little boy's little finger dangling, swinging by a flap of skin, a tiny chicken neck.

For more of this, I would refer you to the Plaintiff's affi-davit, but I was always totally determined that I would not abandon either my brother or my son although in this I had an inflated idea of my rights. For apparently, it was not for me to choose, but rather a judge with a Pierre Cardin tie who made the Brothers Bones the subject of a restraining order and I finally saw that padlock in a clearer light.

So you will now perhaps understand that, when the gorgeous Marlene Leibovitz said she would get me a show in Tokyo, my first thought was not of her moral character—not a quality you can ever look for in a dealer—but of Hugh. There is always Hugh, and what to do with him.

18

I would not mind a quid for every time the Butcher judged it time for me to piss off to my bed but in the case of Marlene Leibovitz no words were needed, their BUSINESS DISCUSSION being so urgent that I said cheerio before I got embarrassed for them both. God save them. When I stood to go she kissed me on the cheek and said something in a foreign language it must have been good night. I had no reason to get myself excited in spite of how I felt.

Having left them to their NEGOTIATIONS I sat on the stairs between the first and second floors but then Butcher came bursting out like a BAND-DOG who has broke his chain. What did I think I was doing? I could have punched him in the nose but our father had correctly taught us the folly of fighting on a staircase and so I descended until I heard him close the upstairs door and slide his bolt, wad, load, what did I care?

From the time I was cast out of State School No. 28 THROUGH NO FAULT OF MY OWN I occupied a grey steel chair purchased from AR-BEE Supply Company, and on Sunday evenings in the summer I would sit and watch the line of traffic that descended on us from Ballarat and the

Pentland Hills, vehicles made of steel but for all the world like flesh and blood, dogs on heat, each one sniffing the tail of the one in front, an unbroken chain of men and women, boyfriends, girlfriends, the females with their heads on the shoulders of the males, sometimes a slender arm stretched out along the top of the backseat. One after the other they travelled in their mating myriads, their red behind-lights stringing a glowing necklace through the gloaming and depresh. Afterwards I went to the sleep-out which was what we called the part of the veranda Blue Bones walled in with asbestos sheets now generally against the law. Nothing much there after my brother ran away—steel bunks, old brown sticky tape the only evidence of the missing HOLY PIC-TURES by Mark Rothko the one who passed away.

On Bathurst Street I carried my JERRY-BUILT chair to the bottom of the stairs all the time feeling the great BLAME of the Butcher settling on my neck and that got my engine churning, pumping, and all the muscles in my forearms began to ELECTRIFY and then I must take a little stroll. I do not like the dark but had no choice. I pushed through the boys and girls, the drunk men shouting suck my dick. Cast-out angels, imps and demons of the bottle dark. Did I make them? Was it my fault they were there?

On another subject—I know not what the Butcher did to his missus but who could blame her for tiring of him in the end? She was not like anyone you might meet if you were a Bones. She was always kind to me, or was until I gave her reason not to be. Also she delivered up a magnificous little boy a MUCH-IMPROVED MODEL of anything the Butcher could have done of his own accord. And I was promoted to be the MAJORDOMO, the factotum, the dogsbody, the nurse, the doorman, the butler, the waiter, the chief bottle washer, and my SIBLING often got it in his head that this was an insult to me to be a servant but he had no idea of who I was, bless me, I was now busy, from dawn to night, continually occupied in useful labour until suddenly GODDAMN ME. That's enough.

In any case.

Was never so busy as when I was Uncle Hugh.

That's enough, although I wish they had cut my throat and buried me that's it.

Not being a brave man I was alive and so I fled from the fornicators on Bathurst Street and I pushed down through the WINE-DARK crowds towards the Quay and soon the footpaths were lonelier and I liked it much better though keeping an eye skinned, as instructed, for THE HOMOS. If I had half a brain I would have returned to the safety of our Development Site but I can be a COMPLETE BLOODY MORON and headed into the criminal shadow of the Cahill Expressway and then the tomato sauce and stink-water of Circular Quay where the deckhand was about to withdraw the gangplank from the Woolwich Ferry. I arrived on board so urgently the plank sprung up in the air, crashed down like a clown-stick on the wharf. The deckhand was thin and ugly with a tattoo on his nose but he shook his head like he was SOMEONE OF IMPORTANCE. Thank Jesus the Butcher was not here to take offence.

I could not go home. All that was lost to me 600 miles away. Even before we were round the corner of Dawes Point I could smell the bilgy oily air blowing from the container ships moored behind Goat Island, and the seagulls were like a white-ant hatch swarming around the pylons of the bridge, also the angry traffic locked in noisy upset above my head. Thus—the ferry—calm and clear, and the North-East wind lifted the shirt clear off my skin as if I was a human clothes-line, no other burden on my soul. For a moment I was happy and then, suddenly, that's enough.

That's enough.

I folded up my chair and walked to the lower deck the big diesel engines never ceased beneath my feet, sending me

back to places known to Bill Bones and me, into our OLD
HAUNTS.

Best not thought of.

Having rashly jumped aboard I had no more choice than
dishwater down the giddy drain. The first ferry stop was the
Darling Street Wharf at Balmain East and here the WELL-
KNOWN CRIMINAL had always had his waterfront mansion
with canvas blinds. Before the COURT ORDER I often came
here with Butcher's little boy and lifted him up to spy across
the wall although we never saw a living soul certainly not the
criminal himself. From here we might walk to the market up
on Darling Street or return to the wharf and catch a SILVER
BREAM or board a later ferry to LONG NOSE POINT and
there visit STOREY AND KEERS the shipyard and if there
were no COMPANY DIRECTORS in the office our mate
would permit us aboard the FOREIGN SHIPS or on to the
low brown WORK BOATS and we were once smuggled out to
Cockatoo Island, Billy Bones and I, where we could have
been gaoled for TRESPASS. Here we illegally visited the
island power station which was like the inside of a valve
radio, purple light, sparks, and also a TOP SECRET tunnel,
cut by men from one side of the island to another. Billy had
the Bones constitution he never tired. If I was a servant I
was happy. Every day was something new. We might take the
ferry to Greenwich and go swimming in the baths—BELLY
WHACKERS and JELLYFISH and the bloody wonders of the
good old DOG PADDLE. It does no good to remember. Better not. Stupid for me to have gone to Circular Quay.

By the time the ferry was coming into the Darling Street
Wharf I did not trust the UNFRIENDLY DECKHAND to permit my escape. I jumped before he got a rope across the bol-
lard, did not even glance at the CRIMINAL HOUSE but
instead rushed up the Darling Street hill with my chair
under my arm. Doubtless I looked like some kind of lunatic
speeding up the hill into Balmain, my goodness, my blood

must have been vermilious. The streets were empty of all but DRINKERS spilling from the pubs like innards from a mortal wound. There was not a street that did not hold a memory Bill Bones and I built the biggest Lego house ever constructed just there, in the park by the emergency ward where I took him when he burnt his little hand through no fault of his own.

Outside the Willy Wallace they were drinking their SCHOONERS on the footpath and I did say sorry when I bumped, but then I departed rapidly with the chair held tight a SHIELD AGAINST THINE ENEMIES. I knew exactly where I was, bee-pop, shee-bop—the smell of gas and cat's piss and oil from Mort Bay all around—when the drinkers confronted me I was close to the site of the 1972 payroll robbery. I had taken young Billy there more than once A HISTORIC SITE where the bagman danced around the bullets RAT-TAT-TAT.

My brother says I draw trouble on myself but how could I attack myself from behind? Being set upon, I was compelled to smite my assailants with my shield. CAN'T STAND THE THINGS THEY DO TO ME. WON'T WAIT FOR JESUS TO PROVE TO ME. The thugs ran limping and howling down the street like curs wombats possums vanquished pudding thieves. As far as I heard later they never lodged complaint or charge and there would have been no trouble but for the actions of that very same unfriendly deckhand—this is not proven but how else were there police waiting for me at the Quay. These officers wished to learn how I got so much blood on my shirt and chair.

All's well that ends well by midnight I was home in bed. It was Marlene Leibovitz who cleaned my chair with Windex. In Butcher's version I was his cross to bear, God bless me, I must be an IDIOT SAVANT, a bloody big disaster.

19

I owned not so much as a Band-Aid but there was no short-age of Corio whisky to disinfect my brother's bleeding chin and on this whiskery site the toilet tissue caught, leaving behind little flowers like sheep's wool on barbed wire. Watching Marlene gently collect and flick away these blos-soms, I could not have cared if she had stolen a painting or robbed the State Bank of Victoria. Of course we had made 'love' already, but what was happening here was serious— Hugh was finally no obstacle to happiness, the opposite, and he drew from her everything that was and still is admirable, that is, her passionate sympathy for everyone strange or abandoned or living outside the pale.

That this unexpected tender heart might also benefit the wounded Olivier Leibovitz did not yet occur to me. The truth? I did not think of him at all. I was like a teenage boy, without harness or restraint, never considering where my ignorant heart might carry me, not understanding that this surge of blood might affect what I painted and where I lived or even where I died. Likewise I did not spare a moment to wonder about the consequences of drifting into the poison-ous orbit of Le Comité Leibovitz. I was in love.

Jean-Paul would soon decide that my affair with Marlene was 'really about' my show in Tokyo. My so-called 'mates'— so bloody psychologically acute they would make you want to die—all thought the same, but if they had even glimpsed this lovely Rembrandt woman reaching out to swab Falstaff's dark abrasions, they would have understood everything she did thereafter, or some of it at least.

Soon all three of us were sleeping on the same floor and I

held Marlene against my chest while Hugh, three feet away from us, snored like a half-blocked drain. She fitted against my shoulder all through the night, still, calm, trusting, showing—even in her sleep—a sweet affection which would never jibe with her public reputation. The westerly blew until the early hours, rattling the sashes and causing the clouds to scud across the lovely shivering moon. Next morning the air was still and I saw first water blue, then ultramarine—her clear wide open eyes, the sky of dirty Sydney, all its poisons blown away.

We had no shower available but my lover drenched herself with cold tap water, and then was perfect. She was twenty-eight years old. I had been that age once, the toast of Sydney, long ago.

Down on Sussex Street there was a louche basement café which I had crossed off my list due to Hugh's tendency to claustrophobic panic. Here my bruised brother was soon happily spreading his baggy arse on a fake-leopard-skin stool. 'Pan-oh,' he announced, drumming his chewed fingers on the counter. 'Two pan-oh chocolate.'

While Hugh distributed his breakfast on his shirt I bought three big bowls of coffee. Marlene was all business.

'Give me this fellow's number.'

'Whose?'

'This man who has your painting.'

'Why?'

'I'm going to get it back for you, baby.'

So American.

'Blumey,' Hugh whispered as she used the proprietor's phone. 'Keep her. Bless me.' And the bugger kissed me on the cheek.

Marlene returned, her upper lip taut with mischief.

'Lunch,' she said. 'Go-Go Sushi in Kellett Street.'

Finally she sipped her coffee, coating the aforementioned lip with sugary foam. But then I saw the secret triumph in her narrowed eyes, and I suffered a jolt of panic e.g., Who the fuck are you, Wonder Woman? Where is your fucked-up husband?

'Oh Butcher Bones!' She drew her fingertip across my upper lip.

'Don't you have a job?'

'I need to pick up some old Mitsukoshi catalogues from my flat,' she said. 'You'll like them, if you want to come. Then, if we've got time, we'll go round to the police and we'll talk to that tricky little shit. We're going to get both your paintings back today.'

'We are?'

'Oh yes.'

Her flat turned out to be in one of those pre-war buildings near the bottom of Elizabeth Bay Road: no lift, just battered concrete stairs at the top of which you might be rewarded, finally, with a view of the bay below. If you are a Sydney painter you will already be familiar with this real estate—Gotham Towers, Vaseline Heights—German cockroaches, encrusted kitchens, deco ceramics, ambitious art, but this was a very different visit to my usual and as Hugh charged upwards, bashing his chair against the chipped green railing, I was finally anticipating the cuckolded husband who had been, until this moment, the baby in his bare-breasted mother's arms. The front door was thick grey metal, showing signs of a recent violent burglary. Inside, there was no sign of the man, or anything that might suggest the son of Jacques Leibovitz, nothing that I might identify as his, except a subscription copy of *Car Rally* and a naked half-eaten peach abandoned to the ants beside the kitchen sink. This latter item Marlene Leibovitz dispensed with and I soon heard it crashing like a drunken possum, careening off the cabbage-tree palm, descending through the rubber trees below.

'That was a peach,' said Hugh.

'A peach,' she said, and raised an eyebrow as if to say—
I had not the foggiest. Hugh lurched towards the kitchen
window and his chair would likely bash something so we had
a little tussle, so vigorous on his part that I guessed he might
be jealous, and by the time I had set him up safely in the
middle of the room our hostess had retrieved a pile of glossy
catalogues from a twisted filing cabinet which seemed to
have been attacked by someone with a crowbar.

'OK, we can go.'

'This is very nice here,' Hugh pronounced, his injured
hands locked on to his mighty knees. 'Very clean.'

Clean, and strange—almost no indication of what you
might call *art*. There was a single Clarice Cliff vase which
had been broken and rather brutally restored and, apart
from that, only a line of small grey river rocks lined up along
the top of a bookshelf.

'Almost all our stuff is still in storage.'

Our?

'We came in a big rush. Olivier was sent out to save a
client from local poachers.'

And where was he now? I could not ask.

My brother turned excitedly. 'Who lives here?'

'What?'

'Who lives here?'

'Mad people,' she said. 'Quick. We've got to go.'

20

In the Marsh life was very slow as I recall although no BOWL
OF CHERRIES, bitter wind from the Pentland Hills then
cold rain all winter, also my neck four times bruised with

hailstones not to mention the frost on the windscreen of the Vauxhall Cresta like crushed diamonds in the freezing light. This last was Butcher's observation and he was never forgiven his POETIC EXPRESSION which was immediately deemed to have come from the German Bachelor. Crushed fucking diamonds, said our father, as was his custom, I mean his custom to be sarcastic when the pub had closed at six o'clock. For Blue Bones' birthday that year Butcher invented a defroster with rubber cups sucking to the inside of the windscreen. God help us it ran the Vauxhall battery flat and then the HONEYMOON WAS OVER as they say. Crushed fucking diamonds, my father said. Fuck me dead crushed diamonds.

Life not always perfect I admit, but relaxing in its way, decent spaces between one thing and another as between the ants in a procession across the footpath. Between Darley and Coimadai there would be, at intervals, a decaying possum or a myxomatosis rabbit on the road. Blowflies are the hourglass of the bush. Fuck me dead the hourglass of the bush. Our father's whispery voice never silent after all these years.

So that is the point: breathing space between things, no matter how bad the thing itself might be.

But Sydney, bless me, it was like CHINESE JUMPING JACKS on Guy Fawkes Day bang-bang-bang-bang without relent and all these explosions caused electrification in my longer muscles and I would truthfully prefer those Sunday afternoons in Bacchus Marsh with Mum crying in her room WHEN EVENING COMES DO NOT DARE TO PROMISE YOURSELF THE DAWN. Time very slow in those days, nothing to do but steal the ice from the cool room and feel it melting secretly inside my pocket. In the dusk of Sunday watch the ants crawl across the footpath down into the drain, who knows what they thought of sunshine, shadow, the headlights on the road to Ballarat?

But in Sydney, Lord save us, no sooner had I bashed the

louts than I interrupted Butcher ON THE JOB with Marlene Leibovitz and after THE SANDMAN came it was another day and we were flooding the blood with CAFFEINE and I was the gerbil on the wheel.

Nothing was said but I had no doubt that Marlene's apartment had been broken into and you could smell the FORCEFUL ENTRY but Butcher like a MORON rushed around admiring stones and broken vases though it was clear to anyone of AVERAGE INTELLIGENCE that some criminals had done damage with a crowbar jemmy sledgehammer that's not all. Even the front door looked like a MURDER VICTIM. I was very worried about how we would protect our new friend with the lovely eyes, a smile so often hidden in their corners.

In order to help Marlene get the CATTLE-DOGS, as we like to call them in the Marsh, I wrenched open the filing cabinet. This had also been assaulted, the tumbler removed, the whole thing like a TRAFFIC ACCIDENT, a mailbox backed into by a garbage truck.

Very neat, I said. This was COMMON COURTESY. That is how I was raised e.g. when my father threw the leg of lamb so hard it broke the plaster sheet and lodged there, thigh first, leg bone pointing right at me, we did not mention it. Eat your dinner.

Just the same, my childhood normally very quiet and calm, nothing alarming to report. I could sit in front of our father's artistic whitewashed sign LOCALLY KILLED MEAT and look at the Christmas trees tied to the veranda posts of the Courthouse Hotel. These were called PINUS RADIATA, no more friendly term being available in those years. These Pinus Radiata wilted in the heat like prisoners executed, not pleasant, but not hectic either, not much to think about but the pulse in the neck and the click in the back of my head although more at night than in the morning.

Butcher showed no curiosity about the Japanese cattle-dogs until he had us all crammed in the sandy ute. The motor was running and my ears tickling due to the distinctive high-pitched whistling of the Holden water pump. We were on our way to the NEXT THING, help me, a mighty DIFFERENCE OF OPINION with the police which Marlene and Butcher seemed pleased about, explain that if you can. The turning indicator was flicking ticking at an awful rate like the heart of a sparrow or a fish—how can they bear it? But then he asks the lovely woman please can he see the catalogues and as a result there is suddenly a great NOXIOUS SPILL of foreign ink, an odour like MUSTARD GAS, and if not that then other alien substances in no way like the smell of art the foreign printers claimed to represent.

Marlene asked me, What do you think, Hugh?

I said it was very nice and to be fair it may not have been these chemicals that hurt my head. In the apartment I had detected the odour of my father's .22 after detonation—CORDITE—the rabbit still writhing on the ground before I stretched his neck. As I said, there was generally the perfume of an INTRUSION but if this was legal or not I could not say. I knew the cattle-dogs were the THIN EDGE OF THE WEDGE to an exhibition in Japan and when I saw how Butcher stroked the pages he was like a dog himself, licking his dick in the middle of the road in dire danger of being run down by a truck.

Before you could say JACK ROBINSON we were in the RECEPTION AREA at Police Headquarters and Butcher must have thought he was playing in the Grand Final at MADINGLEY PARK because he darted over to the wing imagining he could drive up towards the goal but he was out of bounds and we were instead required to fill out our names at the front desk. I didn't like to pay attention in these circumstances. The smell of floor disinfectant very strong.

Detective Amberstreet no longer with us.

That was the news we were finally given and all Butcher's

previous politeness was revealed as so much bad milk floating in a cup of welcome tea, but just as he commenced his rant, Marlene took his receipt from him THANK THE LORD and showed it to the WELL-SPOKEN SERGEANT at the desk. She said we wished only to collect property that had been held in a case now settled.

The well-spoken sergeant offered to escort Marlene.

Thank you, she said, but I know my way.

In the lift her colour was rising and as she had a SCAN-DINAVIAN appearance this was very attractive although a puzzle, never mind.

Up on the third floor we saw 'ART' written on the wall as Butcher had already described and inside there was a police-woman, also a sergeant with a huge SCHNOZZ like an anteater which she lifted expectantly towards us. Bless me, save me. HUGE NOSTRILS. Behind her was a great mess looking more like Eddie Tool's lube bay or Jack Hogan's overnight express service which our father once used to send meat to America although that was ONE DREAM GONE SOUR as the saying is. All manner of art in crates and boxes, and loose items protected by paper, bubble wrap, poly-styrene beads never ending, indestructible until the dead rise up. Also quite similar to the spare parts department in Waltzer's Garage. Stewart Waltzer had fan belts, coil springs, but also snakes in formaldehyde, magnetic letters, bookends manufactured on his workshop lathe. Butcher had no interest in Stewart Waltzer or Jack Hogan. The Marsh was dead to him and he surrendered up his receipt to the ser-geant who poked her nose into the contents of the cage, turning over this or that item, peering sadly at the labels. I was already electric in the forearms but when I witnessed Butcher enter the cage WITHOUT PERMISSION I became light-headed as the saying is.

The brain is a funny thing, the way it works, always seek-ing the most polite explanation so when I saw the Butcher dragging out a black soft item my brain thought it was one of those foreign rugs which he is in the habit of carrying from one woman to the next. He looked like a big old dog tugging a smelly blanket but as he and Marlene began to spread this item on the concrete I heard his cries of distress and then I saw it was a work of art brutalized beyond belief. LORD SAVE US. This was my poor brother's painting. It was our mother's words, black as the pupils of her eyes, and here it had been treated like some off-cut underlay, forgive them, shoved in the dumpster by the carpet layers and the nose woman was saying YOUSE DON'T MAKE IT BETTER FOR YOURSELF BY SHOUTING AT ME.

She was like a clerk at the post office a LITTLE HITLER checking the receipt number against the tag stapled cruelly to the corner of the black canvas. My mother's words rising from the night of Main Street. The Nose matched the tag against a REGISTER but she did not know who she was dealing with. She was not an anteater but an ant, a blowfly on the wall of the palace of a king, and when my brother smoothed out the canvas I had once cut for him so perfectly, he was as FURIOUS and TENDER as he had been when we laid out our mother and placed the pennies on her eyes POOR MUM dear Mum she could not have imagined the path her life would take. Blue Bones had been a HANDSOME MAN the FULL FORWARD of the Bacchus Marsh XVIII and how could she have seen ahead, no more than a pretty hummingbird or willy wagtail beside the Darley Road. My brother was now laying out his canvas on a carpet which was the exact same NICOTINE BROWN as in our motel outside of Armidale $28 a night COLOUR TV. The thirty-inch-by-twenty-inch GOD once glued flat on to the middle of the skin was now torn away in a great flap. My brother held up this blasphemy in loud complaint, his own face crumpled like an unmade bed. THE FUCKING RECEIPT SAYS CONFISCATED FOR PURPOSE OF X-RAY.

YOUSE NOT MAKING IT EASIER.

FUCK ME DEAD DO YOU KNOW WHAT YOU HAVE DONE?

She said he would be fined six hundred dollars for obscenity if he didn't watch himself. This threat made my brother create a shower of slippery twenty-dollar notes which was confusing to us all. Then, bless me, he gave us all a lecture. The Summary Offensive Act allows a man to say what he bloody likes if there is reasonable excuse. And he never saw such REASONABLE EXCUSE in his life than the behaviour of ignorant Croats—what was that? I did not know—ignorant Croats who had ripped his work of art apart. Was this the result of X-rays? He laughed nastily. He would have Amberstreet locked in gaol.

She said Amberstreet was overseas.

He said he did not give a flying fuck. He planned to X-ray him so severely the semen in his testicles would lose its wiggly little tails.

If I could have found my way out of the building I would have run away but instead I picked up the money he was wasting and then I assisted Marlene, carrying the canvas towards the lift while the sergeant was left with the receipt. My brother was not himself. Finally he came and wrenched the painting from us and threw it across his shoulder and this was obviously not the right mood to begin a BUSINESS LUNCH with Jean-Paul.

21

Even at four years of age my son was very serious about his duties in the studio and you could give him a pair of tweezers and set him to picking up dust and hairs and finally he would leave the paint as slick and unperturbed as melting ice. Children raised on Space Invaders and Battlezone will tire quickly of this stuff—no enemy to destroy, no gold coins to collect—but my Bill was a Bones deep to his bloody marrow and he worked beside his dad and uncle, solemn, frecklefaced, with his lower lip stuck out, his tongue half up his nose, and there were many days in East Ryde when we had been all three silently engaged in the sweet monotony of such housekeeping, hours punctuated by not much more than the song of blackbirds in the garden or a loud friarbird with its wattles hanging like sexual embarrassments on its ugly urgent face. Of course my apprentice was also a boy with his own employment, climbing the jacaranda, falling, howling, hooked by a branch stuck through his britches, suspended twenty feet up in the air, but Bill loved Hugh, and me, and the three of us could labour side by side sustained by nothing more than white sugar rolled in a fresh lettuce leaf and never called to dinner until we called ourselves, our stomachs sounding like the timbers in a clinker boat finally riding at anchor for the night.

On the day we carried the injured canvas into Bathurst Street, Bill was there, and not there—the normal phantom pain of amputees. The flesh of my flesh had been chopped off by order of the bloody law and the entire city of Sydney, roads, rivers, railway lines shrunk around my missing son like iron filings making contour lines around a magnetic pole. But he was in residence, as a shadow, as a mirror, and most fucking particularly because Marlene Leibovitz made the same shape in the sonar of my feelings, something very like Bill, benevolent, generous, blessedly in need of love thank Jesus.

I entered Bathurst Street a wild ass of a man, carrying my own corpse across my own shoulder—*I, the Speaker,* now as diminished as a Bugatti abandoned in a West Street parking garage, recovered with dust and feathers and pigeon shit, its battery flat, a dull sickening click, no light at all.

Marlene went off to call Jean-Paul, and Hugh helped me clear the second floor, although my recollections are doubtless filled with all the errors of eyewitness testimony, that fiction used to hang so many innocents. Who knows what really happened? Who cares? The Bones boys were Marines on the last day of a war, throwing helicopters overboard, dragging mattresses to the landing, sending them tumbling down the stairs. Of course I destroyed my private bedroom, but sex was not the point. We found a straw broom as stubby as a good Dulux brush, and I swept urgently, opening the windows to both street and lane, and all the while the tragedy lay folded and rumpled, dead as bloody doornails, on the landing.

Hugh has a reputation for being quiet and shy but the old bugger's normal medicated state is as continuously noisy as a kettle—bee-bop and shee-bop—and as we—phtaaa—unfolded the canvas on the floor he set up a sort of vibrato. My brother had become a car, God help us, a Vauxhall Cresta at eighty miles an hour. These things get on your nerves, but we endure, continue, and I may have looked sour and he may have appeared retarded but we worked like a team of carpet-layers tugging and stretching, battling the stiff unsupple canvas, each victory celebrated by a small explosion as we stapled the fuck to Arthur Murray's resistant hardwood floor. Hugh was soon down to stinky socks and khaki shorts, all his rosy venous imperfection, a sweaty shining Rubens double-declutching on the S-bends. *I, the Speaker* reached almost the length of the room but the width was not so easily accommodated and stapling on the long sides was like playing tennis on an indoor court—the damn baseline too close, but never mind.

'Bill,' he said.

This was not a useful thing to say to me although there is

not the tiniest bloody doubt that—forget the idiot Court Guardian with three pens in his shirt pocket—Bill had the skill to use the staple gun. Instead of which we two dangerous men must work alone, two steps forward, one step back as the canvas—having been wet very bloody judiciously— surrendered a millimetre here and a millimetre there.

I invented a steamer based on a Birko kettle and made a cunning nozzle to direct it. I bought a cheap syringe and, having filled it with GAC 100, lifted the cracked impasto exactly, precisely, as if I were controlling a bloody molecular jack. On the first day we did not quit until the light from the west caught the edge of St Andrew's and filled the upstairs room like single malt, Laphroaig, Lagavulin, God bless the distilleries of Islay. I did not drink until after eight o'clock.

The next hung-over morning I woke to confront the great dead whale still beached upstairs and in the geometric centre, this vast trauma still confronted me. The rectangle of collaged canvas was not 30 × 20½ but it was too late to argue. This single vital patch of gooseturd 'GOD' had been pulled back from one corner to reveal the same answer they had gotten from X-ray and infrared i.e. there was sweet fuck-all to see, some underpainting, but certainly not the missing *Monsieur et Madame Tourenbois*. God knows how long they spent on the X-rays, but this final assault must have taken the cops all of five seconds, more than enough time to stretch and tear the underlying canvas and leave five lines of weft behind. I will not bore you with the surgical operation needed to remove those threads. For a conservator or a surgeon it might have been a lot of fun. For me, forget it. There was no reward in this, no risk, no discovery, nothing except the growing conviction that I was destroying what I had made, sucking out the holy deadly light I had created as a high-wire artist, guided by God, flying blind, my head between the legs of angels.

I was about to have a great show. I could not have a show.

I was about to have a love affair. I could not think about it. I was in a rush. I could not rush. At this teetering moment I was everything that makes an artist a hateful loathsome beast. That is, I stole, I grabbed, I sucked love like phthalo green sucks light. I accepted the most monumental kindness from Marlene who appeared off and on, like a series of surprising gifts, through every day, like a six-winged seraph, her colour high, her eyes narrowed in blessing, offering, for instance, a great lump of wax and an iron with which she intended I should affix the injured collage when it was flat and straight again. Everything about this gift was touching but the most weirdly painful thing was the iron, a Sunbeam steam iron, pale blue plastic, at least ten years old, an instrument that made me think of Saturday afternoon races on the radio, our mother ironing in the musty sleep-out. Life in the half-light of the pit, so far from art.

I've known dealers and gallery owners and authenticators half my bloody life, and not one of them would have thought to give me the wax and the iron. For a refugee from the Benalla High School she was very well informed. And sometimes, in that first mad week, with my own bedroom given over to the *Speaker*, while Hugh snored on the floor, Marlene and I simply shared the Japanese catalogues. She talked. I stroked the pale illuminated hairs on her tanned arms, terrified by happiness.

About her husband, I did actually enquire, but she held her private life so fucking tightly, like a tourist clutching a handbag on the A train, and I learned no more about Olivier Leibovitz's present life than you might deduce from sheet lightning above a ridge line. I would put myself to sleep inhaling her.

On most mornings she was light and easy, but twice a single blood vessel rose in that supple subtle forehead and on both of these occasions she departed abruptly, leaving me with nothing but her dirty teacup in the sink. Off to see the husband. It could have driven me insane, and yet I will never forget the tenderness of that week we worked together on the *Speaker*, a whole country that must be healed, swabbed, patted, cleaned, like blowing air behind a lover's ear.

The rhythms of the restoration were affected by rainy weather which meant the air became suddenly colder and damper and the paint dried more slowly, but by the time the Nor'Easterly returned the *Speaker* was once more a very serious fucking entity. By the fourth evening I had removed the daggy bits of thread and sanded the broken interstices between mother canvas and collage. On the following morning the collage section was stapled to its own distant corner and in this way, with a touch of steam here, and a brutal tug there, we got it flattened and its warp and weft realigned. By the seventh day, I had the iron, the wax, the flat unrumpled 'GOD' released from its torture on the hardwood floor. Gently gently catchee monkey.

'Mate,' I said to Hugh, 'I was planning to take Marlene for dinner.' I gave him two chicken sandwiches, and a big bottle of Coke. Receiving these suck-up tributes, he appraised me, his old red eyes as cunning as a crocodile's.

I raised an eyebrow.

He made a small rocking movement as he considered my request. He said nothing but I observed that telltale muscle, his slippery obtruding lower lip, and then I knew that if I stayed out late there would be big bloody trouble.

I told him we would be around the corner at 'the Chinaman's' a reference to the only restaurant in the Marsh.

Hugh studied his watch very carefully but did not look at me again. Pathetic, both of us. But ten minutes later all my silent rage was gone and I was sitting beside a gorgeous woman at Bukit Tinggi, not Chinese at all, as if it matters.

She was tired, her eyes hollowed.

'Don't ask,' she said. 'Feed me.'

And that is exactly what I did, and we sat side by side like children, and I fed her beef rendang and fiery curried fish and wiped her lips with the tip of my thumb. She talked about the many weirdnesses of Japan. It was all we discussed, but the subject had never seemed the point.

'We'll stay in Asakusa,' she said. 'It's kind of sleazy but there's a very funky inn.'

'I'm broke,' I said. 'I couldn't afford the bus to Wollongong.'

'They'll pay,' she laughed. 'You're such an idiot.'

'And you too?'

'An idiot? No, I'm part of the package, baby.' She cupped her hand around my jaw and stroked my ear. 'I'm the facilitator.'

'What's a facilitator?'

'Japanese. It means buys the drinks.'

I could not tell her but this could only be a fantasy for me. I had never left Australia and I never could. I could not abandon Hugh again. I could not even stay long at the Bukit Tinggi and by nine o'clock I was escorting poor Marlene back up the dismal stairs in Bathurst Street. There is always Hugh.

Opening the door I surprised him, a fucking paintbrush in his hand.

As I rushed at him, he took a step backwards—the moron—itching his big bum, a great goofy grin on his unshaven face.

'What have you done?'

The answer was: the dipshit had painted on my work. I could have killed the prick. I howled at him.

'Shush,' said Marlene but I was deaf with fury at everything I had lost, would lose, my son, my life, my art. He retreated, afraid but not afraid, nodding and waving his arm as if I were a cloud of smoke.

It is my job to see better than you can, or John bloody Berger, or Robert fucking Hughes, but confronting my brother's red assassin's eyes, I saw only that he was a moron and I was therefore slow to notice he had painted only on that portion of the canvas which would, tomorrow, be covered for ever. On that virgin rectangle where the Leibovitz had been suspected of hiding, he had written a mad artless note, like something on a dunny wall.

THE VANDAL AMERSTRIT DID THIS DAMIGE
FEBRUARY 7 1981. NEXT TIME YOUR EERS
WILL BE RIPPED OFF AND EATEN.
PROMISED BY HUGH BONES MARCH 25 1981.

Marlene later said I snarled like an animal. Certainly my sixteen-stone brother cowered, but he was also, at the same time, grinning, a small sharp-toothed de Kooning thing, and he was rocking, just a little, from the waist.

'Lead,' he said.

'You cunt!'

'Lead.'

'Lead *paint*?'

His grin made no sense at all.

'Why did you *do* that, you idiot?'

He tapped his head and grinned. 'Up here for dancing.'

'Shush,' Marlene whispered, stroking my arm.

'Show,' said Hugh.

I snatched the brush out of his hand and threw it out the open window.

'Stop it,' Marlene said. 'It can be read by X-ray.'

She was a quick study, the first to understand that Hugh had written a secret letter in lead paint, words which would only be seen if the painting was X-rayed.

I remember still those eyes, wide with astonishment. She would not forget this, ever. She would never make the mistake of underestimating my brother as a witness to a work of art.

At last I got it too, and then I embraced the huge smelly ridiculous thing, holding his bristly neck while he squeezed the breath from me and cackled in my ear.

Who could explain the dark puzzle of Slow Bones' folded brain?

22

All my life I was Slow Bones unless someone OUTSIDE THE FAMILY was present to explain my jokes. Oh, my brother said at last when THE PENNY DROPPED and he understood my painting, you clever bugger.

I could not return the compliment.

By next morning the repair was concluded, but there was no DAY OF REST and we had another ruction i.e. Jean-Paul had gone to New Zealand for a conference and this had obviously been planned solely in order to inconvenience my brother who wished to retrieve his painting for Japan. It was well known Butcher was too afraid to leave Australia or go to any place he was not known. So who could explain why he was in such a rush now unless he had an ANXIOUS PERSON-ALITY surely that could not be true.

Marlene had never met our benefactor so all she knew of him was from my brother e.g. Jean-Paul was not French but Belgian, not Jean-Paul Milan but Henk Piccaver, and it gave the Butcher a lot of pleasure to tell us that MR PICKOVER was in New Zealand or WANK WALLOON had elevator shoes. Yet our benefactor had saved us many times and when Butcher was gaoled for stealing his own paintings from his wife it was Jean-Paul who was THE GOOD SAMARITAN although he was very frightened of me thinking I was a VIO-

LENT TYPE. When my brother was TAKEN DOWN to the cells it was Jean-Paul who gave me a room in his Edgecliff Nursing Home. AND ON THE MORROW WHEN HE DEPARTED HE SAID TAKE CARE OF HIM, AND WHATSO-EVER HE SPENDEST MORE, WHEN I COME AGAIN, I WILL REPAY THEE. This was not a text my brother would have ever pinned upon his wall.

At the nursing home I made a friend of Jackson the night man a very interesting fellow a PIGEON FANCIER who brought in his patent racing clocks to show me. Better to be Slow Bones than be a bird.

Did Butcher reveal to Marlene Jean-Paul's kindness? Of course not. He said that his patron's Cartier watch cost $40,000. This justified him attacking the DEVELOPMENT SITE with saws and hammers and staple guns and he did not pause to think that he was damaging a dance floor of a qual-ity our parents would have never felt beneath their feet. Only in death were they more peaceful than when joined in the FOX TROT. It would make you cry to see how gently my father held his swollen liver-coloured hand against my mother's little back.

With the rain finished the weather once more turned hot and muggy and being unable to wait a single day without thinking of himself the Butcher began to MAKE ART. Better he be active I suppose but everything turned torrid and he was soon in an uproar not only with the COMMON HOUSE-FLIES who came to smell his underpants but also the smuts which floated through the window. Oh Hugh would you mind if I closed the window? That's a joke. He slammed the windows closed and when I once opened them at night he nailed them shut for ever. Here, have a chicken sandwich. Oh thank you very much. PHTHAAA!

Soon he had two huge paintings ON THE BOIL one upstairs and one downstairs leaving barely room for me to sleep. When you see him work you do appreciate the better side of him the TALENT the German Bachelor was the first to understand. Of course the foreigner was later cast aside, abandoned in West Footscray teaching ADVERTISING GRAPHICS at the Tech.

In Sydney, Butcher used his remaining funds to buy new paint and he must have got a bargain price. These tubes were so old he had to unscrew the caps with pliers. I held my nose. Sure enough the bacteria had been feasting on the extenders in the paint, bless me, we had this trouble once before. The reds were now all related to the CESSPIT family, the blues smelled like rotting peaches. Soon the Development Site was very WHIFFY, hot and rotten, the chemistry of BODY ODOUR was brought in to assist.

So I had to walk—nowhere to go—not yet—but while polishing my chair I recalled that nice white flat belonging to Marlene Leibovitz. The smell of FORCED ENTRY would soon be gone and I did not imagine anyone would try that trick again, not if the Brothers Bones were standing guard. Of course I was not yet invited.

Just the same.

Just the same I had seen a great deal of LOVEY-DOVEY and Marlene had been very DIPLOMATIC about the bad smells of Bathurst Street, not once but three times, so I reckoned I would teach myself how to get to Elizabeth Bay.

I am never good with maps just as well or I would have left Sydney many times and if my needs had not been SPECIAL I would have been on the road to Melbourne where the dog SHAT in the tucker box nine miles from Gundagai. This is not what the FAMOUS AUSTRALIAN SONG says it makes out that the dog SAT on the tucker box. What morons. You could not make a song about sitting. I would know. Butcher once drove me past the actual statue of the dog but it is based on what they call MISINFORMATION and the dog is therefore sitting on the box the work of a MEDI-

OCRITY OR LESS as my brother observed whilst speeding past.

If members of the GENERAL PUBLIC have a map then they can go directly to their destination. In my case it is different I must do a great deal of circling and going around the block to make sure I can get back home from where I have arrived, and I do this when I am halfway there or a quarterway or just a block from home. So what may take the GENERAL PUBLIC twenty minutes walking according to a map might take Hugh as much as three hours but once learned it is never forgotten, burnt into my brain, set fast, like red molten metal cooling in a deep-cut channel. My brain is then HARDWIRED as the saying is. To find Elizabeth Bay I must first proceed by trial and error. Very time-consuming, no point in denying the upsets, frights, alarms, the blood roaring in my ears, the electrics firing in my limbs as I go scuttling back the way I came from. Not so bad to look at as it feels. The MAN IN THE STREET would assume I was running for a train or dentist appointment. Some innocents I hit by accident but very few. Having got up the top of William Street I followed a pair of HARD CASES with no bum inside their trousers, red skin on their elbows. These were identical to the DRUG ADDICT in Bellingen so I knew they must be going to Kings Cross. I should have returned to Bathurst Street but the addicts were a blessing, walking very fast and I stayed with them past the Kings Cross Police Station and then I saw the sign Elizabeth Bay Road.

Onwards, as my dad would say, onwards Captain Pillock. I wrote down where I was and then proceeded. Say not the struggle naught availeth.

At the bottom of Elizabeth Bay Road, past the shop of the BAD-TEMPERED GREEK and the ALL-IMPORTANT bottle shop, there is a big grassy park with TREES FROM THE COUNTRIES OF OUR FORMER ENEMIES and the minute I got there I set up my chair and I was as good as home, with Marlene's flat three minutes away and I knew how to get back to Bathurst Street and my arms were soft as pretty putty.

It was a very pleasant place to sit having very little traffic except the taxis, and big Moreton Bay fig trees sometimes filled with dirty old FLYING FOXES the same as would travel west above the Bellinger River hour after hour all through the dusk and deepest night squadrons of them as if on their way to a war we could not know the rules of. No flying foxes this particular morning. I took off my shirt to feel the sun. Very calm, nothing alarming to note other than the rich person's automatic gate opening and closing without DUE CAUSE as they say. WE ARE ALL OBSERVED—my brother's mad belief—he could not live if he was not watched, his shiny head a request for admiration. I had my eyes shut but soon heard the familiar sound of the HOLDEN WATER PUMP which revealed itself to be a police car come to tell me I could not sit here. I was sure they did not have the right to move me but they perhaps misunderstood my underpants and I had never forgotten Butcher being TAKEN DOWN to the cells. I replaced my shirt and folded my chair and as I did so Marlene Leibovitz arrived in a yellow taxi.

Hugh, she cried, oh dear Hugh. The police were powerless before her. PHTHAAA. She took me up those flights of stairs and I decided I would not leave her flat now because it was very quiet and clean and when you opened the window you could hear the rigging on the yachts smacking against the masts and see the water from Rushcutters Bay dancing on the white ceiling, a swimming pool of air. Poor Mum could never imagine this when she dreamed of God Almighty never thought there might be so many yachts or time to sail them and this sound she never heard, I know it, breeze, light, slight slap of stainless steel in the eternal afternoon.

Would you like to live here, Hugh?

I said I would.

She said she would go and fetch Butcher too. I wished she loved only me, held my face in her dry light palms nine miles from Gundagai.

I asked her what about the mad people who had been living here before. She said there was only one but he was gone. She threw something out the window. I heard it crashing down through the trees but I had my chair and the breeze and a light moving like a 20-amp net above my head. It was the first time I really liked Sydney since poor Billy's finger broke our life, forgive me.

23

Olivier Leibovitz existed outside our frame, tugged and tacked around the edge of life and yet from that offside position he would always exert his influence, creasing his wife's brow by remote control, twisting up my own when, to give a for-instance, I opened Marlene's wardrobe—*my* wardrobe I was told—and discovered his suits and shirts—all different whites like fairy dust. I would have hurled them out but took the more cautious path.

The bedroom was a cabin with space for nothing but the sole essential item. Thirty-year-old steel windows opened on to a sixth-floor garden of white river stones and split-bamboo awning. The bedroom was tiny but one wall was filled with sky and although the stones produced a blinding glare by day, in moonlight we lay face to face inside an abalone shell, rumpled shadows like Ingres, a range of whites washed in pearly pink and green.

Hugh had not begun sleeping on the roof. So the almost-famous actor downstairs was not yet complaining about the crunching pebbles above his head and we were not only spared Hugh's intrusions but the neighbour's phone calls of complaint. We could, for three blessed bloody weeks, leave all the shutters open and lie in the moonlight and, finally, be unhurried in our lovemaking. Her eyes. They were what is called baby blue, that is the precise colour of a baby's eyes before the melanin arrives and here was a pleasure even greater than her taut young skin, a clear view of her naked soul—a deep kind of transparency without a single speck or flaw or smut. The weather remained warm and we lay above the sheets with the yacht rigging playing chimes through sleep and half-sleep. There was nothing in the room but us, no past, no wardrobe, nothing of anyone else excepting the fingerprints of amateur glaziers held by the lumpy Pompeii putty in the rusty window frames.

We were alone, until we were not.

I woke suddenly one Sunday night and there it was, something, looking down at me. I was not drunk, but I had been very deep asleep, and now, Jesus, there was, at the foot of the bed, a whatchamacallit, a creature dressed in a pearly gown. Then it was a man, tall, handsome as a movie star, with heavy-lidded eyes and lips so bluish violet, they must have really been bright red. What I had thought a gown then became a suit or shirt covered in dry-cleaner's plastic and this membrane caught and held the moonlight like a floating lethal thing in an aquarium.

'Olivier?'

Who else would have a key? He sneezed, a sudden noise like ripping curtains, and there was a crumpled rush of light, and in a moment the front door had slammed and I heard his oddly unhurried leather soles descending the stairs.

Ten years earlier I would have made a big bloody scene and even now I was inclined to wake his wife, but it's no good getting old if you don't get cunning, and after a tumbler of Lagavulin, my nerves settled and my outrage subsided. I woke with the incident fresh in my mind but then Hugh burnt his socks while attempting to dry them on the toaster and I saw that Olivier Leibovitz was too big a subject for this kitchen. I collected my thermos and my sandwich, saying I would change her lock that evening when I returned.

Marlene was cleaning the injured toaster but she paused, clocked me with those transparent eyes, rubbed her nose with the back of her wrist, and nodded.

'OK,' she said.

We both thought we knew what the other meant.

Indeed, in bed that night, she began to tell me how she met Olivier Leibovitz in New York and she lay with her lovely small head on my chest and stroked my head. The lock produced the story, that was clear to me.

When she met Olivier Leibovitz on Third Avenue she was only four years out of Benalla, that is she was just twenty-one years old, and she had never tasted French champagne and certainly had not the least bloody idea of who Olivier was, nor had she ever heard of his father or Miró or Picasso or Braque or even Gertrude Stein who is reported to have said of the newborn Olivier, 'I don't like babies but I like this one.'

All the evidence available at McCain Advertising—from the size of his office to his place in the distribution list of the conference reports—made it very clear Olivier Leibovitz was no one of particular importance. He looked after a decidedly peripheral group of Garment District advertisers and had only one real national client, a family business based in Austin, Texas, whose executives, Mr Tom, Mr Gavin and Mr Royce, exhibited both slavish respect for their grand-father's ugly pink packs of dental adhesive, and a creepy fas-cination with Olivier, their international Jew. But as I said, she was only twenty-one, and from Benalla. She had never met a Jew before. All she knew was that he was very cute and he kept a horse in the Claremont Stables on West Eighty-ninth Street and rode it on the bridle path in Central Park each morning. So there was always this lovely perfume about him, beneath the talc, the smell of horse, which to her mind was aristocratic, a word she might have also applied to Cary Grant, an impression strengthened not only by Olivier's physical grace but his clear separation from the general desperate ambition which marked McCain Advertising then and probably still does now that it has become McCain, Dorfman, Lilly. But Marlene, of course, was Australian, and Olivier's refusal to push harder than was absolutely necessary never seemed lazy, the opposite, something on the very, very acceptable side of arrogant.

She herself was absolutely no one, an assistant to an assistant, a typist with a hot red IBM Selectric, its entire font contained in a dancing ball that spun and slashed at those pages headed CONFERENCE REPORT. She wore Bill Blass blouses and Paco Rabanne shoes with fuck-me heels but she lived in a hot stuffy walk-up on the scary edges of West Fifteenth Street, bathroom in the kitchen, number 351, only four houses away from Ninth Avenue, and she stayed in the office in the evenings because it was cooler and no one was urinating on the stairs or anywhere but where you might expect. Olivier Leibovitz often worked late, and once, having gone to steal Finepoint pens from the McCain art department, she discovered him operating a Lazy Lucy, one of those huge tracing machines worked by wheels and pulleys, which enlarged and reduced images in the days before computers.

Only later did it occur to her that he was an Account Executive and therefore had no more business being in the art department than she did. At the time she registered his embarrassment as a puzzle.

'You didn't know I was an artist?' He raised an eyebrow and smiled. He had the most charming accent, not French, but not American either.

She took a step towards him, but only to hide the box of sixty black Finepoints behind her back. I won't tell, she smiled back.

'Here, look. I'll show you.'

He moved aside so she might step up on the low platform and then they both poked their heads through the curtained hood, like a couple making funny faces for an instant picture at Penn Station. What did she expect to see?

'Dentures,' she told me. 'Denture adhesive.'

There was a sheet of illuminated tracing paper, and—breathing that very heady smell of talc and man—Cary Grant would surely have smelt just like this—she saw projected on the paper the most unexpected thing. It was, in fact, an image of *Chaplin mécanique*, from the collection of the Musée Leibovitz in Prague. All this she would learn later. Now Olivier, as artful as a tennis coach, leaned carefully around her in order to rack up the flatbed a notch. It was August 1974 and Marlene Cook had never really seen anything even vaguely like the tumbling cans, the shimmering pearly pyramids, the scary charming moustached child beaming in the window frame. It was an angel or the devil, who could know or tell?

'It's nothing,' he said. 'I'm just cropping it.'

'Is it modern art?'

He looked at her quickly, with a peculiar sort of attention.

She frowned, feeling foolish, but certainly not only that, something stubborn and excited too. For this was clearly, totally, in no way fucking nothing. Later she would discover that she had an eye, but even now she had something which told her that this was immense. Of course she did not know what to say, and her confusion, and her embarrassment at her own ignorance, got mixed up with his smell and the feeling of that arm brushing against her while it slowly turned the wheel of the machine.

'Do you really have a horse?'

He turned to her, the pale palette of *Chaplin mécanique* washing across his cheek, reflecting in his eyes.

'Indeed I do.'

'Oh.'

'And do you ride?'

'Not very well I suppose.'

Outside the black velvet curtain he appraised her very frankly and confidently, and she thought, We Australians are really shit. We know nothing. We are so bloody ugly. Almost everything about him was perfectly proportioned, and the things which were not, like the heavy eyelids and the slightly thicker lips, were what gave his face its extraordinary distinction, made it both surprising and familiar, something one wished to return to again and again.

'Have you eaten?'

'Not really.'

'We could go to Sardi's. Do you like Sardi's?'

'*The* Sardi's?'

'*The* Sardi's,' he said, returning with amusement to his machine.

She pushed the Finepoints away as if she were simply making room to sit on the filing cabinet. After a few minutes, he turned off the machine, retrieved a very small rather scratched transparency and, holding it up to the light, showed her how he had traced its tiny heart, so he could wrap a part of it—the grinning maniacal boy—around a coffee mug.

'What then?' she asked. It was the slight smell of horse that made him seem so familiar.

'I take it to my little Russian on Thirty-first Street and he produces one hundred and twenty thousand of them at twenty-three cents each.'

'Why?'

It was an endearing smile, tight and turned down at the corners, suddenly, unexpectedly shy. 'Let's say, not for my wife.'

'Oh,' she said, 'I thought you were divorced.'

He put a long finger to his lips. 'Exactly. This is my horse money. It's a secret.'

It was years before she understood he always ate at One Fifth and he would have taken no one else to Sardi's which he thought a joke. His invitation had been, if not exactly cynical, then very well judged, for he impressed her hugely, but lazily, sweetly, even shyly, and if she had not been so embarrassed by the battered bath in the middle of her kitchen he would have been welcome to have come home with her that very night. And she was not fast. But she could not take her eyes off him, the loping walk, the heavy eyes, the sense that all of life was a wry and complicated joke.

Soon afterwards he left for vacation in Morocco and in the sudden and unexpected absence she had plenty of time to discover Jacques Leibovitz was his father, and other stuff besides. McCain Advertising was on Third Avenue at Fifty-third Street and the New York Public Library was on Fifth Avenue at Forty-second Street and this was an easy enough walk at the end of those stinking August days. She was no student, anyone in Benalla could tell you that. She was a dunce, or if not a dunce then a troublemaker, but the dear old queen librarian with the dandruff on his jacket did not know that, and he led her to Milton Hesse's monograph and to Gilbert's *Stein*, and Philip Tompkinson's *Picasso's Circle*, and to the character Levine the Goat in a novel by Simenon.

Just before Thanksgiving they did go out, two or even three times she recalled, although it always seemed to happen as an afterthought, or at least without any apparent planning, so their outings involved a great deal of walking from one restaurant where they had not booked to another where the kitchen was just closing and the combination of her teetering heels and Abe Beame's bankrupt sidewalks made the evenings perilous or irritating or both. She let him, finally, drop her home outside her real apartment and on two occasions they made their farewells in the backseat of a taxi while the skuzzy life of West Fifteenth Street continued in cars and doorways all around them. She had no idea that she was living with the ghosts of painters, that Marsden Hartley had rented in that same address, that Ernest Roth had a small back room around the corner at 232 West 14th Street, the famous art rookery. I myself did not really want to know any of this shit, not Marsden, not Roth, certainly not the son of Jacques Leibovitz sticking his tongue down her throat and his hand up her skirt. I smiled and nodded. Fuck him. It makes me sick to think about, even more now than before.

24

Butcher bought a plastic wading pool and then constructed a metal crossbar and once this was bolted to the floor we would drag the canvas like a reluctant beast through a cattle dip of paint. One on each side, we brothers took the canvas by the ears and pulled it through the DUNNY CAN, across the bar, then lay it out upon the floor so the Butcher could argue against it with a plumber's trowel. He now talked only of Japan and his breath was like a dead SHAG stinking of raw fish and suddenly it was *DOMO ARIGATO* and MUSHY MUSH although he had the greatest TIN EAR ever nailed to a bald head and he had failed Intermediate French and had been INCAPABLE of learning the language of the German Bachelor except the word BOW-HOUSE which was where the German had studied before being forced to enter Bacchus Marsh his tail between his legs.

Would my brother dare leave Australia? I did not think so.

I spoke no syllable of Japanese and no one suggested I should learn. This meant one thing or it meant another. Where Marlene and Butcher went I followed. Wheresoever they turned AS THE BIBLE SAYS then I was there, my ear attentive. At Go-Go Sushi in Kellett Street Jean-Paul came to allegedly negotiate terms for lending Butcher's painting for the show in Tokyo. Butcher bought Krug champagne but then John-Paul refused the TWO-HUNDRED-DOLLAR BAIT so Butcher ordered SASHIMI DELUXE $15 and they quickly agreed Jean-Paul would lend the painting for Tokyo and that the catalogue would be printed in the same quality as for the recent Barnett Newman show and that Jean-Paul would be permitted to see the proofs for purposes of CON-SULTATION ONLY that is, he did not have the right to MAKE A NUISANCE OF HIMSELF and that the painting *PHFAAART* would be attributed to the Collection of Jean-Paul Milan and his address and phone number would be provided for the benefit of the Japanese punters. Not once did Butcher say that he would actually leave the country.

Jean-Paul began to make WILD GUESSES about how much the show might be costing and what the paintings would be sold for. It was clear he was trying to get a SLICE OF THE PIE and he suggested he could help with both the airfares. Whose airfares he did not say. I remained still and shiny as a stone. My brother turned on me suddenly, loudly demanding to know if I liked the raw fish because that was all people ate in Tokyo.

I asked was I going to Japan.

For answer he forced me to consume sea urchin, it was very slimy, as disgusting as shark vomit and I gagged. I looked at Marlene and she was a BEETROOT and I suddenly saw I would be abandoned in Sydney and she would be able to FUCK HER BRAINS OUT as the saying goes.

In the Marsh there once lived Muldoon and also Barry, an Englishman who wore a wig which was often remarked on in the Royal Hotel. Muldoon was the rope-skipping champion of Victoria before his motorcycle accident which was when he went into PARTNERSHIP with Barry. It was never clear exactly where they slept, but soon they opened two shops, one up by Geelong Road, the other down by the Royal Hotel and every morning they would meet to have a little chat by the post office. Everyone knew this was WINDOW DRESSING and the fellows used to tell them, Why don't you get on the phone if you want to talk. But it was a joke as they were HOMOS. Then Barry decided to open a third business in Geelong and Muldoon hanged himself in public, from the veranda of the post office where they used to meet.

The point is people often get CARRIED AWAY with their own plans so I asked where I would sit on the airplane. And then the conversation ignited like PENNY CRACKERS bursting open and scraps of red Chinese paper flying in the air and Jean-Paul remembering shearing sheds for NO GOOD REASON and next thing we were discussing Armidale and then the river Styx and there were brown snakes everywhere and the COW COCKY was telling Butcher, If you get bit by a brown, don't bother wearing out the horse. Just write down what you want done with your things ha-ha.

Ha-ha. Fuck you.

I was shocked to learn the heartless buggers would abandon me so I would no longer DIGNIFY them with my presence and I took my chair out to Kellett Street to watch the punters enter and depart from the brothel across the road. My so-called friends MADE NO COMMENT about me but soon they relaxed and I could overhear them scheming like PUDDING THIEVES sharpening their knives over a grinding stone.

Also FYI the Japanese killed many of our boys. Buddy Guilline was tortured by the Japanese, also Moth White—if there's a light on he'll be there. Moth White was beheaded in Penang. Why would I wish to go to suck up to the

Japanese if I could be at home making sausages, that was a job they were always happy for me to do, until our father purchased the hydraulic filler. I was also required for such unpleasant tasks as cooking tripe. Hit the dead white stomach with a stick, good boy Hugh, BEAUTY BOTTLER, but no one would trust me with the knife. They gave the scabbard to my brother. In return he would forget our boys and kowtow to the Crown Princess of Japan. PHTHAAA God save him. He is lucky that his father's dead.

At night my brother would now lie beside Marlene and I would hear them agitating the mattress and when they had finished with that they would talk, on and on they went I do not grudge them a NATTER of course not. Out on the terrace it was very pleasant, and I lay down quiet as an old cow on the gravel my bum up in the air HEAD DOWN AND ARSE TO THE BREEZE as my father always said. Sometimes afterwards I wrote down certain of the comments I overheard by chance, or just an individual word like a stone in your shoe or a knife pressing between the ridges of your spine. Sticks and stones, vertebrae, pigs' knuckles, for amusement, flicked in the air, caught on the back of the hand.

25

If you come from the Benalla Coffee Palace it will never occur to you, not in your fucking wildest dreams, that you might ever possibly talk to someone who wrote a book, so when, in the New York Public Library, Marlene read the young Milton Hesse's monograph on Leibovitz, she was naturally slow to understand that its author was living down the road. It was her friend the gay librarian who showed her the ad in the *Village Voice*—DRAWING LESSONS FROM AMERICAN MASTER. MILTON HESSE. There was an address on Allen Street.

'That's him?'

'Indeed.'

The F train is just minutes from the Reading Room. Delancey Street is seven stops south. Marlene found Milton Hesse off the Bowery, in charge of twenty filthy windows above a shirt factory. Here he was in the process of becoming that creature we all fear the most—a bitter old painter whose friends are famous, whose own walls are now stacked with twenty-foot-long canvases no one wants to buy.

Milt was a few years under sixty, a short dark bull with almost black eyes and a rumpled creased forehead.

'Do you have a folio?' he asked the visitor. He had a dripping strainer full of lentils in his broad and chalky hand.

'I'm from Australia,' she answered.

He left the lentils to pool water on a table, dragged out a splintered easel, and set up the visitor with some cubes and spheres on the window ledge. He provided a pencil and watched. Who knows what he was thinking? Even at this age, even in this defeated situation, Milt would say almost anything for the sake of cunt.

'Gorgeous, you can't draw worth a damn.' He laughed in astonishment, deep in his chest.

'I know.'

'Oh, you *know*.' He raised his thick eyebrows and bugged his eyes.

'I'm sorry.'

'I can't give you talent, doll-face.'

'I need to learn about Jacques Leibovitz. It's personal,' she said.

That stopped him. 'Ah!' he said.

She coloured.

'Don't tell me it's the useless son?' Again, he was delighted. Beside himself. 'It's the playboy?'

'I'll pay,' she said, now very red. She must have been so fucking cute or he would have kicked her out of there.

'Where are you at college?'

'I'm a secretary.'

'Well, aren't you something!'

'I don't know.'

'Can you afford ten dollars an hour?'

The answer was no, but she said yes.

'Why not,' he laughed. 'Why not! God bless you!' he cried, and tried to kiss her on the cheek.

Of course this was not how he talked to his fellow painters, part-time scroungers and dealers who he ran into at the auction houses—then every single one of them had sold out, then he alone had not licked ass, and he would tell them, still, after all these years, how to paint—if you wished to *see* you had to become *wood* and if you were going to remain *flesh* you would never see anything, on and on, as if he could still elevate himself, raise himself up to the pantheon by pushing them down into the mud.

Yet even to those who now steered clear of him, it was accepted that his passion for Jacques Leibovitz was the genuine article and whilst almost every other painter in the world was still—in Milt's mind anyway—his competitor, he remained an acolyte to Jacques Leibovitz. In the toilet of his studio he had a shamelessly framed letter from the master: *vous présentez un peintre remarquable. Milton Hesse est un américain, jeune, qui possède une originalité extraordinaire.*

Two years later, visiting with Marlene, I was encouraged to go to the toilet, first gently and finally, when I stubbornly refused to understand what I was required to do, with very explicit directions to read the fucking letter on the fucking wall. And of course French is not a language spoken in the

Marsh and so Milt had the added pleasure of having me unhook his letter and deliver it to him so he might, sentence by sentence, recite it to me in both French and English. He adored Jacques Leibovitz as if he were still twenty-six years old, in Paris on the GI Bill, at the great man's feet.

When a woman tells you a man is her 'friend' you know the description will finally be exposed as so much worse. So I didn't like Milt when I heard about him.

Introducing me at last, Marlene said, 'This is Michael Boone, he's a great painter.'

Milt looked at me as if I were her pet cockroach. Sixty-two or not, I could have smacked him across the shoulders with his Mahl stick. But I am stuck with imagining the horny little toad, and not because he doubtless fucked my beloved sideways on his drop sheet, but because he changed her life.

Two times a week, he and the secretary went to the Met, the Modern, up and down Madison Avenue, and he never asked again why she would wish to know what he was teaching her. Interesting—his silence on that point. Did he fear he was a whore working for a whore? There is so much fog around the moral high ground. He could never have seen exactly who she was or what he caused to happen.

He said she should not worry about her ignorance. You should, doll-face, treasure it. He taught her that the only secret in art is that there is no secret. Nor should she imagine that there is a hidden strategy. Forget about it. Real artists don't have strategy. When you look at a painting never look to see who did it. Keep your mind open. Good art cannot explain itself. Cézanne could not explain himself, nor could Picasso. Kandinsky could explain everything QED Looking at pictures, he said, is like a prize fight. You should eat well and sleep well before you begin. He quoted Joyce and Pound and Beckett, and bought Pound's *ABC of Reading* for his protégé. He quoted Rimbaud, Emily Dickinson:

'When I feel like the top of my head would come off, I know that's poetry—is there another way?'

It was his fate to have become a part-time dealer. He hated dealers and their clients even more than he hated Marcel Duchamp. ('He played chess because there was no television. If there'd been TV, he would have watched it all day long.') There was nobody, he said, who would lie and cheat like an art dealer. There was no one so frightened of being made a fool of as a rich client.

Sometimes he charged only five dollars. Sometimes nothing at all. That's all we need to know.

MoMA had four Leibovitzes, only three of them ever displayed. The fourth was generally known to have been 'fixed up' by Dominique and this was, from Marlene's point of view, more than fortunate. Milton had spent a lifetime sucking up to curators and board members and administrators and although he had not yet had anything more than a lithograph accepted by MoMA he was able to get Marlene downstairs where they could look closely at the doctored canvas and it was through this single work, no more than eighteen inches by twenty, since destroyed, that she became so familiar with Dominique's messy brushwork, so different to Leibovitz's solid grouping of parallel hatching. Of course this was not clear at first but in the end she wondered how she could ever have failed to see the way Olivier's father had so carefully constructed a sense of visual mass with each parcel of brushstrokes.

Of course I am only repeating what she told me. I was not there to check the facts. I was in Sydney, in East Ryde, with a scabby-kneed son and apples rotting in the summer grass and—anyway—it doesn't matter why anyone did anything only that, by accident—let's say—the Benalla High School dropout came between the orbits of two men, one beautiful and damaged, the other an egotistical monster and, within the confusion of their gravitational pulls, somehow managed to slide upwards and sideways, so although she remained an assistant to an assistant, and continued to live three houses from the corner of Ninth Avenue, she quietly, triumphantly, entered a completely unmapped ocean, and was gobsmacked, like Cortez, or like Keats himself, to see what the conditions of birth and geography had hidden from her i.e. the true wonder of bloody everything, no less.

26

Having once become a German for the sake of art, Butcher now wished to convert into a Jap. I watched with interest as he removed the down pipe from Marlene's gutter and replaced it with a length of chain, all so the storm water would flow down along the links AS SEEN IN a so-called masterpiece of Japanese Cinema. Did this mean he would go to Tokyo where no one knew his name? That'll be the day that I die.

Just the same, I silently observed how everything was now turned oriental without relent, resulting not only in raw fish and parasites inside his bowels but also the FAXES growling through the night, hot paper falling, curling, not inches from my aching head.

Until I heard the fax machine I never understood the expression MILLS OF GOD but as this nightmare roared inside my brain I saw my mother as she embroidered THOUGH THE MILLS OF GOD GRIND SLOWLY, YET THEY GRIND EXCEEDING SMALL; THOUGH WITH PATIENCE HE STANDS WAITING, WITH EXACTNESS

GRINDS HE ALL. Poor Mum, she could not breathe without imagining her end.

After she died Butcher got in an awful rage with Jesus, throwing handicrafts on the Darley Tip, but our mother's life had already been absorbed into our blood, five quarts of memory pumped through our bodies, spewing out across my brother's canvas, forgive him, Lord, a dickhead in your sight.

Butcher and Marlene were in the bedroom with the door shut, her eyes always alight when she looked upon his ugly face his GORMLESS COUNTENANCE. When I inquired of Butcher if she permitted him to put it up her bottom he smacked me across the lughole. I WAS ONLY ASKING. Many mothers with boys at Sydney Grammar are happy to oblige. The autumn rain made it impossible to overhear them talking, even from the garden. The FOUNTAINS OF THE GREAT DEEP were broken up, the WINDOWS OF HEAVEN were opened and the cord of water from the roof was ducking and diving along its ARTISTIC chain and splashing the walls and flooding the actor downstairs who lost the part of KENNY in *The Removalists* as a result.

Were they leaving me? I could not hear.

One sunny morning we three travelled in contravention of the court order across the Gladesville Bridge, Marlene's arm lay across his shoulder, her fingers playing with the hog's bristles at the base of his thick neck.

This was to do with Japan, that's all I knew.

Out the back of Jean-Paul's house the shade was deep as dirt and in the green shadow of the palms and bougainvillea there were HINDOO GODS with black-and-white checked coverings on their stone particulars. Dead wasps, bless us, in the swimming pool. All light waving, nothing constant.

The collector was wearing a bathing suit to show himself to best advantage.

Will I be left behind?

Marlene explained to the patron that there was a green cast on the Japanese reproduction of *I, the Speaker* and she was taking PERSONAL RESPONSIBILITY for its correction.

Jean-Paul had begun by admiring Marlene's legs but now his eyes turned as dead as the grey wood of his own back fence. He would not sign his MONIKER until the colour was corrected.

Then words were spoken HALLELUJAH. I thought, That's it, it's over, thank the Lord. Watching Jean-Paul attempting to scoop the proofs out of his pool I thanked God for my brother's temper.

Alas there was soon a SECOND ATTEMPT at the Sushi Go-Go on Kellett Street and even before Jean-Paul arrived I had a very bad feeling because my brother tried to once again prove that I would hate Japan, insisting I eat LIVE sea urchin from its shell a soup like monkey brain or worse.

I sat before the vomitous creature waiting to hear my sentence. Instead I saw a man, no more weight than a streak of GUANO as the saying is. It was the vandalizing policeman my brother had vowed to fold and staple to a hardwood floor.

Marlene clocked Detective Amberstreet, her eyes lowering as she smiled and blushed.

Butcher leapt up and I thought he was going to murder him, but instead he laid his hand on his shoulder like they had been best mates from school. My brother beaming, Detective Amberstreet all creased with smiling like a lizard in the mouth of a dog.

So, the policeman says to Butcher, meanwhile tucking his satchel underneath a chair. So, I hear you and Marlene are going to Japan.

So I learned my fate.

27

Having shoved his arm inside my painting and pulled it inside out, you would expect Detective Praying Mantis to be afraid, but in spite of his scaredy-cat haircut, his eyes showed no more agitation than might be caused by the sight of something nice to eat. And no, it did not help to have my moron brother smashing his fist into his open palm. Marlene moved away. Hugh followed her. I did not even pause to think of why they should. I was wholly occupied by this little vandal with the creased-up eyes. After he sat down he constructed an 'X' with the chopsticks and then retrieved one in order to wag it in my face.

'Michael,' he said.

'That's me.'

'Michael.' He ducked his head, and used the chopstick to construct a 'V'. 'Michael, and Marlene.'

'Oh, you are a clever boy.'

'That's right, Michael,' he said, using my first name in a style beloved by the New South Wales police. (Now pull over, Michael. What do we have, Michael? Have you been using drugs, Michael?) 'I've got an MA, Michael,' he said, 'from Griffith University.'

'I thought you left the force.'

He blinked. 'No mate, you're not going to be that lucky.'

'How do you know I'm going to have a show in Tokyo?'

From beneath his chair he produced a cheap canvas satchel, a design I would later recognize as being popular with elderly single visitors to the Museum of Modern Art. From this he conjured up a recent copy of *Studio International*, an issue not yet available in Sydney.

'You've been overseas?'

He blinked twice rapidly but held my gaze, and I was so concerned with combatting his character, whatever that might be, that I was slow to see the full quarter-page ad he was sliding out towards me: 'MICHAEL BOONE,' I finally read, 'Mitsukoshi, Tokyo. August 17–31.'

My mouth, I'm sure, went slack.

'Congratulations, Michael.'

I was mute.

'You've gone international, mate. You must be proud.'

Well I was. No matter who was saying it or why. Beyond description. If you are American you will never understand what it is to be an artist on the edge of the world, to be thirty-six years old and get an ad in *Studio International*. And, no, it is in no way like being from Lubbock, Texas, or Grand Forks, North Dakota. If you are Australian you are free to argue that this cringing shit had disappeared by 1981, that history does not count, and that, in any case, we were soon to become the centre of the fucking universe, the flavour of the month, the coalition of the willing, etc., but I will tell you, frankly, nothing like this had been conceivable in my lifetime and I did not care there was a dirty green cast across the reproduction—I should have cared, but I am saying that I did not give a fuck and on the facing page there was a late Rothko. Do you understand? I mean—how far this was from the life of reproductions taped to the sleepout wall? From Bacchus Marsh? From the life of a celebrated Sydney painter?

'Everything all crated is it?' he asked.

'Oh yes.'

'But not through customs yet.'

'I think it may have gone.'

'No, mate, not yet.'

The little fuck was grinning like he'd just won the trifecta.

'Marlene set this show up for you, Michael?'

'She did, yes.'

He smiled at me and began flipping through the *Studio International*.

'"Rothko's death changed everything,"' he read out loud. 'That's what they're saying here, Michael. It transformed the meaning of his work, gave every encounter with his painting a terrible gravity. That's how they're reading it, like *True Confessions*. I don't see it that way, not at all. I don't think you would either.'

He closed the magazine and beamed at me.

'I'm so pleased the Japs are into the work. In all sincerity.'

My work, I thought, don't you talk about my work.

'Who's doing it, the crating?'

'Woollahra Art Removals.'

'Fantastic, mate, no one better. Here, I can see you've got your eye on my *Studio International*.'

I received his magazine without caution, unprepared for the three typed yellow pages which slid out of it and came whispering like weapons across the tabletop. '*Jacques Leibovitz*,' the first page read, '*Monsieur et Madame Tourenbois. A Condition Report*.'

I thought, you cagey little cunt. What are you up to?

'Read,' he encouraged. He wiped his bloodless lips with the back of his hand. 'Very interesting,' he said, 'in my opinion. Did you ever look at a Condition Report before?'

It was a strange document, very distinctive, bright yellow with a band of pink across the top. I wondered was this the report from Honoré Le Noël. If so, it was very credible, like a dentist's record of the most fastidious inspection, and this one began with the gums, so to speak, the frame, describing how it was constructed, what—in the case of *Monsieur et Madame Tourenbois*—the condition had been before it was removed and abandoned by the thief beside the pancake mix on Dozy Boylan's kitchen countertop. It gave me bloody goose bumps, to read how Leibovitz had made 'a light-duty strainer of bevelled construction'—those were the actual words—'with no structural element touching the surface of support'. The corners were half-lapped, glued and nailed with small brads. The back of the strainer was labelled in paint: 25 avril XIII.

'What's avril?'

'April,' he said. 'Spring.'

There was so much more. The support was of close linen weave, estimated to be of commercial preparation with rabbit-skin glue, or words to that effect. The policeman watched me closely as a cat, but I was inhabiting a space he would never reach, not even if he died and went to heaven.

On the back of *Monsieur et Madame Tourenbois* were three labels, the first put there by Leibovitz or perhaps Dominique or even Le Noël himself, assigning it a number 67, and an address at 157 rue de Rennes. This was undated. Next to that was a label from an exhibition in Paris at Galerie Louise Leiris in 1963, nine years after the artist's death. There was also an envelope containing a four-by-five-inch photograph taken by Honoré Le Noël.

The policeman pushed close. I moved my chair away, though not beyond the whiff of the carbon tetrachloride rising from his shiny suit.

'Short-sighted,' he said. 'You read out loud.'

'Fuck you. You do it.'

To my great surprise, he obeyed.

'"There are numerous and intermittent *abrasions*,"' he recited, '"showing loss of paint and material at the top edge from the left centre to the right-hand corner. They extend into the painting approximately three blah-blah. Ultraviolet examination was made . . . blah blah . . . The examination revealed . . ." Here we are, young Michael Boone, here it is. "The loss of paint and subsequent replacement of an area 13 millimetres by 290 millimetres from the top left corner to the centre point. Brushstrokes measuring between 4 and 6.5 centimetres thus out of character with artist's known work." You see this? It's bloody wonderful. See, see . . . here . . . "Subsequent X-ray analysis has revealed that the upper lay-ers cover what appears to be a work similar to that produced by the artist after 1920." You understand that, Michael. *Monsieur et Madame Tourenbois* is dated 1913 but it can't be 1913, because it's painted on top of something done in 1920. I smell a little ratty, don't you? A little ratty rat.'

'How?'

'If it's 1913 it's great Leibovitz. It's worth a fortune. If it's 1920 . . . well, forget it.'

'Come on, mate, this one is in all the books. It's also in the Modern. Everyone knows it.'

'*Was* in the Modern, Michael. So why do you think they got rid of it?'

'And why are you showing this to me?'

'I would think that was obvious.'

Obvious? All that had ever been obvious was the little creep had stolen my canvas and then ripped it apart. Now he handed me the Condition Report and said, 'I think the forensic significance of this is very clear.'

'You know, Barry, frankly, I don't give a shit.'

'I know,' he said, 'but just imagine if you'd authenticated this, Michael. You might just want the canvas to disappear. You might want to smuggle it to Japan, say, where the rules are different.'

'Oh.'

'Oh,' he said, folding his big white hands across his crotch.

'You think this is what my show is all about?'

'Michael, I'm very sorry.'

'You know, Barry, why is it when an Australian does well outside the country everyone thinks it's a scam? What if I was a great painter?'

'You are a great painter, Michael. That's why I hate to see you used.'

I looked up to see the authenticator herself moving towards us. I pulled a chair out for her, but she leaned across my shoulder and then, suddenly, violently, snatched the paper from my hand. Turning, I could hardly recognize her—the cheeks made into hard angular planes, eyes narrowed in fury.

'This is crap,' she said to Amberstreet. 'You know this is crap. It's not even your property.'

'It came into our possession, Marlene.'

'Yes!' She sat beside me, looked around wildly, ordered a glass of water, stood and drank it so rapidly that it spilled down the front of her dress. 'Yes, it came into your *possession*,' she said, returning the glass loudly to the table. 'Because you burgled my apartment and stole it from my files. You've been hanging out with art dealers too long, my friend. Do you know who actually wrote this criminal shit? Do you really seriously believe it was ever X-rayed?'

Amberstreet lifted his head as if expecting to be kissed.

'We explore all avenues,' he said. 'That's our job.'

'Then piss off,' I said. 'Explore that avenue.' And when I turned I saw Hiroshi, the owner, and I ordered a bottle of Fukucho sake and when I had done with that I discovered the detective gone, Marlene in tears, my copy of *Studio International* gleaming in the summer light. She saw me reach for it and, bless her, smiled.

'Do you like your ad, my darling?'

How do I love thee? Let me count the ways.

28

Yes sir, no sir. My brother persisted in sticking his PROBOSCIS up the policeman's arse. Yes sir, no sir, be-bop-a-lula, it was a blessed wonder he could breathe at all. No sir, I don't mind you destroyed my art. He was ALL PISS AND WIND as our father said when my brother would not fight ALL MOUTH AND TROUSERS what an ugly picture that made. I departed urgently with my chair to Kellett Street it was no wider than a lane but connected to bigger streets and highways so the shortness was not soothing as you might expect. Also the footpath was narrow my chair IMPEDED THE RIGHT OF WAY, no place to rest. Near by was Elizabeth Bay Road an ACCIDENT WAITING TO HAPPEN although I had previously travelled that way to the GREEK MILK BAR and the ALL-IMPORTANT bottle shop, but sitting was locally ILLEGAL and the police were VIGILANT.

Across from Go-Go Sushi was a green brothel popular with UNSAVOURY CUSTOMERS I have watched them come and go but even when I was most particularly upset I was never such a reckless fool as to have my BRAIN IN MY DICK. I turned left in the direction Marlene had taken, past SPORT ITALIA where the COLOURFUL RACING IDENTITY was shot in the neck by a KNOWN ASSOCIATE OF CRIMINALS. Thank God I had no gun myself. A very short distance beyond this BLOOD-SPATTERED CRIME SCENE was Bayswater Road which would make you giddy with bridges and tunnels and cars descending and rising and crossing the abyss not a LIVING SOUL God save us all. What will happen to me? I searched for Marlene, back and forth between Bayswater

Road and Elizabeth Bay Road, the narrow footpath causing both dents and bruises which would later bloom pink yellow green the colour of SWEET BREADS. I was making a map. Too late. This was how I should have learned a bigger territory, like the children singing their times tables.

In the Vauxhall Cresta I was six years old fighting with my warty brother. I did not start the war but neither could I stop and suddenly Blue Bones pulled up the car by the salt pans at Balliang East.

Get out, he said.

It was just on dusk when I obeyed and my father reached back a long wiry arm and slammed the door shut. Then he drove away, the taste of the salt dust, crows cawing, the taillight red as it proceeded into dark, sixteen miles towards the safety of the Marsh. It was well after the moon had risen before the OLD MAN returned to find his bawling boy. It learned me, as he told me more than once.

As chance would have it I heard Marlene's voice calling from beneath the grapevines of the crime scene and looking into the shady garden I saw she and Jean-Paul at a round green table with the dreadful catalogue laid out before them. They were IN CONFERENCE RE JAPAN. I easily got my chair untangled from the garden gate and I sat between her Jasmine and his Brut de Brut where I was informed that Jean-Paul had agreed *If You Have Ever Seen a Man Die* would be picked up by Woollahra Art Removals that very day.

I began GRINNING LIKE AN APE as the saying is.

Jean-Paul asked me how was Butcher.

My face was hurting very bad.

I heard Jean-Paul ask me would I like to get a job but he had no understanding of my situation. If I am GAINFULLY EMPLOYED the social services will stop my disability pension and when I finally lose my job I will never get the pension back for having LIED TO THE GOVERNMENT. If Butcher had been here he would have explained it properly but Jean-Paul did not believe me. I said I was no good at jobs and would not stand being shouted at as he might have reason to recall.

I mean, he said, off the books.

Whatever it was OFF THE BOOKS made my stomach sick. I pointed out that the social services were LITTLE HITLERS sometimes they came to inspect our garbage to see if I had a job and was buying Tasmanian Pinot noir for instance.

No, he said, they don't do that.

I smiled at Marlene like a dog. She placed her hand on me, it had no more weight than a cabbage moth upon my shoulder. Off the books, she said, means Jean-Paul would not tell anyone you were working but he would give you money.

But Butcher had been in prison and it nearly killed him. I began to explain his continuing difficulty with Detective Amberstreet but Marlene prevented me, resting her hand light as a whisper on my lips.

Would you mind helping out Jackson at the Edgecliff Nursing Home?

I asked her, Do you know Jackson?

No, she said. Jean-Paul tells me you were mates when Butcher was in gaol. You raced his pigeons.

But no one understood anything.

You were his friend, the night man.

I touched his pigeons, that's all.

Would you like to help him be the night man for a week or two? For money? Off the books?

I asked her if she thought I should.

She said yes, so I said I supposed that would be OK.

Marlene then stood. She said she had to CATCH UP with Butcher at Go-Go Sushi and that she would see me in a minute and then she walked raising fine white dust from the gravel with her lovely sandalled feet.

I smiled at Jean-Paul but began to gag.

He pushed his chair away from the table and said, You would sit at the door all night and if anyone is sick you pick up the phone for the duty nurse.

I asked him, Was this so my brother did not have to take me to Japan?

He said, Yes that was so, he would not lie.

I asked when this would start but the truth is I could not even hear him any more. God knows what damage I might cause if left alone.

29

The Plaintiff had a horse at one time, a very flighty Arab named Pandora and by the time Pandora had ripped her fetlock on barbed wire and then, three weeks later, thrown the Plaintiff, thus breaking six bones in her so-called art hand, I was pretty much retired from horses.

That is to say, I have not the least interest in the horse Olivier Leibovitz kept on West Eighty-ninth Street and I never enquired as to exactly what sort of animal it was, only being sure—because Marlene told me—that it was absolutely not one of those Claremont Riding Academy horses from the same address, notorious bitter nags which had the habit of crushing their riders on the walls of the transverse on 102nd Street. The riding-school horses were as close as Marlene got to Manhattan equestrian life, and her own feeling for horses was not really the point. For she loved Olivier and she loved Olivier on a horse, how he looked and smelled, and most importantly, how happy it made him.

Contrary to what I thought when she walked across my paddock carrying her alimony-whore shoes, Marlene was extraordinarily kind to those she loved and it was completely typical of her to go out of her way to give me pleasure by arranging the ad in *Studio International* or to butter raisin toast for Hugh or read aloud from *The Magic Pudding* and, years earlier, when Olivier's divorce left him so broke that he had to sell his horse, it was a case of fuck the court and all of 60 Centre Street. He would get it back, the horse, she would make sure of it.

At first Olivier's stable expenses had been covered by his pathetic efforts on the Lazy Lucy, that is, licensing small slices of three Leibovitzes. These were not works chosen with any care, just scratched transparencies that had been left to float around in the company of paper clips and pencils and bits of art-related correspondence. Most of the latter was in French, a language he spoke fluently but which he affected to be unable to read.

At the time when Marlene first surprised him he had imagined he was hiding his tiny licensing profits from his wife's lawyers, a fantasy of course—his possession of the Leibovitz *droit moral* was no secret and it was naturally deemed to be part of Marital Assets and he was forced to cough up every cent he made from his tacky souvenirs. His only luck, which was not clear until later, was that the lawyers, being philistines and ignoramuses, valued the *droit moral* in terms of the profit he had previously gained from it: i.e. sweet fuck all.

By the spring of 1975, which was when he lost the horse and stable, Marlene was his secretary and had therefore been granted the care of that rat's nest of paper he referred to only as 'the French Material'.

She asked him, 'What shall I do with it?'

He looked into the grey metal cupboard with its bulging files, its ribbon-bound sheaves, its single orphaned pages, yellowed, browned, creased. He shrugged, a Gallic gesture, so it seemed to Marlene Cook.

'Is it about the art?'

'Yes.' He startled, smiling. 'Absolutely! About the art.'

He could have had no clue that she was already half drunk on her learning curve. She would have been far too shy to tell him that she had read Berenson and Vasari, Marsden Hartley and Gertrude Stein but at the time she asked, Is it about the art? she knew the importance of such correspondents as Vuillard and Van Dongen, and she had eaten enough hot dogs during lunch at Phillips and Sotheby's to wonder if this rat's-nest archive might not cover his horse and stable costs entirely. He had no idea how she loved him. She thought herself below him in every way, in grace, in beauty, in sophistication. He hadn't noticed that she was his angel, repairing him, dressing all his bleeding wounds.

So she turned to raging old Milton Hesse who was, for his part, smitten with her. It is easy enough to decide that she was using the poor bugger but I doubt either of them would have seen it quite like that. She knew that Hesse despised Olivier, and knew she could not change his mind but she shopped for Milt at Gristede's. She made him Tuna Casserole with a recipe from *Australian Women's Weekly*. And she paid him, always, at least five dollars every week.

'Bring me the letters then,' said Milton. 'Let's see what you got.'

'I'll have to ask permission.'

'Permission! Bullshit. Just borrow them, doll-face. No sense making a fuss if they're worth nothing.'

So she schlepped two heavy boxes down to the F train and sat with the weight cutting into her thighs all the way to Delancey and it was in his freezing studio, while she made lentil soup, that the old man read stuff that made his eyes bulge more than usual. For at that moment, in 1975—this was what the most recent letters showed—the following paintings were on the market, or would be once Olivier Leibovitz was nice enough to authenticate them: *Le Poulet 240V* (1913), *Le*

Déjeuner avec les travailleurs (1912), *Nature morte* (1915). The total value of these works today would be at least 10 million US dollars. You will find them in all the books now, but at that time they had no official existence, having been omitted from Dominique's shoddy catalogue raisonné and traded and stored in God knows what shady circumstances.

'The Dauphin never replied to these letters?' asked Milton who, for the first time, had abandoned his water-front-bull persona and, with his tufts of eyebrows, and his rimless glasses on his forehead, was more like an old Jewish scholar, very foreign, very far away from anything Marlene could even half imagine.

'How could he have?' she asked. 'He really knows nothing about art. He doesn't care to.'

'It takes no knowledge, toots, just his own birth certificate.'

'He can't.'

'Baby,' said Hesse, 'it is not so complicated. If you can recognize Maman's wet and sloppy brushstrokes, which you can, I know, you simply say, ah—this one stinks. No one likes to think this, but it really does not help to go to Cooper Union. You could do it now, today. It's not rocket science.'

Marlene Cook, hearing her future described, did not understand she was no longer a dunce. 'Would you do it, Milton? You could advise him.'

'No.'

'Please.'

He folded his spectacles and snapped them inside a metal case. 'It is not the relationship I have with Jacques.'

She liked him too much to think him pompous. She smiled at him and at first this produced no more than his assistance in repacking the cardboard boxes, but then he opened up his spectacle case once more.

'Here, read this,' he relented, 'from Monsieur L'Huillier in the sixteenth arrondissement.'

'You know I can't read French.'

'Then I'll translate. If Mr Olivier Leibovitz can introduce Mr L'Huillier to a buyer for a Leibovitz presently owned by Mr L'Huillier, then Mr L'Huillier will split commission with Mr Leibovitz.'

'But Olivier does not know people who buy art.'

'Of course. He's an idiot, forgive me. But he does not need to know anyone. Listen, baby. This is code. L'Huillier already has the buyer. But he needs—listen to me—he needs the painting authenticated. He's saying, just confirm that this is a Leibovitz and I'll give you a pile of cash, in a leather suitcase if you like. This is what art has been reduced to. These are the most larcenous people on Earth. In France this is even recognized in law, that dealers are the lowest of the low, beyond leniency.'

'Oh my God,' said Marlene Cook. 'I've been a perfect dill.'

'So do you understand?' asked Milton who, in laying his broad square hand across her own, was putting quite another, much sadder, question.

30

When my brother left to suck up to the Japanese, Jackson was my friend and gave me money OFF THE BOOKS. Jackson was not going nowhere, believe him mate. Jackson was here to stay, no worries. Jackson was wired like a generator, so he said, sparks came from his fingers in the night. Once he had been a RAWLEIGH'S MAN, travelling hundreds of miles a day. White dust on the blackberries beside the roads, purveying tonics FOR MAN OR BEAST. He had seen many

women with nothing on beneath their dressing gowns a
GREAT BIG BUSH between their legs. As a YOUNG BLADE
Jackson had bright red hair and even now it was a GOOD
THICK CROP which he combed as often as time permitted.

After years of living in an Austin A40 van and many bad
frosts especially in the southern highlands he returned to his
trade as a FABRICATOR. In the city of Warrnambool, Victoria, Jackson invented the shopping cart for supermarkets.
This was the first in the world, and has been proven.
Warrnambool is where the famous Fletcher Jones trousers
are made in a huge factory i.e. you can get very rich in
Warrnambool. The shopping cart was constructed from a
FOLDING CHAIR with two wire baskets Jackson borrowed
from the bicycles of TWO SPINSTER TEACHERS at the
high school. I was Slow Bones, never understanding the
possibility of the folding chair although I was SITTING ON
A GOLD MINE all those years. When not in use Jackson's
carts could be stored against the supermarket wall and the
handbaskets were stacked like dishes in the sink.

At this time there were no supermarkets in the so-called
LUCKY COUNTRY otherwise he would have been a rich
man rather than be gaoled for larceny of two baskets not
his own.

Jackson was married twice and has the photos including
plaintiffs, bridesmaids and many stories, also snapshots of
five dogs including two of them run over by the same truck
in different years. At the nursing home Jackson slept in
Room No. 1 and worked from eight o'clock till breakfast, on
the SHIT AND WANDER shift. He brought his best racing
pigeons to be stroked by patients out of THE GOODNESS
OF HIS HEART but there was a complaint about BIRD LICE
by people with eyes so bad they would not be able to read
their own death notice.

When there were medical emergencies and lost memo-
ries, Jackson took MATTERS IN HAND and was not always

thanked as he should be. He also made arrangements with the SAFEWAY MANAGER when the patients took those carts down the hill and left them on the lawn outside Jackson's office. Many is the evening he pushed the long line of carts up the hill on Edgecliff Road, a cruel punishment, he said so often. Fate had spurned him. All God gave him was a big dick FOURTEEN INCHES LONG you would never guess it to look at his skinny freckled arms.

I had my own folding chair and was now EMPLOYED OFF THE BOOKS to push the carts instead of Jackson. I was happy to spare him all that pain. Also, in the parking lot of the Safeway, I was fortunate to come across an abandoned pram, a story too sad to imagine so I blocked it from my mind, the child and mother, who knew where they were?

Just the same, the pram was waterproof in very good condition and I could fill it with crushed ice and then set my Coca-Cola in the ice and my chicken sandwich in the top and in the days after my brother ran away I was not afraid but lived in the lap of luxury in front of the nursing home.

The police came but soon they knew I was a LOCAL CHARACTER and when Jackson found me the PSYCHE-DELIC GLASSES then the police liked me even more and soon they would stop for a chat and look at what I had inside the pram which was always dripping. They once bought me a DISPOSABLE DIAPER for my Coke bottle. They knew that I could take a joke.

Edgecliff Road is fast and winding. It might make your electrics fire off like jellyfish stingers through your hair, to see all the cars screaming around the bend and tradesmen's trucks losing bricks off their loads at 4 p.m. I never thought there could be a local character in such a busy place but soon I was that very thing.

What a BLESSED RELIEF it turned out to be so far away from the constant raging about art, and all the world trying to prevent my brother having the publicity to which he was entitled. Strange to say, I never knew such peace as camping on the shore of Edgecliff Road, a river in flood, roaring with rubber tyres and bricks and blasphemies.

I truly hoped my brother was happy eating raw fish and fucking himself stupid. His broken promise was his own to suffer bee-bop, shee-bop, it hurt me not at all.

31

I have said some dreadful things about Business Class, some in print, but I am an artist and I had often need to make myself at home amongst the purchasing class. I let the lackey fill my glass with, as it happened, Tasmanian bloody Pinot noir and after the last chocolate and second Armagnac Marlene lay her head upon my chest and we slept damn near all the way to Narita. Even with a bursting bladder, I was as weightless as an astronaut.

Of course I would be punished for this trip, but that would be later and this was now and not since the bawling screaming murderous year I ran away to study life drawing at Footscray Tech had it ever once occurred to me that it might be possible to ever be *free* of my brother's bony elbow, his stinky breath, his sweaty sudden arrivals in the middle of my sleep. During the Boeing's descent, and then through all the wait at Immigration, on the train, through the following days, I continued to feel so high and happy. Forgive me, I did not worry about Hugh. Not for a second did I try to imagine how he felt.

In Tokyo they are intent on concreting themselves to death, but I found the city beautiful, a three-dimensional representation of my neon leaping heart.

As Marlene had predicted, my paintings had been delayed in Sydney while Amberstreet and his fellow geniuses ripped the crates apart. Why else send my paintings to Japan if not to hide a stolen Leibovitz? Go suck my dick!

Of course they failed to find the *Tourenbois* so they spent a few hundred taxpayers' dollars to crate them up again. By some miracle they didn't hurt my canvases, which I saw unpacked at Mitsukoshi only two days late.

I would normally have driven the gallery nuts with hanging and rehanging, but I found myself agreeing to leave matters in their hands, and for the next three days we did the honeymooner special, and I will spare you the cute postcards of Asakusa, and the cries of the caged birds who staffed the front desk at our hotel. I was happy in Japan, happy with Marlene, happy to wake and look at those clear bright inquisitive, mischievous eyes.

To do the simplest thing with her was a pleasure, to look at anything, to drift, light as gossamer down a lane, to be confused by the labyrinth of Lego-coloured subway symbols, to discuss the gauze of August light falling across the billowing curtains of construction sites. We finally arrived at Mitsukoshi just as the white-gloved greeters began their morning work, and on the thirteenth floor we found my paintings and even if my name was spelled BONE I did not care, even if they had lit each canvas so fastidiously there was no spill of light on to the wall and there was, let us say, a slightly precious decorated element which was a very fucking long way from Bellingen, I did not care. The work could still bite your leg off and spit the crunchy pieces on the floor.

Marlene was so close, a shadow, a touch of sleeve, a whisper of hand, a living breath of kindness on my cheek.

'Do you see that?' she asked me.

'See what?'

'That.'

She indicated, I thought, the general way the gallery was

arranged—five rooms, nine big canvases, impossible to see more than one work at any time. The numbers and titles were placed away from the work, on the adjoining wall where it was both clearly attached but also separate.

'The titles?'

'You moron, Butcher. Look.' Beside each of the titles was a small Japanese character, black on white. 'Here,' she whispered. 'This is the Japanese version of a red sticker. It means no longer available. Sold, yes. You've sold out, my love.'

And there, in the middle of the empty gallery she leapt on me, pinned her legs around my waist.

'Shit.'

'Yes, shit. Congratulations.'

This was what Amberstreet could not get his provincial little head around. The show was not even open, and I had sold it without a suck-up dinner or dangerous conversation with a critic. This was so much better than Australia. Even in my good years I had never had a sell-out before the drinks were poured and while I kissed her soft, wide mouth, I was— forgive me—doing calculations, multiplying, subtracting. I had two hundred bloody thousand dollars after commission and freight. Just like that.

Later there would be the opening celebration about which there is nothing much to say. Certainly, in the country of Hokusai and Hiroshige I did not expect an introduction by lesbian trick riders, but by then much stranger things had happened.

It was to a printer's shop we went a few days later, carrying a professionally wrapped bottle of Lagavulin. We were to pay our respects to Mr Utamaro who had printed the catalogue for my show. That was all I knew about him, and that he had his offices at the end of a blank-faced lane in Ikekuburo. God knows what the other buildings were, warehouses or something else—I have no idea. Mr Utamaro met us at the elevator in a canvas printer's apron and led us into one of those very simple rooms you might normally expect to find at a framer's. His steel windows were so close to the expressway you could see no more than five speeding Hondas at any time. Below the windows and around the room were deep wooden studio drawers, each one neatly labelled, not in English naturally. With infinite courtesy, he removed a poster for Pollock, a catalogue for Matisse, and with the freeway rumbling in our ears, set them carefully upon the pale scrubbed table which occupied the centre of the room.

The old codger was handsome, strangely freckled, with a high forehead from which he swept his mane of silver hair. There was a delicacy in his mouth and a softness to his hands that soon made it clear that he was a great deal more than a common printer. I never, for a second, underestimated him, but he was very hard to understand and—also, by the way—I had not expected an extended visit. It was not until my face was aching from politeness that I helped myself to the second glass of Scotch. Well, fuck it, I was Australian. What else was I meant to do?

When the cars on the expressway turned on their lights, we were still stuck with Mr Utamaro and then the glow of the passing faces, all separated in their own cocoons of life, reminded me of the melancholy parade that cut the Marsh in half on Sunday nights. I topped up my glass again, why not?

Mr Utamaro rolled down a soft grey cloth on the wooden table and on top of this he placed a glassine bag. Then, having looked up expectantly at Marlene, he slid out a very ordinary brochure, maybe eight inches by six inches, black-and-white, glossy but discoloured with age.

'Michael!' she cried, but although she reached for my hand, what she was looking at was the brochure, on the cover of which was, so I thought, the painting Dozy Boylan had bought years later.

Marlene made a dove noise. 'Oh.'

Mr Utamaro bowed.

'Christ,' I said. 'It's *Monsieur et Madame Tourenbois*.'

Mr Utamaro smiled.

'No, no, shoosh.' Marlene's colour was very high, a sort of aspen pink. She pointed at the title and dimensions which were, in the midst of all the Japanese, in English. 'It's a different work,' she said.

Well I already knew she had an eye but I have one as well, and I had grown up with a black-and-white reproduction of *Monsieur et Madame Tourenbois*.

'No, it's the same.'

'Yes, darling,' and she stroked my hand as if to soften the contradiction. 'Except it's smaller. It's twenty-eight by eighteen inches. A study.'

Having had my own painting ripped apart by morons because a piece of collage was allegedly thirty by twenty-one and a half inches, I was not likely to forget the number.

'See,' she said, 'the title of this one is *Tour en bois, quatre,* "*Wood-lathe, number four*".'

If I was somehow irritated by this coincidence, I had no good reason to be—artists can do twenty studies for a major work. In fact it was not even a coincidence, but somehow this thing pissed me off.

'*Tour en bois*,' I said. 'I know what it means.'

'Shoosh baby. I know you know. But look anyway.' Watching her slip on a pair of white cotton gloves you would swear she had spent twenty years working at the Tate. She held the old catalogue in her open palms and sniffed it like a rose. Then, softly, deftly, she brought it back to the grey cloth and Mr Utamaro, having gravely bowed, returned this ridiculously ordinary item to its glassine bag.

By now dark had fallen and the cars ran past the window in such a way that the whole wall became like a canvas by the great Jim Doolin who had been driven out of Melbourne in 1966. Now, surely, we could go, but no, we moved to a small alcove where Mr Utamaro formally refilled my glass and I learned the story of *Tour en bois, quatre* which had come to Japan as part of an exhibition of works by Dumont, Léger, Leibovitz, Metzinger and Duchamp organized by Mitsukoshi to introduce the Japanese public to cubism. This was in 1913. Mr Utamaro's father had photographed the paintings and met with M. Leibovitz himself. And bless me, if there was not one more exhibit—a very solid-looking Japanese gentleman side by side with the old goat in a fancy restaurant with heavy black Empire chairs.

'Do you know who this is, Michael?'

'Of course I don't.'

'This is Mr Utamaro's friend, Mr Mauri, who bought *Tour en bois, quatre* in 1913.'

I nodded.

'Michael, you know his son.'

I don't think so.

'Michael! His son is the gentleman who bought your entire show. I told you,' she said, colouring intensely enough for me to realize she was not excited but upset.

'I'm sure you didn't say the name.'

'Oh, never mind,' she said, and was suddenly fond, stretching out her hand across the table to hold my arm. 'So when we do meet him, baby, perhaps he will show us *Tour en bois, quatre.*'

I looked to Mr Utamaro and bowed from my chair. I hoped that would be polite enough for a hairy barbarian.

Marlene stood. Mr Utamaro stood.

Thank Christ, I thought, that's over.

I was, as they say, mistaken.

32

Marlene said, You must be over the moon with your success.

I said it was a damn good feeling. It was a dirty lie, but it is completely unacceptable to tell the truth—that it is very bloody unpleasant to have all your paintings hoovered out of you by strangers. If it had been a museum, OK, that's completely different. But the punter was someone I understood to be a corporate Japanese. Buy the Empire State Building, you're welcome. Take every Van Gogh you want. Have a Leibovitz, why would I care? But what the fuck was this Mr Mauri going to do with *I, the Speaker*? The so-called Plaintiff had all the 'precommencement' paintings and now this bugger had the rest. Was there a faster way to be erased from history?

All of these nasty ungrateful thoughts I kept buttoned up for at least twelve hours, until, that is, we were sitting on tatami beside forty Japanese men drinking beer and eating raw fish for their breakfast.

When I said the unsayable, Marlene leaned across to touch my butcher hands, and held each ugly sausage finger as if it had been, individually, miraculously, responsible for *The Last Supper*. And then, without for a second interrupting this particular series of caresses, she very quietly drew my attention to the benefits of my situation. For instance, she revealed that she had authenticated a Leibovitz for Henry Beigel, a South African millionaire and had learned, in the process, that the fucker had squirrelled away 126 works by the American painter Jules Olitski. Beigel was a total bastard, she said, but he had an eye, she said, a real eye, and he was slowly driving up Olitski's prices and he, like

Mr Mauri, had been known to buy a damn show. So, she told me, her very long eyelashes delineated like pen strokes in the ever-present neon light, if you were Jules Olitski you would know your prices were protected and that your best work would end up in a good museum. You would have your future underwritten, not by some flake like Jean-Paul but by an educated, greedy art collector, no one better.

Fine, yes, Henry Beigel, but Mr Mauri, who the fuck was he? I did not mean to be abrasive. I was happy, of course I was bloody happy. I was grateful. I loved her, more than the eyelashes and cheeks, her tenderness, her generosity, and— even if this sounds weird—her guile. I was at home with her, with her light, slight body, her bottomless eyes.

That morning, after breakfast, we both returned to the scene of the crime at Mitsukoshi. I expected I would feel better when we entered. We both expected it, I think. But instead my work seemed lost and alien, almost meaningless, like wretched polar bears in a northern Queensland zoo. What did these punters think? I asked a fellow with a blond streak on his head, but that was later, after lunch. I had been drinking, and Marlene shooshed me and we went out in the streets and walked a little, not stopping at the bars.

The faxed invitation from Mr Mauri was waiting at the so-called Ryokan. It consisted of two pages, the first a delicately drawn map, the second a very formal letter that read like a comic translation from *The Government Inspector*.

I decided that I would be a gentleman and stay away from Mr Mauri.

To this very generous offer, Marlene made no response, not until we were inside our tiny room. Even there she took her time, removed her sandals, and squatted quietly before the little table.

'All right, Butcher,' she said, 'time to cut the crap.'

She fixed me with her snake eyes.

'First,' she said, 'this man is a very important collector.

Second, I do a lot of business with him. Third, you are not going to disgrace me now.'

In my ugly early life this would have been the starting point for a fearsome row which might have run into the early hours of the following day and ended with me alone in some Ukrainian bar at dawn. To Marlene Leibovitz I said, 'OK.'

'OK what?'

'OK I won't disgrace you.'

I was embarrassed, I suppose, to give in without a fight. I could easily have worked myself into a fury, but when I slipped into my Armani jacket she reached up to tie my tie.

'Oh,' she said, 'I do love you.'

With Marlene I was always in a foreign country.

Of course everyone but me knows about Roppongi. It was here apparently, in High Touch Town, that Mr Mauri's father had the famous bar where American spies and gangsters and visiting movie stars would hang out all night long. It was Mr Mauri's father who claimed to have turned the pinball machine Japanese, by setting it on end and—having made sure a lot could fit into a small space—devised a sly system, involving soft stuffed toys and very fucking narrow alleyways, where it became pachinko, a gambling machine. Some dispute this, but no one argues that Mauri San was both a thug and a very serious art collector, well before the war. The son was filial to a fault. So to enter Mauri's office you had to walk through the ancestral shrine, the bar, the chalkboard menu featuring shitty pizza and Italian meatballs, leftovers from the cowboy years of occupation.

At that hour, before the famous lighting did its trick, Mauri's Blue Bar had all the fusty dullness of a theatre with the house lights on, and it really took a lot of imagination to understand how anyone would pay twenty dollars for a martini in this joint. This was where my art had always been headed for, how depressing. We entered the lift and ascended to the eighteenth floor where young Mr Mauri ran something called the Dai Ichi Corporation, *dai ichi* meaning 'number one'.

The receptionist was a very dour long-chinned lady with a helmet cut and dull grey suit, but she did not punish us for long and soon we were brought, through an anteroom, to my new collector's office which was as dull as ply and aluminium can be made to be. Nothing suggested taste or sensitivity at all, and I was taken aback to find myself treated with such veneration by Mr Mauri who appeared to be an earnest, even studious man of thirty.

Our interview was conducted on either side of his big empty desk on which there was a folder containing not only my press file, but a considerable number of transparencies and these my new patron or owner occasionally held up to his desk lamp, speaking about each at some length. I could understand almost everything he said, and often recognized the sources of his sentences, some praise for me from Herbert Read (1973), a little from Elwyn Lynn (1973) and Robert Hughes (1971). I sat, thinking about the Japanese education system, the benefits of learning things by rote. I looked to Marlene but she would not catch my eye. She sat on the edge of her chintz-covered chair, her hands upon her lap, nodding from time to time.

Once more I was in a room watching the dark come down in Tokyo, the sky outside the uncurtained window filled with pink and green neon advertising bars and go-go and Bang-kok Massage. Mr Mauri finished with his dissertation and led us into another room, much more comfortable, with overstuffed armchairs and a number of early twentieth-century paintings—there was a very plausible Matisse.

One of these, reflecting so much quartz halogen from its shrieking gold perimeter, was *Tour en bois, quatre*. If I experienced a lurch of disappointment, it was not because this was the study, but because, at this momentous meeting,

Leibovitz appeared to be a smaller talent than the one I knew when I was a jerk-off teenager with no more data tha n a black-and-white sixty-five-screen reproduction. I had imagined something ethereal, transporting, mythic, colours glowing with layers of obsessive underpainting.

'My goodness,' said Marlene and she was straight at the canvas without any Japanese preliminaries. Mauri was beside her too, a pig at trough, I thought, his gold-rimmed spectacles twirling like a spastic top in the hand behind his back.

'Oh my God,' she said.

Is that all there is? I thought. The canvas was almost homely, a chip missing from the blouse, a slight grubbiness on the surface of the cadmium yellow. All this—little things, easily repaired in restoration—was exaggerated by the gaudy criminal frame, and it took a real act of will to escape the pin-up of my youth, to actually see what was in front of me, the lovely witty squirrelly brushwork of the lathe, and, more generally, the brave decisions the old goat had made at a time when no one, certainly not Picasso, had entered this particular arena of non-synthetic cubism. Here, in the products of the lathe, in cylinders and cones, there was a clear straight line from Cézanne to Leibovitz.

'May I?' Marlene asked.

She lifted the work off the wall and turned it over. 'Look,' she said to me. Mr Mauri bowed me forward so I could see the shadowy secret discoloured canvas, the tracks of staples from its loans and travels, the Japanese characters stamped upon the stretcher which, I guessed, marked its appearance at Mitsukoshi in 1913. There was also a desiccated Stalk-eyed Signal Fly, I might not have noticed if I had not spent so many nights drawing the enemies of art. This little bugger had freshly hatched, and found itself behind a Leibovitz, and here it had been caught and died but somehow never eaten. This sad little death would continue in my mind for days.

'Perhaps a problem,' said Mr Mauri, 'I do not wish to sell it in Japan.' He smiled painfully. 'Japanese people don't like so much.'

'Of course.'

'St Louis perhaps?'

I was slow to realize what was happening in front of me. Mauri was asking her to sell this work. I looked to her but she would not catch my eye.

'The first thing', she told him, cool as ice, 'would be to get it to New York.'

'Not Freeport?'

'No need.'

Mr Mauri paused and looked at the painting. 'Good,' he said.

He bowed. Marlene bowed. I bowed.

And that, I realized, was it. It was done. Presumably there would be paperwork, a signature from the owner of the *droit moral*, but the painting was now all but authenticated. That much I got completely.

I had expected Mr Mauri would wish to discuss his clever strategies for driving up the price of my nine paintings, but nothing like that occurred and a few minutes later we had passed through the famous Blue Bar and were on the streets of High Touch Town amongst the jostling crowds. Marlene took my hand and swung it high, literally skipping down the steep stairs to the Oedo line.

'What happened?' I asked as we fed our coins into the ticket dispenser.

'Oh baby, baby,' she said, 'I am so happy. I love you so.'

She turned to me and lifted her chin and her eyes were glowing, clear as water on the subway stairs.

'I'm on to you.'

'Sure you are,' she said and we kissed there, before the turnstiles, in front of the white-gloved ticket collector, beside the flood of High Touch girls and gaijin hopefuls who pushed around us, buffeting us, not knowing what worlds they were connecting to, threads of history joining us to New York, Bellingen and Hugh, always Hugh, sitting on the footpath with his dripping pram.

33

Jean-Paul came to visit in shirt cuffs and perfume. He was very cross because Marlene Leibovitz had wired him fifteen thousand dollars. What had offended him? He lit a cigarette and blew smoke at me.

He had spent the MORNING WITH LAWYERS. Christ Almighty, Marlene Leibovitz had tricked him into signing over the right to sell *If You Have Ever Seen a Man Die* in Japan. This painting was his PROPERTY. It had been NOT FOR SALE AT ANY PRICE so Marlene was an EMBEZZLER and a CON ARTIST. He said he would report her to INTERPOL as soon as he could find out how.

I thanked him for being so kind—suck up suck up. Immediately he asked to see my room and I was sorry I had spoken but my FEW POSSESSIONS were in their proper place including the wreath and radio given me by the police. Jean-Paul turned very thoughtful. He put his cigarette under the running tap and said he was worried for my safety. I said Butcher would soon return to fetch me and he gave me a look so full of pity it made my stomach turn.

MINUTES LATER I was informed by Jackson that my bed was needed for a new CLIENT and I must remove my pram and second trolley to the utility room where I would live until my position was made clear. My brother was IN ARREARS. What would happen to me now? My brother had once forced me to live in the back of his FC Holden. I had been LEGALLY IN HIS CARE in the streets of St Kilda, Mordiallac, East Caulfield and other places he was drawn to by his pursuit of women who would hold his ugly head between their breasts. Yellow streetlights, redbrick flats, designated parking, oil stains on the concrete, no soul alive except, every now and then a single REFFO or a WOG or BALT each man driven from his place of birth condemned to roam the Earth at night.

The FC Holden stank of wet cigarette butts, potatoes sprouting in the damp rusting floor, piles of newspapers mouldering and all this FLOTSAM meant the LAYBACK SEAT could not be lowered, all sleep denied.

At East Ryde, even Bellingen and Bathurst Street I had thought those bad days over but the utility room had been always waiting at the end of the L-shaped hallway, down five steps, beside the laundry, the sour smell of cleaning rags worse than the smell of AUSTRALIA'S OWN CAR. I asked Jackson was there a nicer room. He said no, and then he tried to give me money off the books but I dare not take it.

He said suit yourself.

Not wishing the clients to know I was being paid I had never talked to them. Now they thought I was Jackson's friend so naturally they did not like me. It was my own stupid fault I was all alone. I missed my brother and could not think how he might ever hear my voice.

And Samson called O LORD GOD, REMEMBER ME? He said, I PRAY THEE, ONLY THIS ONCE. AND HE TOOK HOLD OF THE TWO MIDDLE PILLARS, ONE WITH HIS RIGHT HAND, AND OF THE OTHER WITH HIS LEFT.

It was wrong they should upset me thus.

34

We fled the subway at Shinjuku and then zigzagged down a lane of bars and she was bright as silver, a fish rising in the night, up a set of stairs until we were—4F—in this huge dark shouting place—*Irasshaimase!*—where they cooked mushroom, shrimp, lumps of dogshit for all I knew, but they kept the sake coming and Marlene sat beside me at the horseshoe bar, her face washed by orange pops of flame, starry night, Galileo blazing in her almond eyes. As she lifted her sake to me I was reminded of how she sniffed the catalogue in the glassine bag. This thought was not so sudden. I had been seeing that fast sniff all day long. She clinked my glass. Cheers, she said. She had had a coup. To victory. She had never seemed stranger, more lovely than right now, with those long threads of mushroom in her mouth, all alight, her neck was warm and fragrant, and I was bursting with desire.

'Exactly why did you sniff that catalogue?'

Her mouth tasted sweet and earthy. She wagged her finger and took another sip, then she laid her hand on my thigh and rubbed my nose with hers. 'You figure it.'

'1913 ink?'

She was *beaming*. The shouting cooks sliced squid and hurled it on to the metal plate where it leapt like something in my mother's hell.

'The catalogue's not old at all? That old bugger, Utamaro, he printed it for you?'

Instead of contradicting me, she grinned.

'Look at you!' I cried. 'Jesus, look at you!'

She was keyed up, adorable, her lips glistening. 'Oh

Butcher,' she said, shifting her hand to my upper arm. 'Do you hate me now?'

I have told this bloody story so often. I am accustomed to the expression on my listeners' faces and I know there must be some essential detail I omit. Most likely that *detail* is my character, a flaw passed from Blue Bones' rotten sperm to my own corrupted clay. For I can never have anyone really *feel* why her confession so thrilled me, why I devoured her slippery soft-muscled mouth in the dancing light of country barbecue near the Shinjuku railway station.

So she was a crook!

Oh the horror! Fuck me dead!

Yes: she had a dodgy painting, or one with a murky past. Yes: she invented a history with a bullshit catalogue. Yes: it's even worse than this. Well: my complete abject fucking apologies to all the cardinals concerned, but the rich collectors could look after themselves. They would steal my work when I was desperate and sell it for a fortune later. Fuck them. Up their arse a squeegee. Marlene Leibovitz had manufactured a catalogue, a title too as you'll soon learn. She had turned a worthless orphan canvas into something that anyone would pay a million bucks for. She was an authenticator. That's what she did.

'There was really a cubist exhibition in Tokyo in 1913?'

'Of course. God is in the details.'

'You have the clippings? Leibovitz was in it?'

She nestled against my neck. '*Japan Times, Asahi Shimbun* too.'

All through this, the pair of us were smiling, could not stop.

'Of course this particular painting of Mauri's was nowhere near this show?'

'You hate me.'

'There were no contemporary reproductions, were there? And of course, newspapers don't report the size of paintings.'

'Do you hate me?'

'You are a very bad girl,' I said.

But the art business is filled by people so much worse, crocodiles, larcenists in pinstripe suits, individuals with no eye, bottom feeders who depend on everything except how the painting looks. Yes, Marlene's catalogue was fake but the catalogue was not a work of art. To judge a work, you do not read a fucking catalogue. You *look* as if your life depended on it.

'You don't hate me?'

'On the contrary.'

'Butcher, please come with me to New York.'

'One day, sure.'

We had been drinking. It was noisy. I was slow to understand she did not mean one day. Also, once again, she was astonished that I had not understood something she thought had been clearly said. Hadn't I heard? Mauri had asked her to sell the Leibovitz? She had asked him to ship it to New York. She hadn't had a choice.

'You heard me, baby.'

'I guess,' I said but nothing was so simple. There was Hugh, always Hugh. And I know I said I didn't think about him in Tokyo, but how could anyone believe such shit? He was my orphan brother, my ward, my mother's son. He had my brawny sloping shoulders, my lower lip, my hairy back, my peasant calves. I had dreamed of him, had seen him in a Hokusai print, an Asakusa pram.

'He's in good hands.'

'I guess.'

'He likes Jackson.'

'I guess.' But it was not just Hugh either. It was Marlene. How had this painting turned up in Tokyo? The fake catalogue said it had been there since 1913.

'Tell me,' I said. I held both her hands in one of mine. 'Is this Dozy's painting?'

'Will you come with me to New York if I tell you the truth?'

I loved her. What do you think I said?

'No matter what I tell you?' Her smile had a gorgeous rosy lack of definition you might more normally explain with paint, a thumb, a short and stabby brush.

'No matter what,' I said.

Her eyes were bright and deep, dancing with reflections.

'How big is Dozy's painting?'

'This one's smaller.'

She shrugged. 'Maybe I shrank it?'

'It can't be Dozy's,' I said.

'Come, Butcher, please. It's just a few more days. We'll stay at the Plaza. Hugh will be fine.'

About Leibovitz, Milton Hesse's high-school drop-out had become completely, improbably, expert. In the case of Hugh, however, she had not the faintest fucking clue. I could not have the same excuse.

35

It was in the reign of Ronald Reagan, at three o'clock on a September afternoon, that we arrived in the heart of the imperium. For a moment it was more or less OK, but then, at the limo counter, everything began to come undone. Marlene's Australian bank card was rejected by a tall black woman with rhinestone spectacles and a thin wry mouth. 'OK,' she said, 'let's try another flavour.'

It had been an eighteen-hour flight. Marlene's hair looked like a paddock of hail-damaged wheat.

'Any card at all, Miss.'

'I've only got one card.'

The dispatcher examined my travel-soiled beauty, slowly, from top to bottom. 'Uh-huh,' she said. She waited just a moment before holding out her hand to me.

'Oh, I don't have cards.'

'You don't have *cards*.' She smiled. You don't *have* cards.

I was not going to explain the terms of my divorce to her.

'You don't neither of you have no credit card?' Then, shaking her head she turned to the man behind us.

'Next,' she said.

Of course I had two hundred thousand dollars coming to me, but I didn't have them on me. As for Marlene's credit, something had fucked up at Mauri's office or his bank, but it was three in the morning in Tokyo and we could not find out. Well, fuck that, I phoned Jean-Paul from Concourse C, and I did reverse the charges but we had just wired the little bugger fifteen thousand bloody dollars—my entire gallery advance— for *If You Have Ever Seen a Man Die*, so he had made a profit on the painting he had lost. It was five in the morning in Sydney, early, yes, but no reason to scream into my ear about all the litigation he had planned for me. It was his phone bill so I let him rant. He calmed after a while, but then he started in on Hugh who he claimed was smashing up his 'facility'.

'He pulled the washstand off the wall.'

'What do you want me to do? I'm in New York.'

'Fuck you, you thief. I'll have him locked up for his own protection.'

After the nice patron slammed the phone down in my ear we found a bar and I drank my first Budweiser. What a jar of cat's piss that turned out to be. 'Don't worry,' Marlene said, 'it'll be all right tomorrow.'

But it was Hugh I was thinking of. And although I held Marlene's hand, I was alone, rank with shame and weariness as I was led on to the bus to Newark Station where we caught New Jersey Transit to Penn Station and then changed to an art-encrusted loony bin to Prince Street. It was SoHo but not the SoHo where you bought your Comme des Garçons. I had no idea where I had surfaced, only that I had destroyed my brother's life and that the sirens were hysterical and cabs would not shut the fuck up and that, somewhere, near here, there was a place to stay. I wanted a gin and tonic with a great fat fistful of anaesthetic ice.

At dusk we finally arrived on Broome and Mercer, that is at an hour when the sheet-metal factories were dark, the power was off, the ageing pioneers of Colour Field and High Camp Anaesthesia were presumably crawling into their fucking sleeping bags while the web of fire escapes was weaving a last lovely filigree of light across the factories' faces.

On the corner of Mercer Street, Marlene said, 'I'm going to stand on your shoulders.'

I obediently held out my hands, and Marlene Cook climbed up me like a full forward in the goal square in the Melbourne Cricket Ground. This was the first time I glimpsed the size of what might be still hidden from me. With her big handbag still across her shoulder my intimate companion leapt from my hands to my shoulders. Only one hundred and five pounds but she departed with such force that my knees bent like tired old poppy stems and by the time I steadied myself she was pulling herself up on the rusty ladder, then zigzagging through the filigree to the fifth floor. I heard a resistant window break free, a kind of pop, like a locked-up vertebra achieving independence. Who was this fucking woman? There was a police car approaching, lumbering slowly along the broken street, headlights up, headlights down. And who the fuck was I? My money was all Japanese. My passport was with my bags in a locker in Penn Station. A silver key fell from the night and bounced across the cobbles. The police car braked and waited. I entered the spotlight, picked up the key, retreated. Then the car lumbered onwards, dragging its muffler like a broken anchor chain.

This was not Sydney. Let me list the ways.

'Come on up,' my lover called. 'Fifth floor.'

On the other side of the door it was pitch bloody dark and I made my way slowly up the stairs, feeling my way past a landing filled with disgusting smoke-damaged carpet and another with cardboard boxes and then on the fourth floor I saw the flickering light of candles spilling from behind a battered open metal door. 'How's this?'

It was a loft, almost empty, almost white. Marlene stood in the centre. Her big black handbag was on the floor behind her, beneath the big deep-silled window, amidst the mess of wooden splinters which announced her entry. Abandoned on the sill was a fucking Stanley Super Wonder Bar, a heavy-duty piece of steel with a ninety-degree-angle claw for pulling nails and, at the other extremity, a deadly point.

'Honey, is this yours?'

She took it from me without a word.

I observed how familiarly she hefted it. 'Whose place is this we're in?'

She was studying me closely, frowning. 'New South Wales Government Department of the Arts,' she said. 'They have it for artists-in-residence.'

'Where is the artist?'

'You?' She approached, a supplicant, her shoulders bending to fit against my chest.

I snatched the pry bar from her. 'Who lives here?'

I had hurt her hand, but she smiled, soft and bruised as peaches in the grass. 'Baby, we'll have money from Tokyo tomorrow.'

'Tomorrow I have to fly home.'

'Michael,' she said. And then she broke apart and she was weeping, Gaudier-Brzeska, Wyndham Lewis, fractured, her beauty divided against itself by cracks and fissures, a pit, eyes like animals, God have Mercy I threw the bar away and held her, so shockingly tiny against my chest, her little head within my hands. I wanted to wrap her tight inside a blanket.

'Don't go,' she said.

'He's my brother.'

She turned her big wet eyes up to me.

'I'll bring him here,' she said suddenly. 'No, no,' she said, jumping away from my nasty laugh. 'No, really.' She joined her palms and did a weird sort of Buddhist thing. 'I can do this,' Marlene said. 'He can come with Olivier.'

Oh no, I thought, oh no. 'Olivier is coming here?'

'Of course. What did you imagine?'

'You never said a thing.'

'But he's the one with the *droit moral*. I can't sign.'

'He's coming here? To New York?'

'How else could I do it? Really? What did you think?'

'I thought this was some little romantic tryst.'

'It is,' she said. 'It is, it is.'

For this I had betrayed my mother and my brother? So fucking Olivier could be witness to adultery?

'Don't you fuck with me, Marlene.' I was Blue Bones' son and don't know what else I said. I certainly kicked the nasty wonder bar against the wall. 'What's that?' I roared. 'What the fuck is that?'

'I don't know.'

'Bullshit you don't know.'

'I think it's called a pry bar.'

'You think?'

'Yes.'

'And you really carry this in your purse?'

'I had it in my suitcase until Penn Station.'

'Why?'

She shrugged. 'If I was a man you'd never ask me that.'

That was when I walked out. I found a place called Fanelli's up on Prince Street where they were nice enough to let me pay a thousand yen for a glass of Scotch.

36

One Sunday in the Marsh.

One Sunday in the Marsh there came a bishop walking out of the vestry like a crab he had been in Sydney that very morning but before that time he had been tortured by Chinese communists. He had his back split open by whips and his flesh had hardened rough and raw as a Morrisons road full of dried tyre tracks after heavy rain. Following the first Psalm he explained why no one should vote for the Australian Labor Party and then he removed his vestments in full sight of the CONGREGANTS and my mother said Lord save us but when invited to respond my daddy wished to know what time did the bishop have his breakfast in Sydney.

What was the question?

How long did it take to fly from Sydney?

One hour, said the bishop.

My mother kicked my father but he was Blue Bones and he did not give a tinker's damn about the opinion of the men in the vestry and he certainly would not modify his behaviour on account of a size-four female shoe. Our father was a well-known MARSH IDENTITY. The flight from Sydney was a bloody miracle as far as he was concerned, so he wanted the bishop to answer him—was it rough or smooth?

The bishop told him smooth.

Lord knows what my father would say now if he rose from the grave to find me prisoner in the utility room of Jean-Paul's nursing home. No doubt give me the STROP to punish me for destroying PRIVATE PROPERTY. Fair enough. Only when justice had been done would he understand that

Butcher had flown all the way to New York, had abandoned me again.

That would get my father straightaway. Ah, he would ask, how long would that take?

Thirteen hours.

Good heavens.

My daddy was a REAL CHARACTER, as the saying is. Everyone remembers him. WHY HAVE YOU FORSAKEN ME?

The police are little Hitlers according to Butcher Bones but when I was in arrears at the Nursing Home they did not charge me with a crime. As long as I remained inside the utility room everything was hunky-dory. They brought me interesting objects they had discovered in their travels including a bear used to advertise a doughnut shop.

My father was a hard man living in an age of miracles and wonder. I would come upon him in the night as he contemplated the wonder of REFRIGERATION. Before refrigeration he drove his wagon to Madingley to meet the Melbourne train, then back to fill the ice chamber. Then came the fridge EUREKA you would think but the GENERAL PUBLIC did not like cold meat and would only buy what was hanging in the shop THE MORONS as my father said. He was always for progress, including widening the main street even if it meant we had to kill the trees. My father was a well-known REALIST. The leaves blocked up the gutters anyway, as he said more than once in the public bar of the Royal Hotel.

I was sitting on my chair in front of the shop. This was several years ago, bless me, Blue Bones had not been taken from us. Two Melbourne fellows came by travelling in a Holden which was a new BRAND never heard of before that year. One had a pinstripe suit the other tartan shorts you would split your sides to look at him. The one in the suit asked may we take your picture. Not being certain of my GROUND I fetched Blue Bones and I could see from his face he agreed they were a pair of POOFTERS but he did not mind if he and I posed together father and son. The poofters had what is called a POLAROID. When the photograph was taken, we stood around and I watched myself appear like a drowned man floating to the surface of a dam.

Look at this, my daddy said. See, this didn't work at all.

I saw his point immediately, but it took some time for the poofters to understand my father's objection which was you could see no more of Blue Bones than his apron. They then agreed to take a second Polaroid and he could keep it, welcome to it, no trouble to them at all.

When they had made a portrait to Blue Bones' satisfaction they presented it to him and then SKEDADDLED. Who can ever imagine where they went to?

Fancy that, my father said, studying his likeness as it bloomed before him. He had a face like a hatchet and angry red eyes but when he placed the Polaroid on the mantel he was a different man. Fancy that, he said. He cocked his head. He almost smiled. Fancy fucking that now.

Later the Polaroid began to fade and then it got much worse because within a week it had completely VANISHED. You would expect our father to get into a whipping rage, but he never did, not once, and the Polaroid stayed on the mantel for as long as he lived and sometimes I would see him checking on it as if it were a barometer or clock. Then he died, everything gone and weeds coming through the floor of the sleep-out.

I stayed in the utility room for many days waiting for my brother to deal with the ARREARS. It was an ugly room with a basin and a bucket and a gas hot-water service that roared to life in the middle of the night. WHOOMP. WHOOMP. It would put the fear of God in you. I arranged the bear and the wreath and turned on the radio and although it would not play its green light was always comforting.

I opened my eyes one morning and saw steam from the

laundry, sun streaming through the clouds and the HEAV-ENLY CREATURE was there even though he was a MALE he was as beautiful as the famous painting by FILIPPINO LIPPI—his suit was a dusty white silver like the underside of moth wings when they are dying in the holy light.

And thus the stone was rolled away and I followed him along the hallway where the old people came out to tell me I would trip on the cord trailing from my radio and it must have been before eight o'clock because Jackson was still sitting at the desk.

The angel creature said, Give him his money.

Jackson gave me an envelope. He said no hard feelings.

In the street outside there was waiting a white Mercedes-Benz as if it was a wedding. I got in next to the angel creature. He had dark ringlets glistening, freshly blessed. He said I am very pleased to meet you. He said, It appears we are travelling together. Good grief. Where to? Suddenly I was afraid.

He said I am Olivier Leibovitz and you and I are going to New York today. Forgive me, all I could think was my brother was ROOTING his wife. Should I tell him? What would become of me? I told him I did not have my chair. I said I must return for it.

There are many chairs in New York, said he. I'll buy you one at the Third Street Bazaar.

At Kingsford Smith International Airport Olivier took a pill. Here, he said, you better have one too. He gave me a Coke and two pills. I took them both and soon after that I discovered I had a passport. I never knew I had one, or what one looked like. When I went into the airplane I was thinking of my father.

I asked Olivier how long it would take to get to America.

He said thirteen hours to Los Angeles, Bless me, bless my poor dead darling daddy. He could not have borne it, to see Slow Bones sitting in his seat.

37

There were only two bars in SoHo in those years. One of them was Kitty's and the other was Fanelli's, and it was here that a swollen-eyed Marlene found me thirty minutes later. She arrived at my back-room table, light as a moth, carrying two Rolling Rocks, one of which she placed circumspectly before me.

'I love you,' she said. 'You have no idea how much.'

Being filled with raw emotion, I did not trust myself to speak.

She slid on to the opposite bench, raising her bottle to her lips. 'But you can't love me unless you know what it is you've got yourself involved with.'

As this was exactly what I had been thinking I lifted my beer and drank.

'So,' she placed her own beer, carefully, on the tabletop. 'I'm going to tell you.'

She paused.

'You know, when you saw me first . . . in those ridiculous shoes that got you so excited.'

'I hated the shoes.'

'Yes, but don't hate me. That would be unbearable. Don't worry about Hugh. I'll look after Hugh.'

I snorted at this, but I must tell you, it touched me. No one had even *lied* to me about this sort of thing before.

'Olivier authenticated Dozy Boylan's painting,' she said finally. 'I had been away. By the time I was back in Australia he had done it. Jesus! So dumb. Boylan was a friend of a client of Olivier's and Olivier was too embarrassed to admit he didn't know a rat's arse about his father's work.'

'It's a famous painting. Where's the risk?'

'If he had looked past his nose he would have discovered it had been deaccessioned by the Museum of Modern Art. In other words, dumped.'

'I know what it means, baby.'

'I know you know, but shouldn't that have been a red flag? Why would they have dumped it? Even Olivier should have thought of this.'

'But you said it's fine. It's almost the first thing you ever said to me. "The good thing is that Mr Boylan knows his Leibovitz is real."'

'Shoosh. Listen.' She took ahold of both my hands and lifted them to her lips. 'Listen to me, Michael. I'm telling you the truth.'

'His Leibovitz is not real? Is that it?'

'In my opinion? It was an unfinished postwar canvas that Dominique and Honoré removed the night the old goat died.'

'Fuck, Marlene!'

'Shoosh. Calm down. This was not a valuable painting, but they doctored it. They dated it 1913. Then it was a valuable painting. MoMA snapped it up as soon as it came on the market in 1956. It came straight from the estate. It had a perfect provenance and it was commonly reproduced. But it was a fixer-upper. Honoré, of course, knew *exactly* how much and in what way it had been tampered with. He didn't need an X-ray. He probably watched Dominique do it.'

'But you found the paint receipts in the archive? Oh shit. You printed the receipt yourself?'

'Baby, please don't hate me. I really wasn't always a crook. We should have just taken back the Boylan canvas, but who would have loaned us the one and a half million US dollars we would have had to pay? No one.'

'So you faked a receipt for titanium white.'

'That was just plugging a leak with chewing-gum. For

about two days the painting was legit again. But before too long there would be a real X-ray and then we would be, excuse me, totally fucked.'

So now I understood. 'It was insured. You arranged to have it stolen.'

Her eyes were a little puffy and the light from Prince Street was soft and blue. For all the time she had told the story she had seemed dejected and I was therefore slow to spot the shadow of a smile which was now showing in the corner of her mouth.

'You *personally* stole it.'

'Well, Olivier was not going to do it.'

'You walked a mile through the bush at night?'

In New York it had begun to rain, great fat drops which struck Fanelli's window and cast dance-floor shadows on that lovely rather lonely face as she explained, checking my reaction constantly, how she had paid cash for a pair of nipple-tipped gardening gloves, a set of screwdrivers, carpet knife, wire cutters, wood chisel, nail pullers, a flashlight, a roll of duct tape and a Wonder Bar. She lived for two days in a Grafton motel and when she knew Dozy had left for Sydney she drove along those lonely back roads to the Promised Land. The rental she parked on an abandoned logging road and from here she walked along a ridgeline through scrubby country, and although she had some difficulty locating the pole, she climbed it easily and disconnected both power and telephone.

'How did you know how to do all that?'

She shrugged her left shoulder. 'Research.'

By the time she arrived at Dozy's front door the night was a shower of crystalline stars in a velvet sky. Working with no more than moon and starlight, she used the Wonder Bar to remove the mouldings on the glass panes in the door. This was something I remembered from the press report, the local detectives saying the robber had been a 'neatness freak'. Marlene had left the mouldings tidily stacked on top of the dishwasher.

Dozy had already shown her exactly where the painting was and how it was secured. Now she used a bolt cutter to sever the cable, and carefully removed the frame which had always offended her. She covered the painting with a number of pillowcases, wrapped the entire thing with duct tape, and walked up through the bush.

'What then?'

Her lowered eyes were suddenly wide and hard. 'Do you still want to have anything to do with me, baby? That is really the question.'

I should have been scared, but I wasn't. 'I'll have to hear the whole story.'

She raised an eyebrow. 'You want a written confession?'

'The whole story.'

'Oh really. Indeed,' she said, a little rattled.

'Do you remember, when you first came to my place and you saw what I was working on?'

'I've never lied about your work. Never. Ever.'

'I don't mean the paintings.'

'Yes, you had some lovely drawings of insects.'

'Flies, wasps, some butterflies.'

'I remember thinking, Thank God, he can draw.' She coloured. 'I was ahead of myself.'

'Well, the Stalk-eyed Signal Fly, for instance . . .'

'Michael, you did tell me this before. It's called Borobodur. It's rare except that Boylan found it near his house.'

'*Borboroidini*. That's the Wombat Fly.'

'I know.'

'When we were looking at *Tour en bois, quatre* in Mr Mauri's office, there was a Stalk-eyed Signal Fly caught in a spiderweb on the back. That's a very local insect also.'

It took her a moment, but when she got the point she seemed almost pleased.

'You're a very clever man.' She smiled.

'I am.'

'So, my sweetheart, tell me how I made it smaller?'

'You tell me.'

Just then someone turned the light off in the bar, and she leaned across the wet laminated table and kissed me on the mouth.

'You figure it,' she said.

Fanelli's was closing and we stumbled out, down along the slippery cobbles to the big dark loft. We said nothing much really, but when we made love that night it was as if we wished to tear ourselves apart, to death, devour. Hide inside the secret wonder of the other's skin.

38

The aircraft seat too narrow the roof too low but then Olivier gave me two more yellow pills and soon it was very nice to be above the clouds. My father never saw this sight. Not in all his life. Nor the Kings of England. No one in the Holy Bible witnessed such a thing unless views are granted in the process of ASCENSION. Blue Bones could not have imagined me, his DISAPPOINTMENT, suspended above the earth, angels and cherubs all around, my heart and arteries clearly seen, being bounced through the heavens like a ping-pong ball inside a gumboot.

At night the eternal river of the sky, my soul like blotting paper dropped in ink. Olivier could not look out the window he said it reminded him that he was nothing. Then he said he wanted to be nothing. He said he only wanted Marlene. He didn't care she had burnt down the Benalla High School.

It had been a shock to discover but it made no difference to him now. He was all for burning down.

The waitress asked him would he like a drink. He said he was already at 30,000 feet. I had a beer.

Olivier smelled of perfume and talcum powder like a BABY'S BOTTOM. The waitresses had been ALL OVER HIM since our arrival and when his lovely white jacket passed between them I saw a slight silver shimmer, a creature flown out of the night to cling to the wall above a woman's bed.

He whispered to me that he did not care his wife had turned out to be a PSYCHOPATHIC LIAR but he wished she would not pity him. Why could she not be like a normal woman and dump him in the street?

He said Marlene either loved my brother or his work, who could ever tell which one? She was a romantic fool and had no idea of the bad character of artists.

I said I understood completely.

He said he understood completely from the day that he was born.

I said it was the same for me. Exactly. When he said his father was a selfish pig I reached to shake his hand.

The waitresses brought dinner on a tray and Olivier thought he might have just a CHOTA PEG which was only whisky in the end. I had a beer.

TWO FOUR SIX EIGHT BOG IN DON'T WAIT.

Olivier nibbled at his RABBIT FOOD but then got bored with it and arranged his bottles like checkers on the tray.

He asked did I want him to tell me his pills.

That was OK with me.

He praised TEMAZEPAM he said the ATIVAN was also good and would I like a GENERIC VALIUM. There was much more than this. These are the ones I knew the names of at the time but he must have had ADDERALL as well.

He took a CODIS tablet and one or two assorted capsules

and then a sip of Tasmanian Pinot noir saying the wine would POTENTIATE the pills by golly.

You must not think me a sot, old Hughie. See I am in agony. I love her but she is a terrible, terrible woman.

I did not know what to reply as Marlene was my friend and she and my brother had been ROOTING LIKE RABBITS with my full knowledge. I was an ACCESSORY AFTER THE FACT for all I know. Many is the night I had to put my head beneath the pillow to block the noise.

Ask me how many women have I been to bed with, Olivier said.

He was like a film star with his red lips and curly black hair the skin of his eyelids was soft as a penis freshly bathed. I said ten.

That made him laugh. He patted my elbow and rumpled up my hair and said there was not one of them like his wife. Just the same it had been a RED FLAG to discover she had burnt down the school. He had learned this in the most dreadful way, being told at dinner by a client of his advertising firm who knew only that Olivier's wife came from Benalla.

How old is she? asks the client.

Why twenty-three, says Olivier.

Then she must have been there when that Marlene Cook burnt down the High School. What's your wife's name?

Geena Davis, said Olivier.

Like the movie star.

Same, exactly.

I will not easily forget the day I was declared too slow to return to Bacchus Marsh State School number 28. I would have burnt them to the blessed ground if only I had had some damn good pills to stop me being afraid of punishment. God bless me, save me, I have been made good by cowardice nothing more.

Olivier said I might as well have another beer. I had the weight to soak it up, he said so. He asked me did I know Marlene was a thief. I said she was my friend.

At this he moaned, saying she was his friend too, God help him. Soon he was saying the most frightful things and it took a while to understand he had switched the subject to his mother a very nasty woman. He was happy she was dead. He got a rash when he remembered her.

He was called away by the waitress and I thought he must be in trouble for his violent language but then he returned with airline socks which I must put on. Everyone must obey this rule. He MINISTERED UNTO ME, kneeling to remove my sandshoes and whiffy socks which he tied inside a plastic bag. He said it might be better if I LIMIT MY FLATULENCE to the rear of the plane where it was needed, and then we laughed a lot.

You should have been rich, old chum, he said. You could employ me to change your socks every day.

The waitress brought us each a brandy and put my socks and shoes in the locker overhead.

Olivier said he could have been rich easy enough but his mother was a thieving whore who stole everything from him and it made him sick to think of what she'd done. He would like to be rich and that would be perfect, to look after his horse, to ride like hell, he looked at me and smiled and I knew exactly what he meant—the blood and heart, everything pumping, happy, fearful, the human clock in the river of the day.

She has ruined me, he said. I thought he meant his mother.

Am I her pet dog, he continued, so I knew that was Marlene. You see, that is exactly what I am, he said. She will fill my bowl and brush my coat. I would rather be put down.

I can ruin her, he said a moment later. That's the irony,

old chap. I can destroy her. But what would be the bloody point, old man? If I ruined her she would not rub my ears.

I woke up in the sky above America with my mouth full of dust, scents of fancy gargle, shaving cream, female soap.

That's Los Angeles, he said.

This was my first sighting and I did not know what it could mean, but later I would see the swarms of tiny lights clustered through the night, the cities and highways of America, the beauty of white ants, termites devouring, mating signals glowing in their pulsing tails. Which prophet ever foretold such infestation?

Olivier tapped my knee and said, I am in a state old chap. He offered a pill packet and a sip of his water. He said that if he ate peanuts he would die, if he had oysters his throat would close, but if he did not have Marlene he might as well cut his own throat with a Stanley knife.

I returned his pills. He took one too.

He said, I've just decided I am not going to sign that thing for her.

I asked what thing.

He said, It is completely bogus, so I won't. It's time I had some principles.

I asked what it was.

He said, She would never think I have the nerve. But you watch her old chum. You watch her when I refuse.

I asked would he destroy her.

That made him laugh a long time, stopping and starting and snorting until I feared he had gone mad.

Finally I asked him what was so bloody funny but we were, as they say, PREPARING FOR LANDING and when the aircraft banged itself to earth, my question had not been addressed.

39

The taxis in New York are a total nightmare. I don't know how anybody tolerates them, and I am not complaining about the eviscerated seats, the shitty shock absorbers, the suicidal left-hand turns, but rather the common faith of all those Malaysian Sikhs, Bengali Hindus, Harlem Muslims, Lebanese Christians, Coney Island Russians, Brooklyn Jews, Buddhists, Zarathustrians—who knows what?—all of them with the rock-solid conviction that if you honk your bloody horn the sea will part before you. You can say it is not my business to comment. I am a hick, born in a butcher's shop in Bacchus Marsh, but fuck them, really. Shut the fuck up.

Yes, it is insane to consider educating them one by fucking one, Miss Manners, but when I find a moron leaning on his horn outside my window . . .

So I had to go to the supermarket at a time of night when you would expect the trip to be a swift one, when all the nice Jewish grandmothers should be home in bed or making their special gefilte fish for Rosh Hashanah or whatever it is they do—but perhaps the crowds of grannies in Grand Union were Christians or Tartars, but by God those old women were a subcategory of their own and they would smash you with their shopping carts if you could not match their speed. I was jet-lagged, a foreigner, and I was slow. God help me.

An American supermarket is one thing, Jesus—but a New York supermarket is a complete dog's breakfast—you would have to be born in Aisle 5 to understand its logic. As you have doubtless guessed already, I had come to buy a dozen eggs. At first I could not find them, then there they were, right next to the feta, so many bloody categories of eggs, sizes of eggs, colours of eggs, my fellow shoppers could not wait for me to make a choice. I was blocking their aisle, so they locked wheels with me, crowded in from Aisles 2 and 3, swarmed like gridlocked morons at the entrance to the Holland Tunnel.

I bought brown eggs because they seemed more basic—I really was a hick—but five blocks later, above Mercer Street and Broome, when I stood in the rusty shadow of the fire escape, I discovered the expensive little fucks had shells like concrete. Did I tell you I had been a fatal fast bowler at Bacchus Marsh High School? I still had a good eye and my father's arm but no matter how I swung or spun them, the eggs bounced off the windscreens of the honking cabs.

Marlene, bless her, tried neither to prevent nor encourage me and when I stepped back in through the open window she looked up from the ratty sofa where she was stretched out reading the *New York Times*. 'Come here my genius.'

She was so, so gorgeous, the reading light catching her left cheek, a wash of gold dust, rising from a slate-blue field.

'You are a moron.' She held her arms open and I held her, smelled her jasmine skin, her shampooed hair. Did I say I loved her? Of course I did. I slid my hand down her poleclimber's back, touching every vertebra in that nubbly line of life. She was my thief, my lover, my mystery, a lovely series of revelations which I prayed would never end. It was our third night in New York City. We had money now. The day had been a big success, and not just because of the case of Bourgueil and the bottle of Lagavulin, although that did smooth the edges, but Dozy Boylan's Signal-Fly painting was now stored in an art-world fortress in Long Island City. Its only entrance, Marlene told me, was through a tunnel which was flooded every night. The vaults were filled with Mondrians, de Koonings, and her precious Leibovitz which her wacko husband would come and sign off ASAP.

'Forget the taxis,' she said. 'It's New York. What do you expect? You'll get used to it.'

She was right, of course. I was from the Marsh where Highway 31 ran right past my bedroom, trucks roaring and grinding all night as you waited for them to lose it on Stamford Hill, plough down into Main Street, sheering all the verandas off the shops. I would grow accustomed to the fucking taxis, but what I could not get used to was that Marlene was not screaming at me. By now the Alimony Whore would have called the cops but here I had a quick hit of Lagavulin—God bless the working men of Islay—and as I left to buy some better eggs, she called me an idiot and put her tongue inside my ear.

At this hour in Sydney only the bars would still be open but the entrance of Grand Union was crowded with limping black men who had come to feed empty cans and bottles to an automated machine. Also, new grandmothers had arrived—later I discovered that there was an endless supply of mafia mothers in the neighbourhood and I mention this now because John Gotti's mother was later mugged by some unlucky fuck. What did I know? It was my good fortune that I was polite to all these lethal individuals, and when I tested an egg or two inside the refrigerated cabinet, no one had the time to see my crime.

There are 8,534 taxi medallions in New York, which must mean close to twenty thousand drivers and of course I could not give etiquette classes to them all, but you must believe me when I tell you that my eggs finally made a difference. You think this is ridiculous, but ask yourself: What are all those Sikhs saying to each other on their radios?

I was much happier with my second dozen eggs, large thin white shells which splattered beautifully. We turned off the lights and my beautiful little thief came out on the fire escape to admire my aim.

'You're being unfair,' she said. 'The wrong people are

being punished. Forget the taxis. Go for the minivans with New Jersey plates.'

I was drunk when we came back inside, a little spongy in the legs, and when the next serious eruption of horns arrived, just before midnight, I was ready to say my point was made. But I was standing at the icebox, so it was nothing to pick up an egg, turn off the lights, heave open the window, and burst my yellow bomb across the offending windscreen, a minivan as it turned out, with Jersey plates.

'Come back in. Turn on the light.'

In front of the minivan, whose wipers were now smearing yolk and white across the glass, was a yellow cab from which two travellers were slowly emerging.

Pleased as I was that the minivan was now silent, I was slow to realize that the men emerging from the taxi below were both known to me.

40

In the past many unhappy voices. In the past the smell of stove blacking, Johnson's floor polish, cloudy ammonia, then my father's bloody aprons soaking in the bleach. DEAD BODIES so-called in amber glass—Foster's Lager, Vic Bitter, Ballarat Bertie, Castlemaine XXXX, all those arguments best left in the slop tray but I never did like to hear them. There, I've said it. In the past, there was the main street. There was the butcher's shop. Behind the shop the paddock was filled with boxthorn, then on the hill the vicarage. Happier listening to the bells for evensong. There, I've said it. Happier listening to the kookaburras, watch them tracing out their territory at dusk. Better to know SFA about the kookaburras, God save us from the beak, the congregation of the worms and mice.

Which is to say, NO DISCORD GENTLEMEN PLEASE. Likewise in the modern day I did not like to hear how my brother spoke to Olivier on Mercer Street, New York, the address written on my wrist. DON'T GET ME WRONG—I was very happy for a moment, on arrival, but then Marlene asked Olivier to sign the BOGUS DOCUMENT and within five minutes I had departed for the street. Soon there was a fellow approaching. Who was he? I did not know. He was dragging a loud cardboard box across the foreign cobbles. What did he intend? He was a BLACK MAN with a grey beard and a pair of Mickey Mouse ears or perhaps some other brand of mouse for the ears were small and pink UNNATURAL. Frankly, I liked the cut of him.

He asked, Suspender been by here?

I replied I just got here.

He asked me where I been.

Australia.

Mad Max, he said, and continued on his way down the centre of the street, laughing like a drain. SO WHAT'S THE JOKE YOU DICKHEAD? as my brother would have said. I returned to the safety of the loft but Butcher was busy threatening Olivier with violence, I will break your this, will tear out your that. Home sweet home and OLD LANG SIGN. In his red-faced rage he described plastic buckets filled with Olivier's blood but his voice was shaking like a loose bit of tin on a chook-house roof. I knew he was afraid.

Olivier had remained very still, bending his body into the sofa like GUMBY. When I saw him smile at my brother I knew there would be bloodshed. I once more made my EXIT via the dreadful factory stairs pushing through a forest of SICK-MAKING wet burnt carpet rolls. My arm muscles were firing sparks, and I had a shuddering inside my head. Thank God to get into the air outside but then I understood I must be in the NEW YORK SLUMS, bless me. The door shut beside me and there was nothing more to do but wait and hope I would not be a VICTIM.

I was frightened by Suspender that's the truth. Later, once or twice, I used the name. Who are you? I'm Suspender.

A man rode past on a bicycle, bless me, I had not expected bicycles at all. No harm was done.

Then Olivier appeared.

He said, I have brought your suitcase, but it's up to you.

What?

I can't stay here, old mate, he said.

I asked him where was he going.

Off to my club, but you will probably prefer to be with your KISS AND KIN.

Can I come with you? I asked.

He looked me up and down. He did not want me. I could see.

Assuredly, he said at last. He smiled. He put his arm around me, but once we were in the taxi he drew back into his corner and exploded I HATE THE FUCKING BITCH!

Bless me, save us. The misery of Sundays.

I HATE HER.

Hide the knives, lock the doors.

I HOPE SHE DIES.

Then he paid the driver and we were outside a mansion.

This was the Bicker Club whatever that meant. He said would I wait outside a moment as he would HAVE A WORD with Mr Heavens. I was causing trouble. What else could I do?

I had AMPLE OPPORTUNITY to read THE BICKER CLUB'S DRESS CODE FOR NON-MEMBERS.

INAPPROPRIATE ATTIRE IS LISTED BELOW:
LEGGINGS, STIRRUP PANTS, CAPRI PANTS
SHORTS OR CUT-OFFS

SWEATSHIRTS, SWEATPANTS, OR JOGGING
SUITS
HALTER DRESSES OR SUNDRESSES
DENIM OF ANY TYPE OR IN ANY COLOR,
INCLUDING DRESSES, SHIRTS, SKIRTS, VESTS
AND/OR SLACKS
SPANDEX OR LYCRA GARMENTS
T-SHIRTS, TANK TOPS OR CROP TOPS

Did I have CAPRI pants? What was a LYCRA garment?
Olivier returned, not with Heavens but with Jeavons, a
strange and ugly thing in a PENGUIN SUIT, as sniffy as the
CARDIN JUDGE who gaoled my brother. Jeavons had a bald
head and huge ears and when he spoke he raised an eyebrow
as if sending me private messages. All Greek to me.

Jeavons provided me with a long fur coat but I was a HOT
ENGINE as my mother always said. OUR DEAR V8 she
called me. I said I was not cold.

Said Olivier, the bear suit is not exactly voluntary old
chum.

Then I understood the rude bugger Jeavons wished me
to cover my own clothes. True enough—once my Marshy
body was hidden from the MEMBERS' view I was permitted
entrance to the Bicker Club. You never saw such a place, too
High Church for Mum, stained-glass ceilings, wood carved
like a bloody ROOD SCREEN so it was IN EVERY WAY
SUPERIOR to the place where we had left poor old Butcher
and Marlene where the only chair had been a case of wine. I
kept my coat buttoned tight around me because by now
I was certain I must have a LYCRA GARMENT and when
Jeavons said, You've had a long journey sir, I answered yes.

Then I added, *Mad Max*.

He laughed. I was pleased to have made a joke.

On the way to what you would call an ANCIENT LIFT
we passed a long gallery with a stained-glass ceiling which

was dead as a DODO with no sunlight to drive it. MEDI-
OCRE CRAP hung on the walls and I was pleased Butcher
was not here for he would have got COMPLETELY APE
SHIT, taken a whip and driven the so-called artists into the
park for manual labour. Of course I did not know anything
about Gramercy Park, not the secret tree poisoning, not the
locksmith on First Avenue who will cut the illegal key to its
gate, not the trouble with the committee either and when
Jeavons told me Bowtie Johnson had declared this mansion
among the most beautiful in New York, I did not know this
name any better than Suspender.

Just the same, on my first night in New York City I
understood I was with the CRÈME DE LA CRÈME. I slept in
a bed two feet wide, as snug as a bug in a rug.

41

My first week in Manhattan was spent jet-lagged, twiddling
my thumbs and dozing while Marlene attempted to persuade
Olivier Leibovitz that he should exercise his *droit moral* and
sign the certificate of authentication.

Marlene told me everything, blow by blow, and I was so
free of jealousy, so bloody adult, you have no idea, and it was
only when AT&T asked for my social security number that
I really went ballistic. An hour later, at Prince Street Lum-
ber there was a set-to when they did not understand that
an 'outlet' is what is really called a 'power point'. After that
I was nearly run down on Houston Street. I was a
lonely, unemployed disaster, a two-hundred-pound barra-
mundi flapping on the deck.

That Slow Bones had deserted me in favour of the bloody

Bicker Club was more upsetting than you might imagine. But what could I do? There is always Hugh, an interference on the screen, a hum in the speakers, a nagging ache when there is nothing wrong. So what was I complaining about? I had more money in my pocket than my father had accumulated in the full total fury of his life. So I could visit the Corots at the Met, or finally admit, if only to myself, that I had never seen a Rothko except in reproduction. I had the time. Indeed, the Mercer Street apartment was full of time, a cold metallic blue colour which soaked into every corner, sucking the life from the greys and browns, and once I had stood naked in front of the dusty full-length mirror, confronting the puckering pectorals, I knew it was better to be outside, away from the Lagavulin and my own decay and guilt.

In an empty lot on Broadway, I bought a severely second-hand London Fog from a hostile Korean in mittens. The coat was adequate, or would be for a week or two. Never mind, I hurried into a shop where they understood my accent and I bought a tourist guide and a five-dollar lottery ticket and then I walked beneath all those blunt sans-serif shop signs advertising quality linen and factory remnants, past the Strand Morgue, all the way along lower Broadway, on up to Union Square where I figured out the subway could get me to the Museum of Modern Art. Then, on what we might call a faux-impulse, I cut sideways, across the grey and black gum-speckled sidewalk, down to Gramercy Square. I might just look at this ridiculous Bicker Club. It was in my guidebook after all. Philip Johnson said it was great. Not knowing his work, I went along.

There was also, as there had been on lower Broadway, a certain level of street hollering, so I was not surprised, on entering this lovely garden square, to hear the human voice once more in uproar. Waaaaaa! I shoved my hands into the nasty twenty-dollar coat and peered between the black spiked rails, and there, at the far end of the locked park, I saw a white man running. An ambulance now entered Twentieth Street and was attempting to push its way across to Madison with the force of nothing but light and sound. In the midst of this confusion it took me a moment to see that the white man was the author of that dreadful Waaaaaaa. He was barrelling around the park with his naked legs exposed by cowboy chaps.

Then I saw that the chaps were split trousers and that the man was none other than my brother Hugh.

The thing about Gramercy Park is, you need a key. *But* if you're a guest at the Bicker Club you are entitled to take a stroll, and Olivier, it seems, had instructed the Little Old Butler Figure whose name I will not say, to let Hugh enter. The Little Old Butler Figure, for whatever cruel reason best known to his own twisted tiny mind, had not only admitted my brother but then closed the gate behind him. And although the idiot savant, on finding himself caged, had attempted to explain his dilemma to the street, first to a dog walker, then to a limo driver and then to what appears to have been a group of English models on their way to a photo shoot, none of them—and this may not be the fault of their characters, but of the Australian accent which in Slow Bones' case was rather broad—not one chose to acknowledge him with the result that he became distressed, and therefore more alarming to those later people to whom he delivered his appeals, including—so I heard—a member of the Gramercy Park Community Board, a 'sprightly'—oh save me—eighty-year-old who, having found herself locked inside the park with a 'homeless man', fled to the street and slammed the gate.

My brother, it is alleged, then tried to climb the spiked railing and in order to do this he successfully wrenched a park bench from its mooring, managing to shear four quarter-inch bolts, and then dragged it into a flower bed—

all quite sensible you would think—until the bench sank from his weight at the most unlucky moment and Hugh got an iron railing shoved up the leg of his brand-new grey flannel trousers which then ripped him from cuff to baggy boxers.

Poor old darling moron. I waited for him to arrive back at the gate. And when he saw me, how he began to bawl, clambering, slipping, then embracing me across the spikes. He wanted to go home, just home. It took a moment for him to get his breathing right, and a considerably longer time before I learned how he got in the park and who might let him out again.

Thus I presented myself to the sniffy little snob at the Bicker Club and when he did not seem to like my twenty-dollar coat or the fresh marks of my brother's mucus on the sleeve, I picked him up, this little Butler Thing—there was not much to him, but some was held together by a corset—and I carried him like a roll of carpet through the traffic and when he was finally alongside the gate, I asked him did he wish to release my brother or to join him.

He chose release, so I set him very gently on the sidewalk and watched his huge disturbing hands as he fetched a busy ring of keys and opened wide. Hugh looked at me, blinked, then elbowed me violently aside.

I grabbed at him, but he ducked, running blindly out into the street. He stumbled on the far kerb, then rushed up the steps into the club.

The Little Butler Thing, to his credit, did not scold or threaten. He stooped for a moment, picking at the button of his butler suit.

'You're drunk,' he said.

And then with not so much as a glance at the Armani suit now visible beneath my coat, he walked stiffly back into the mansion.

After that I got a taxi back to Mercer Street, and poured myself another Lagavulin to which I added—fuck the Malt

Whisky Society of Edinburgh—a fistful of crushed ice. Bloody Hugh. Later, when it was morning in Tokyo, I woke, washed my face, and having negotiated the disgusting stairs, made my way down Mercer to Canal Street where I found Pearl Paints. On the fourth floor I bought a sketchbook and a box of ink sticks.

42

The great artist was in an uproar to discover no one but Marlene had ever heard of him. He was NOTHING without his so-called art which was his prop, a splintery length of wood you place beneath the wash line.

Hugh Bones was another matter. I took to the city like a DUCK TO WATER. I sat on the demonstration model folding chair outside the Third Street Bazaar. Except its leg was tied to a chain I might have been a BOUNCER behind a VELVET ROPE. I wore a soft thick Italian coat and a black woollen beanie and I folded my HUGE ARMS across my chest. Then the police came at me. They emerged from McDonald's and walked directly towards my place, guns and batons and handcuffs strapped to their great big bottoms.

I thought, I am a FOREIGNER occupying space on the public footpath in CONTRAVENTION OF THE ACT. But the cops did not give a shit, as the saying is. They had more important business—who knows what it might be?—perhaps looking for a DUNNY ROLL to wipe their GREAT BIG BUMS.

This was when I first noticed the GENERAL LAWLESS-NESS pedestrians disobeyed the DON'T WALK sign on Third Street and the so-called AVENUE OF THE AMERICAS. The Melbourne cops would have pulled the SCOFFLAWS back on to the footpath and given them a loud lecture on their mental health. The police on Third Street gave not a TINKER'S FART, to coin a phrase. They carried their big batties down the street—they should have used a wheelbarrow—and I was still a free man when Olivier came out of the Bazaar with a brand-new folding chair beneath his arm it was $13 black and shiny as a Mercedes-Benz. Olivier put his hand around my shoulder then he took me off to show me why I should be very happy with my life.

This is your town, old boy.

Olivier's hives were calmer since the HYDROCORTISONE only the big welt on his neck hidden by the turned-up collar of his IMPORTED COAT. He was very handsome, a Wimbledon ace returning to the back line, loose in the knees, his head hung down in response to the applause.

Olivier now taught me to never call the Avenue of the Americas anything but Sixth Avenue. Everyone would know I was a New Yorker straightaway. Once this was set in concrete we walked for a while and then turned right into Bedford Street where I learned I could sit outside the Laundromat without a permit. Soon we met a man called Jerry who had a hoarse voice and a handkerchief around his head. Jerry said I could come and bring my chair there any time I liked. He said he always wanted to go to Australia. I said it was a very nice country but do not try sitting in the street without a permit.

After this I sat on Sullivan Street between Prince and Spring. Then I sat on Chambers Street.

Old boy, you are a genius at this sort of thing.

Finally I sat on Mercer Street below the artist's loft Butcher had stolen from the NEW SOUTH WALES GOVERNMENT. I rang the bell but no one was home. Either that or my brother was playing possum.

Olivier now revealed he had to go off now to do business with Marlene elsewhere in the city.

I asked would he destroy her.

This did not make him laugh this time. He stared at me very hard and said he would now teach me how to get from Mercer Street to the Bicker Club by myself.

I apologized for what I said.

Hugh, he said, you're a great man. You're wonderful.

But I feared I could not reach the Bicker Club unaided. I had sparks in my long muscles and a click in my head like a catching latch in need of oil.

Olivier gave me a striped capsule which I swallowed without water. Come old fellow, he said, you're a New Yorker now. He took out a notebook and drew me a map. Like this:

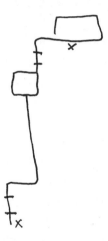

See old chum, he said. Nothing could be simpler.

The pill was not working.

If you get lost, said Olivier, you get in a cab and say take me to Gramercy Park.

I said I would not know what to pay.

Give them ten dollars, he said. Say keep the change.

Then he gave me a roll of notes with a rubber band around them.

When he hailed a cab I folded my chair, but he slammed the door, save us, the taxi drove away. I chased after the tail lights, but it would not stop. I ran back down to the apartment but my brother would not hear the bell, poor puppy, so I ran to the other end of Mercer Street, all the way to Canal Street where I dented my chair by accident against the metal pole. Tail lights receding in the night.

I forgot the name of GRAMERCY.

At Houston Street, I got it back.

Gramercy, Gramercy, Gramercy.

Poor puppy no one heard him bark. I was sweaty, smelling worse than carpet. On Houston Street three taxis tried to run me down. The fourth one stopped.

Gramercy Park, I said.

Which part, he asked. I think he was a Chinaman.

Any part.

As he was a Chinaman, I held the map in my hand to make sure he would know the way but he set off in another direction and in the end he slid shut his window so I could not speak to him.

I was doubtless smelling very WOOFY by the time I looked out the window and saw, by chance, Olivier standing beneath the portico of the Bicker Club.

Stop, I said. I gave twenty dollars. Keep the change.

Olivier now wanted me to walk back to Mercer Street. I asked him what game he thought he was playing. He was my friend and I did not wish to damage him but he fell down.

Olivier then picked up my Dekko Fastback and gave it to Jeavons. Jeavons brushed down the Italian coat. Olivier drew on his gloves.

He said Jeavons should make me a chicken sandwich and bring me a beer in my room.

I asked him how he felt.

Never better, he said. Never better old chum.

As a result of jet lag, I began crying on the stairs.

43

I have never been able to look at paintings with another human being—everyone else too superficial, too solemn, too impatient, too slow. But now Marlene Leibovitz and I moved around MoMA like partners in a waltz. She was the angel. I was the pig, drunk, endlessly enquiring, staring at Cézanne's *L'Estaque*, finally understanding—at my age—that Braque had no sense of humour, getting myself in a tussle with a fucking fourteen-year-old who was wilfully obstructing my view of *Les Demoiselles d'Avignon*.

'Shoosh,' said Marlene. 'Leave him. He's a baby.'

My competitor was a tall pimply boy with a safety pin in his tiny girly ear. I will not say I hated him exactly, but it broke my heart, to think how it might be to stand inside his stinky shoes, to know this masterpiece at fourteen years of age, or argue with it, and do it all as easily as I had once walked along the dull footpath from the shop, up Gell Street, to the sale yards on Lerderderg Street.

'I know,' she said, although I had not spoken, and for this alone I would have worshipped her, but my God—the shape of her face, the bones, the slightly narrowed eyes, the taut lovely funny upper lip.

'How did you shrink the Leibovitz?'

She kissed me in reply.

Did I like New York? I loved *her*. If she had been with me every day, I doubt I would have picked up the ink sticks, but the business of the Leibovitz dragged on. So when my genius little thief went out like a pooka playing tricks, I put on my twenty-dollar coat and took my ink sticks and sketchpad, first down the block on to Canal Street, then on to Chinatown, East Broadway, then the deep charcoal shadows beneath the Manhattan Bridge, and from there to an awful place beneath the FDR at Twenty-first Street, the undercarriage of a crashed machine, abandoned, scabs of rust and concrete falling as I worked.

There were many other places I might have gone to draw, but I did not really question why I drifted further and further from the streets and places I celebrated with Marlene. Now it's clear enough to me—the city scared the shit out of my small-town soul, and it was this that pushed me on and on, a ridiculous effort to somehow conquer, to 'get on top of it', a quixotic quest that finally took me out to Tremont on the D train where I became, it seems, the only human figure on all that cruel Cross Bronx Expressway. And it was here that the Forty-eighth Precinct coppers found me, just before the George Washington Bridge itself, just at the moment where the huge Macks and Kenilworths shift down a gear before descending into the storming bolted belly of the beast itself.

'Get in the fucking car you fucking fuck,' is what the nice policeman said.

As Milton Hesse later told me, I was lucky they did not take me to Bellevue rather than the subway station. I never showed Milt the drawings, but there seems little doubt that they would not have saved me from Bellevue for they were black and dense as soot on a hurricane lamp, a rubbed and broken carapace of dark around the struggling light. These works are very bloody good, but they would have been so much less if I had bought the 'right' materials. As it was, the notebook pages were too small, the paper too fragile for my constant erasures and, on more than one occasion, I wore clear through the stressed-out surface. As is true so often, it was the limitation of the materials that made the art, and they are so filled with a wild ugly sort of struggle which was only made bigger when, finally on Mercer Street, I patched

A over B, and joined A to C, and so on. Anticipating this last stage I had rode the train down to the Village, my hands as black as a coal miner's, eyes cold and mad in my overactive face.

Marlene could see exactly what I had done. You see that is one reason I could always trust her. When she stood in front of art with me, she told the truth. It was Marlene who not only went to New York Central Supplies for more material but arranged—a birthday gift—to borrow two of my paintings back from Mr Mauri.

Neither of us could have foretold the consequences, but the result was that she, with my complete agreement, could bring people to see my work.

This turned out to be a dreadful idea, because the minute *I, the Speaker* and *If You Have Ever Seen a Man Die* were tacked to the wall they could be variously patronized and misunderstood by all sorts of idiots who thought the future of art was being charted by, say, Tom Wesselmann, for fuck's sake.

Their assumption was, I had come to New York City to make my name, that I had arrived at the centre of the universe and so I must want to suck up to a gallery, get a show, meet Frank Stella or Lichtenstein. Nothing could have made me feel worse. It is in any case, a ridiculous proposition, to arrive at thirty-seven years of age. It simply can't be done.

Of course I went to a party now and then, an opening at Castelli, Mary Boone, Paula Cooper. I finally even met the raging Milton Hesse, the first time to be bored by his letter from Leibovitz, the second so he could see my work. What a fool I was. Even now I am embarrassed, to remember how, in front of *I, the Speaker*, he began to tell the story of a fight he had with Guston in 1958. I waited very patiently for him to connect this to his judgement of my work. But in the end it was no more than an association of words and he had no interest in anything to do with me.

The argument with Guston, he said, had been tape-recorded at the artists' club. He wondered—turning his broad and slightly hunched back on the painting—did Marlene possibly have a moment to type it up for him.

And of course I was—just generally—provincial and not up to date, and a part of me was very bloody impressed to sit at Da Silvano and see Roy Lichtenstein and Leo Castelli eating liver and onions at the next table, and if I was as impressed as any hick could be, my reaction was no help to Lichtenstein's art which is already moving rapidly towards deaccession, that is, the point at which curators begin to quietly dump their worst excesses.

New York, it is believed below Ninety-sixth Street, brings out the best in artists, but I cannot say that worked for me. Partly, of course, I was jealous. I knew what it felt like to be Lichtenstein in Sydney, but I could never be Lichtenstein in New York. I was a no one. I went to Elaine's like a tourist and meekly accepted my table by the kitchen. All this I had expected. Why would it be otherwise?

My error was, for a moment, believing that I might possibly be wrong and then permitting the dealers to look at *I, the Speaker*, to see their eyes glaze over, to realize they had never wanted to see it anyway, that they had come because they wanted something from Marlene. Yet, even that particular mortification should not be exaggerated. Artists are used to humiliation. We start with it and we are always ready to return to real failure, the shitty bottom of the barrel, the destruction of our talent by alcohol or misery. We live with the knowledge that, alongside Cézanne or Picasso, we are no one, were always no one, will be forgotten before we are in the ground.

Shame, doubt, self-loathing, all this we eat for breakfast every day. What I could not stand, what really, completely, made my teeth curl was seeing the complete certainty of total mediocrities when confronted with—let's call it 'art'.

For the very same people who cast their glazed eyes on my canvas were often at the auctions at Sotheby's, Christie's, Phillips. And that's when something snapped, when I finally understood, not only their dull complacent certainty, but their lack of any fucking eye at all.

I went, one freezing February day, to Sotheby's. They had two Légers, lots 25 and 28. The first painted in 1912 had six pages of supporting documentation which basically contained reproductions of really good Légers which Sotheby's had once sold for a lot of money. These two were shit. These sold for $800,000. That was the real problem with New York for me. That $800,000. How can you know how much to pay if you don't know what it's worth?

There was also a de Chirico, *Il grande metafisico*, 1917, 41¾" × 27⅞", ex–Albert Barnes, a deaccessioned work. Did anyone think, for a bloody nanosecond, why it might be being deaccessioned? Authentic pre-1918 de Chiricos are rare as hen's teeth. Italian art dealers used to say the Maestro's bed was six feet off the ground, to hold all the 'early work' he kept 'discovering'. But suddenly this pile of crap was real? It was worth 3 million? It made me ill. Not so much the dirty money, but the complete lack of discrimination, the fashion frenzy. De Chirico is in. Renoir is out. Van Gogh is hot. Van Gogh has peaked. I wished I could kill the fucks, I really did.

It was just after this that Olivier finally signed the certificate. I did not enquire as to what had taken all the time, did not ask what acts of kindness were offered, what deal was struck, but my suspicion was that the poor neurasthenic darling had wrinkled his nose and then taken a dirty big slice of pie. Of course he could do whatever he wished, it was not my business. He could be the nursemaid to my brother and be the author of Hugh's hostile eyes. He could steal old Slow Bones from me, if that is what he wished.

Marlene and I stayed on at Mercer Street. At first I

understood this as an economy—why not? It was free—so it took a while to understand that we were hiding. We did have a kind of social life whereby I, by agreement, kept away from dealers, but we made good friends with restorers, authenticators, and one wonderful man, Sol Greene, a tiny little fellow, who ran a family paint business on Fifteenth Street. How much nicer it was to discuss the curious history of, say, madder red, than listen to the drama of the latest Sotheby's circus.

Marlene was scratching around trying to free up some Leibovitzes—there was a collector waiting—but our best days were really just spent walking. Then, in the early days of fall, we began to rent cars, and trawl through junk shops and deceased estates along the Hudson. I won't say it was not interesting to look at America this way, and it was on one of these trips, in a musty barn in Rhinecliff, that I found a mediocre canvas with the perfectly legible inscription—Dominique Broussard, 1944. It was a coarse synthetic cubist work, the type of object you might easily find on a weekend drive from Melbourne—heavy black lines, slabs of sloppy colour—an order of misunderstanding you probably see in Russia too, but hardly at 157 rue de Rennes.

The barn had an earth floor and the canvas was leaning against the wall. It was not art, was less than art. It had been there so long you could feel all the damp of Rhinecliff in its frame, but there was a way in which this neglect was unwarranted for it was as precious as the droppings of a termite until now thought to be extinct.

I spat and rubbed away a little dirt and what I saw then made me laugh because one could so clearly see her character. She was a thief—she had stolen her boss's paint and canvas. She had no sense of colour—in her hands the Leibovitz palette was gaudy. She was complacent.

One could imagine her head held to one side as she admired her own brush moving like a poisonous snake through summer grass. She had no wrist, no attack, no taste, no talent. She was, in short, disgusting.

If this revulsion seems cruel or excessive, it was absolutely *nothing* compared to Marlene's.

'No,' she said. 'No way are you going to buy this.'

I laughed. I did not understand her, had no real sense of the degree to which she was still defending Olivier against his mother. Of course she knew the enemy's brushstrokes, but never had she seen an original work and here was laid bare the complete and awful lack, not only of talent, but of anything at all. Finally grasping the great nothing, Marlene, so she told me later, was physically ill.

In perfect ignorance, I took the canvas into the little office which was set up like a shed within the barn. A pleasant grey-haired woman was watching football on television, her swollen legs exposed to an electric heater.

'How much?'

She looked over the top of her glasses. 'You're an artist?'

'Yes, I am.'

'Three hundred.'

'It's shit,' said Marlene.

'It's our history, babe.'

'I'll burn the fucking thing,' said Marlene, 'if you even try to bring it home.'

The woman looked at Marlene with interest. 'Two hundred,' she said evenly. 'It's an oil original.'

I had, as it happened, exactly two hundred. So I ended up getting it for $185 plus tax.

'You folks married?'

'No.'

'Sure sounds like you're married.'

She wrote her receipt slowly, and by the time she had wrapped my purchase in newspaper Marlene had walked out to the car.

'Now you go buy her something pretty,' the woman said.

I promised that I would, and then drove my lover back to New York City—the Taconic, then the Saw Mill—sixty minutes in icy silence.

44

Olivier signed the bogus document he was so weak he told me he could not even die. He was crawling back to life, old chum, returning to his previous employment at McCain.

They do not like me, Hughie, but I am the perfect bum boy for their client. Bum boy, he called to the Irish barman who said, That's right sir.

Olivier drank a SIDECAR and swallowed a blue capsule.

Here's to honest labour, he said.

Jeavons was standing by his shoulder and now he DISCREETLY passed his big soft hand across his mouth. He had medicine to swallow too.

He said, Thank your mother for the rabbits, sir. This was an AUSTRALIAN JOKE I taught him many days before.

Then I had my capsule. What would happen to me now?

Sitting by the low round table Olivier asked me, Did you ever meet her father, Hughie? He meant Marlene's father.

I said I had never been to Benalla.

He was a bloody truck driver can you imagine that?

Jeavons approved of truck drivers. He drifted away like a man at a ball, his arms out from his sides.

I imagined truck drivers. I saw them all lined up at the Madingley mine.

And that's the thing, you see, that's what I'm up against.

What did that mean? He was sad and silent as he unfolded a map of New York across the little table. With a cheese knife he began to slice it up.

I asked what about the trucks.

She likes big beefy chaps who smell of beer. That's it, really. At the end of it. If you get a redneck who also smells of linseed oil, she's like a cat on heat. Do you follow me?

All I understood was the cheese knife was not the right tool to cut a map and it hurt to watch him botch it. Soon he tore half the map away. The big blue words WEST VILLAGE floated to the floor.

I held my head. I may have made a noise. Who wouldn't?

What's up old chap?

I told him he was making me giddy with Marlene's daddy. I wished he would put the map away.

The map, old chap, will cure the giddiness. So stop lowing. Lowing, he said, that's exactly what you do.

What about Marlene's father?

Dead of lung cancer, he said, but causing trouble to this day.

He removed a lump of map. I caught it floating down but he snatched it back and crumpled it and threw it across the bar. THIS DID NOT CALM ME DOWN.

We have no use for Central Park he said.

But what about her father?

All I'm saying is your lumpen brother is a lucky man.

He tapped the map with a swizzle stick. Now! Remember! Everything is straight up and down except Broadway. Keep an eye on that one, chum. He marked Broadway with his pen. A snake in the grass.

Her father?

Broadway. Also West Broadway. Not to be confused.

To complete my map he ripped across the top at Fifty-fifth Street. World ends here, he said. My office. Top right corner of the map.

Now, he said, test drive.

We set off across to Fifth Avenue where we found a Duane Reade a CHEMIST SHOP where I was introduced to his client's products the denture glue also the bubbling tablets the sufferers used to clean their teeth at night, poor Mum, she was what is called the TARGET MARKET.

On Sixth Avenue Olivier bought SUPPLIES including a flask of Bourbon which fitted nicely inside his coat. This is your town, old mate. Never let them tell you otherwise. He waited while I checked our map. I saw exactly where I was.

Now, old chum, we're going to walk clean off the map. Don't panic. Watch exactly how it's done.

Soon thereafter, on Twenty-fourth Street, we found a group of men outside a church. Not all had chairs like mine, but at least four did. Others preferred the fire hydrant, church steps, SIAMESE CONNECTION. A close similarity to a gathering of PUDDING OWNERS with diseases that swelled their ankles and turned their legs all blue and black.

Fellow professionals, he said. Your peers.

I opened my chair. Olivier was wearing his shimmering grey suit and his poofter shoes. He didn't have a chair but when he took out his flask of whisky he soon made friends.

New York is a very friendly town, he said to me.

The first person to take a swig gave us his business card.

Vincent Carollo
Film musician • *Chelsea Diner*

His black hair was due to boot polish. It made a straight line across his forehead and the hair was all swept back from there. He said call me Vinnie. He had played a banjo in *Chelsea Diner*, a famous film apparently. Also, we should never stay in the West Sixteenth Street shelter, and remember, the soup at St Mark's was better than what they give you at St Peter's. He also taught me never leave my chair unattended and then I sang 'ADVANCE AUSTRALIA FAIR'. He took back his card as he needed it for later. He said I would be in the next film too but when I invited him to the Bicker Club Olivier said it was time to go.

But he had showed me I could make friends. I didn't need him now. That was his whole point. He was going to abandon me. I could not be permitted to sit with him in his office, nor to visit at any hour. He was hoping he could have this rule changed but don't hold your breath, Hughie.

The thing is, old chum, he said, they are very superficial individuals.

I asked could I stand on the street outside.

He said you have UNIQUE TALENT, old chum. I mean, old chum, you do know how to BE.

He meant my talent for sitting on a chair while Butcher flew around in a mad frenzy, a willy wagtail trying to be a king. He did not know I had a TALENT for drawing. When they sent me home from school I did not burn them down. Instead I began to work peacefully with biro on my sheets and by the time Mum LOOKED IN ON ME I had all the Marsh laid out in pen across it. Blue Bones dealt with that one in his usual style.

The Marsh was my place as no other. Not only the chair, the footpath. I knew the drains and culverts, the length of every street and where they crashed together. From Mason's Lane to the Madingley railway crossing was 6,450 heartbeats. In the whole 5000 POP. who else knew this simple fact? Yes it was a talent but I was allegedly too slow to go to school.

When Olivier left me on Monday morning I took the map and laid it on the carpet in the room. Explosions in my neck but nothing bad. I drew the Main Street of Bacchus Marsh down Broadway, and the Gisborne Road across Thirty-fourth Street. Lerderderg Street lying like a ghost along Eighth Avenue.

I felt better. I felt worse. Then I could not stand the map. I left.

Across to Third Avenue and up. That was my plan. Twenty-second Street, Twenty-third Street, and so on. There was no doubt I could reach Fifty-fifth. Heart closer to 200, great red lump of muscle in an uproar, never mind. Reaching Fifty-fifth Street I was denied access to the building by a man in a brown suit.

I walked back downtown. Followed the map of the Marsh and arrived at the Butcher Shop next door to Duane Reade where I bought a pack of Band-Aids it was HIGHWAY ROBBERY.

Olivier finally arrived back at the club BETTER LATE THAN NEVER I gave him the Band-Aids and instructed him to stick one on his window so I could see his office from the street.

Old Chum, he said, I will put up the Band-Aid at exactly ten past one.

When we set up in the bar, Olivier told me he was getting his life back.

Here, he said, have one of these.

He would now divorce Marlene.

He downed a big gin and tonic and crunched up the ice. This will totally fuck the bitch, he said. Once she was divorced she would never authenticate another painting or try to make him sign a form.

Here, he said, have one of these as well.

I pointed out the second pill was a different colour from the first pill. He replied that we were desperados not decorators.

He was on his HOBBY HORSE and galloping. She could go back to the typing pool, old mate, the pond from which she rose and then he listed the names of different SCUM that grew on top of ponds for instance SPIROGYRA.

Jeavons came to have a word.

BLOOD ON HER SADDLE he said the words from a song who knows which one. Jeavons made a sign to the bartender and I understood Olivier was going mad.

Next morning I knew I must take a holiday with my brother. It was his job to care for me. On arrival I requested sausages and eggs. He knew his obligation.

Marlene was asleep on the mattress on the floor. She had a bare leg sticking out beneath her quilt and I could see her batty, bless me, it was so pretty I had to look away. For REASONS KNOWN ONLY TO HIMSELF my brother had purchased a sheet of glass and was grinding pigments, gathering and scraping the pigment with a spatula.

I asked him why he did not buy some nice one-pound tubes.

He said I could go and fuck myself.

Very nice. I sat and watched him until he asked me would I like a try. So I was needed to be the DOGSBODY.

He had no linseed oil but something else called AMBER-TOL. I was pleased to show how well I produced the buttery texture he required. The colour very soothing before he made it into something angry. Oceans of yellow, colour of God, light without end.

So, said he, how is your mate Dr Goebbels?

Who?

Olivier.

I told him Olivier was going to divorce Marlene. I intended to make him happy. Perhaps I did. In any case I heard Marlene shift in the bed but she might as well have been asleep because she did not say a word.

45

The face of Dominique Broussard's dusty canvas was now turned permanently towards the wall, and if there was still a certain tension between the pair of us, it was entirely pleasant.

That is, my baby had a secret—how had she shrunk the painting? And I also had a secret of my own—jars of paint in colours I refused to explain to her. I left these five enigmas in full view on the blistered kitchen countertop, and I made sketches twenty feet away from them, in a corner by the windows, sitting on a wooden box with my back turned to the dirty street. What was I up to? I would not tell her and she would not ask. We smiled a lot, and made love more than ever.

Then she bought a bench press, assembling it in pretty much the same spirit that I worked on my paints and pencil studies. Sometimes I stepped away from my secret project to draw her lovely slender arms, the stretched tendons in her neck. She sweated readily when exercising but in these drawings, which I still have, it is my own desire that glistens on her skin.

It was 1981 and the only rule was DON'T BUZZ IN PEOPLE YOU DO NOT KNOW. But when, late one snowy morning, the street bell rang, I buzzed in the stranger and threw our apartment open to the fates. It was either that or walk down five flights to find no one more interesting than the UPS guy.

On this occasion I accidentally let in Detective bloody Amberstreet.

Marlene lowered her weights.

'What are you doing here?' she asked.

'What are you doing here, Marlene?' said Amberstreet, his white creased-up face protruding from a long black quilted coat. 'That would be more pertinent.'

'Nice shoes,' I said, but he had always been impervious to insult and now he complacently considered the snow-encrusted Converse sneakers protruding from the skirt of his black coat. 'Thanks,' he said. 'They were only sixty dollars.' He blinked. 'The thing is Marlene, this loft is the property of the Government of New South Wales. I hope for your sake that you have permission to be here.'

But then his eye was taken by *I, the Speaker*, and here his snarky manner unexpectedly melted and that strange adoring look crept into his eyes. Without altering this new focus of attention he removed his ridiculous coat, revealing a sweatshirt reading 'UCK NEW YOR', the 'F' and 'K' being hidden underneath his arms.

'So,' he said, hugging the coat against him like a comforter, 'so, Michael, were you a friend of Helen Gold?'

Marlene cast a quick look at me. What the fuck did that mean?

'She's a bloody awful painter,' I said. 'Why would I know someone like that?'

'She was artist-in-residence here.'

'Actually, she was a friend of mine,' said Marlene.

'So, Mrs Leibovitz, you knew Helen killed herself.'

'Of course.'

'So you understand that you have been contaminating a crime scene?'

'Sorry,' she said to me. 'I did not want you getting spooked.'

'It has bad light,' Amberstreet announced, taking in his twenty-eight-inch belt another notch. 'I don't know who would buy a space like this for an artist. Are you working here, Michael? Are you producing?' He peered around, his bristly head darting towards the jars of paint I had lined up on the kitchen countertop.

'A change of palette!'

He squeaked across the floor towards the kitchen. Marlene shot me a warning look, but why?

The detective was like a dog, sniffing here, pissing there, running from one smell to the next. He laid his coat down on the countertop and picked up two jars, one red, one yellow. 'How exciting.' Pant, pant, pant. Then he was pushing his pointy nose towards *I, the Speaker*, squizzing up his eyes, clasping my bottles to his chest. If he had opened one and got a whiff of Ambertol . . . He didn't.

'God,' he said, 'even if the lighting was a little bit too perfect. I mean at Mitsukoshi. A complete sell-out, I mean in the good sense, Michael, of everything being sold. I hope you got some press back home.'

'I don't know.'

'Of course you've not been home either. It was Mauri, right? Hiroshi Mauri who bought the whole damn show. That's a class above your mate Jean-Paul.'

'Yes.'

'An associate of yours, Marlene, would that be correct?'

Marlene had been sitting on the bench, but now she stood, wrapping a towel around her shoulders. 'Oh please,' she said. 'This is so boring.'

'Yes, you know what I thought, Michael?' He immediately gave me my jars of paint to hold. 'You know what I thought when I heard about your show? I thought, This is how Marlene is going to get Mr Boylan's Leibovitz out of Australia.'

It was hard not to laugh at the little fuck. 'Yeah, well you were wrong about that one.'

'No, I don't think so, Michael. I wasn't wrong at all. My, this painting was beautifully restored.' The V-shaped creases around his eyes were deepening like wire cuts in a sandstone block. He cocked his head, and, in what seemed a sort of frenzy of curiosity, twisted his wire arms fiercely around his chest. 'Really, it's no excuse for what we did to it, but it's actually improved, don't you think?'

I looked to Marlene. Amberstreet caught my look.

'I heard, Marlene, that there was a new Leibovitz on the market in New York. Ex-Tokyo. So what I realized, Marlene, was Michael's paintings were a kind of feint. We opened all the crates at Sydney Airport, but you had the Leibovitz in your hand luggage. In your garment bag, I'd say.'

Oh fuck, I thought, she's caught. It's over. It had happened, just like that. But Marlene was not looking caught at all. Indeed, she smiled. 'You know very well it can't be Mr Boylan's painting.'

Amberstreet tipped his head and looked at her, no longer officious or even sarcastic, but, just for a brief moment, showing something close to admiration.

It was Marlene who finally spoke. 'You measured it?'

The detective did not reply but, in an oddly polite gesture, retrieved my jars of paint from me, and returned them to the kitchen where, in short order, he opened a cupboard door, closed it carefully, ran his finger along the countertop, turned on the tap, washed his finger, and then, finally, it seemed he might speak. But then his eye lit on the back of Dominique's dumb little canvas. He turned it over. I held my breath.

'Guess where I was just now,' he demanded.

'Tell us,' I said. I thought, Where the fuck is all this heading?

'With Bill de Kooning in the Hamptons.'

'Yes. So?'

'No one ever told me he was so handsome,' said Amberstreet.

I could not follow him.

'And there's the wife. Elaine. Gone back to him.'

Marlene's eyes showed no concern at all. They were
bright and clear, intensely focused. She handed me my coat.

'Just wait,' begged Amberstreet. 'Please. Just look.'

From the pocket of his ridiculous coat he produced an
envelope from which he removed a two-sheet cardboard
sandwich which, in turn, protected a tiny charcoal doodle.
This he handed to me, cradled in his palm, as fragile as a
butterfly.

'It's a de Kooning?'

'Everyone has to go to the lavatory sometime.'

'You prick,' Marlene said. 'You stole it.'

'Not really, no. It isn't even signed.' He danced from one
foot to the other, his mouth turned down in a rictus of
denial. 'Who would believe that in Sydney?' he said. 'Who
would have any idea? You're both leaving? I'll walk down
with you, but tell me, I wanted to ask you. Did you see that
Noland show?'

No more was said about Mauri or the stolen Leibovitz.

'Well,' he said, as we arrived on the street. 'I'm off to
Greenwich. I've got a map of artists' houses.'

'You mean the Village.'

'You know I'm going to get you, Marlene,' he said.
'You're going to go to gaol.'

And then he winked, the little creep, and we watched him
head up towards Houston with his stupid coat floating like a
squid in the snowstorm.

Marlene took my arm and squeezed it.

'It was a feint?' I asked her. Of course I didn't think it
was, and I should have been furious that she smiled back so
readily. In fact I was simply pleased she had not been caught.
I laughed and kissed her. My friends all tell me I should have

hated her. Oh, what a cheat she was. What a sucker I was, to fall for all that Tokyo bullshit. The best canvas I had managed to produce had been used like a matador's cape. Surely I was angry?

No.

But was it not true that, even as we walked across Canal Street and down into the huge dark silence of Laight Street, amongst the soot-covered ghosts of the former railway-freight terminus, surely as that rat ran across the cobbles, seven of my nine paintings had vanished from the face of the fucking earth? Might they not, for all I knew, be now discarded like pretty paper ripped from Christmas presents, stuffed in black plastic body bags, dumped out on the Roppongi streets?

No.

But couldn't I see my own denial? Had all my boring speeches about my art been forgotten?

No.

But why would I not turn away from her, now, as we passed this scratched-up metal door from under which wafted the inexplicable odours of cumin and cinnamon?

I did not wish to turn away.

So I really believed that a self-confessed liar and cheat really loved my paintings.

I had no doubts. Ever.

But why?

Because the work was great, you dipshit.

As we walked down Greenwich Street, with a bitter wind whipping off the Hudson, sheets of newspaper lifting into the lonely air like seagulls, Marlene made herself small beneath my arm and I was not angry because I knew no one had ever loved her until now. I understood exactly how she created herself, how she, like I, had entered a world which she should never have been allowed into, the same world

Amberstreet crept into when he nicked the piece of paper off Bill de Kooning's floor.

We had been born walled out from art, had never guessed it might exist, until we slipped beneath the gate or burnt down the porter's house, or jemmied the bathroom window, and then we saw what had been kept from us, in our sleep-outs, in our outside dunnies, our draughty beer-hoppy public bars, and then we went half mad with joy.

We had lived not knowing that Van Gogh was born, or Vermeer or Holbein, or dear sad Max Beckmann, but once we knew, then we staked our lives on theirs.

This was why I could not seriously dislike Amberstreet, and as for my pale and injured bride, my gorgeous thief, I wished only to hold her in my arms and carry her. And I could see, even in the dark of what is now Tribeca, the miserable lino on her mother's kitchen floor. It was close to being a vision, watered-down Kandinsky in mad and frightening detail: then the kerosene refrigerator, the chipped yellow Kookaburra stove, the neighbours all called Mr This and Mrs That, none of them with any idea that they were being starved to death. Who is Filippino Lippi, Mrs Cloverdale? You've got me there, Mr Jenkins. I'd have to say I didn't have a clue.

Do not make fun of the lower-middle classes, you can get in trouble, get a ticket, be roared up, reported, dobbed in, cut down to size, come a cropper, fuck me dead. A nation that begins without a bourgeoisie does face certain disadvantages, none of them overcome by setting up a concentration camp to get things started. By now of course Sydney is so bloody enlightened it is impossible to board a train without being forced to overhear arguments about Vasari conducted by people on mobile phones.

Who is Lippi, Mrs Cloverdale? Excuse me, Mr Jenkins, do you mean Filippo or Filippino?

But in the times and places where Marlene and I were born it was different and it was sheer chance that we stumbled on to what would be the obsession of our untidy hurtful lives. Look at all the murder and destruction that led dear little queeny Bruno Bauhaus to the Marsh. And what did he have to feed me when he got there? Nothing but his mad passion for Leibovitz. Not even a real oil painting. There were none for thirty miles around.

From zis shithole, he told me, you must go.

And I obeyed him, the strange blue-eyed miniature. I abandoned my mother and my brother to the mercies of Blue Bones and went down to Melbourne on the train, a bruiser, unlettered, with white socks and trousers to my ankles. I had no choice but to play the cards I had been dealt, and I tried to make a virtue of them, deliberately arriving at life class with blood still on my hands. For what was I judged to be but a kind of raging pig? I had not read Berenson or Nietzsche or Kierkegaard but still I argued. Forgive me, Dennis Flaherty, I had no right to knock you down. I had no right to *speak*. I knew nothing, had seen sweet fucking all, had never been to Florence or Siena or Paris, never studied art history. At lunch break at William Anglis' wholesale butchery, I read Burckhardt. I also read Vasari and saw him patronize Uccello, the prick. Poor Paolo, Vasari wrote, he was commissioned to do a work with a chameleon. Not knowing what a chameleon was, he painted a camel instead.

Well fuck you, Vasari. That was the level of my response. I thought, You went to the finest schools all right but you are nothing more than a gossip and a suck-up to Cosimo de Medici. I was a butcher and I came in through the bathroom window and how could I do anything but hold Marlene? I had never been so close to another human being, not even, forgive me, my darling son. And I kissed my thief at ten o'clock at night, on Greenwich, between Duane and Reade, not because

I was blind, or because I was a fool, but because I knew her. I was on her side, not Christie's, not Sotheby's, not the dead-eyed pricks from Fifty-seventh Street who presumed to judge my paintings and then went out to bid up Wesselmann or some piece-of-crap de Chirico. I kissed her wet smudgy lids and then, in the blue light, with the wind lifting her straw-coloured hair straight up into the air, she smiled.

'Do you want to know why the Leibovitz is a different size to Boylan's?'

I waited.

'Dominique,' she said.

'The catalogue raisonné!'

'Dominique was a drunk,' she said. 'The catalogue raisonné says thirty by twenty and a half inches. It's wrong. I must be the first one to ever measure it.' She kissed me on the nose. 'And I know your secret too.'

'No you don't.'

'You're painting a new Leibovitz.'

'Maybe.'

'You're a very naughty boy, but did you consider, for a moment, how a new Leibovitz might possibly acquire a provenance?'

'You'll find a way,' I said, and I meant it, for I had thought of this so many times before.

'I will,' she said and then we kissed, winding, pressing, pushing, swallowing, wet clay, one entity, one history, one understanding, no air left between us. You want to know what love is?

Not what you think my darling young one.

46

I've been back since, to that corner where we each formally declared our whole-hearted criminal intent. There should be a blue plaque there, but there's only a Korean nail salon, a pet shop, the sort of wine store that sells Bordeaux futures. The streets are filled with thousand-dollar strollers, wheels as big as SUVs', every third one carrying twins. IVF Sci-fi. Doesn't matter. I don't mind. Here I became a counterfeiter, how fucking shameful. Please let me publicly apologize for my fall from grace. Of course Leibovitz himself, as everybody knows, had been part of what they used to call a 'Rembrandt factory'. That was in Munich, in his early teens. He was the pencil man in the employ of a kind of German Fagan, that is, he was the one who went to the ghetto to draw 'characters'. These were then handed to a Swiss who would take them to the Pinakothek and there carefully daub them *à la Rembrandt*. Leibovitz, having walked through ankle-deep mud all the way from Estonia, was just trying to stay alive and his forgeries cannot be compared—morally, artistically, good grief—with what I was making in that cold liquid-blue room above Mercer Street. Here, with the door locked and bolted, I began to prepare that famous lost Leibovitz which had been continually admired by Picasso and described by Leo Stein in his journal. The original hung for a while in the dining room at 157 rue de Rennes, but it is not to be seen in any of Dominique's boring dinner-party photographs. Forty-eight of these survive, each one the same—that is the guests have been required to turn and face the hostess, each one to raise a glass. The painting, I guess, was behind her back, hidden from her subjects and from history.

It's a fair guess that the painting was spirited away on that snowy night in January 1954, and that it went into the garage by the Canal Saint-Martin, but after that, who knows? Everything about it was thought to be remarkable, not least—Stein mentions this—that it was painted on canvas at a time when canvas was impossible to obtain.

So when you read the signature and date—Dominique Broussard, 1944—what does it tell you about Dominique, that she dared to use a square inch of precious canvas for herself?

It is also important to remember that the artist was a Jew in Vichy France and by his very refusal to leave Paris had placed himself in mortal danger. The complete and utter seriousness of his situation coincides with his decision to abandon the popular sentimental Shtetl Moderne style he had drifted into since the heights of 1913.

Leo Stein describes a cubist work, made in the characteristic Leibovitz cones and cylinders which suggests to a reader, sight unseen, his younger oeuvre. Stein however is at pains to make it clear that this was 'an unexpected leap'. The thing that tickled him the most was a raging Golem, 'like a circus beast', a bright yellow robot with wires and a generator and five frightened villagers turning the generator like a windlass. Anyone who has seen *Chaplin mécanique* (1946) will recognize the style here being described, one that owes more to Léger than to Braque while being undeniably a Leibovitz. Writing at a time when *Chaplin mécanique* did not yet exist, Stein beautifully evokes the severe mechanical planes, steely grey, smoke grey, and the armoured victims of the Golem's wrath, 'springs like men, lethal centipedes in terror', tumbling towards the bottom left, nails, screws, washers, all in the most 'elegant geometric chaos of defeat'.

If the buzzer sounded, forget it. Hugh? Come back later. Marlene? She had a key but even she was denied any sight of the work-in-progress, a great deal of which in any case—

took place solely in my head. That is, I sketched and read, filling my Gentile imagination with I. B. Singer's imps and Golems, Marsden Hartley, Gertrude Stein. This was not Leibovitz. I didn't say it was.

I sought out the pre-war loonies, the futurists, the vorticists of whom it can at least be said that they were kind enough to write more than they painted. Not that Leibovitz the Jew would ever have placed himself amongst their number, but because he had always shown a great communist hope for the technological future. I found a ridiculous bookstore upstairs on Wooster Street where, amongst a lot of creepy comics and works by Aleister Crowley, there was Gaudier-Brzeska:

> HUMAN MASSES teem and move, are destroyed and
> crop up again.
> HORSES are worn out in three weeks, die by the
> roadside.
> DOGS wander, are destroyed, and others come along.

I had to somehow feel the past as if it would not arrive until tomorrow, feel it in my gut as it was born, the collision of violent vectors, contradictions driven by Cossacks, Isaac Newton, Braque, Picasso, fear and hope, the dreadful Bosch.

I SHALL DERIVE MY EMOTIONS SOLELY FROM THE ARRANGEMENT OF THE SURFACES, I shall present my emotions by the ARRANGEMENT OF MY SURFACES, THE PLANES AND LINES BY WHICH THEY ARE DEFINED.

You can class all the above as *getting in the mood*. It was not the subject which was . . . paint. If I was to outwit my opponents at Sotheby's I could not be complacent. I prepared the ground with a white lead paint, and on top of this I made a charcoal sketch, the broad cartoon form of the work which would show against the lead with X-ray when they called their buddies at the Met. The work then had to be 'about'—not the Golem—but lines and planes, space fractured and reconfigured by an angel of the future toiling along the road from Mont Sainte-Victoire to Avignon.

Then there was the handwriting, the little stabby brushstrokes which the old goat massed in those groups of parallel hatches. This sounds so bloody easy, I am sure, but it involves more than a wrist and a red-sable brush. It is how you stand, how you breathe, whether you paint flat or on an easel. And there was the very particular modelling of the cylinders and cubes which I aimed to make a fraction—just a fucking smidgen—less confident than the *Chaplin*.

As I worked on my sketches I discovered and then adopted the mad joy in the Golem. He had an electric-light globe burning on his shoulder and blazing blue eyes, spheres of cobalt blue. So although wreaking vengeance, he was—like Stein had said—'a circus animal'. I did not even plan this. It happened, partly a function of the palette, but only partly. *Le Golem électrique, 1944* as I was later free to write upon its reverse side, was like a raging vengeful funfair ride.

I have never minded working in public view, but I would not let Marlene see me walk the wire until I was safely on the other side.

She had the eye, the intelligence, I've said that all before, but at this moment these qualities would not help the task at hand. This is why I went ahead and baked my masterpiece before submitting it for her approval. The canvas fitted perfectly inside the GE oven and I gave it sixty very bloody nervous minutes at 105 degrees Fahrenheit. If I had used linseed oil this would not have been enough but because the medium was Ambertol it set like bakelite. Its skin was dry and hard as if it had stood in air for sixty years.

I left *Le Golem électrique, 1944* to cool like an apple pie on an American sill, and then I took the paints and threw them into a skip, not the one near by on the Prince Street corner, but right over on Leroy Street, almost on the West

Side Highway where the marauding relentless Amberstreet would not bring his pointy red-tipped nose. It was here that I also discovered, along with broken plaster and bricks from a demolished garage, a gorgeous prissy frame, a smoky grey with grapes and garlands in low relief. Too big, but that was better than too small. This I carried home in triumph, down streets which were slowly becoming familiar, Leroy, Bedford, Houston, Mercer. I let myself in, finally comfortable in the darkness of the stairs.

Marlene was still not home. I turned the easel, set the painting on it, angled to catch what little light there was. It was a lovely, lovely thing, believe me, and I was about to celebrate, was searching for a corkscrew on the work table, when I heard the scream. Or not a scream, a screech. Marlene!

47

I ran to the door, no weapon but the corkscrew, leapt into the dark, entered the confusion of trash and carpet, fell, tumbled, broke nothing, and arrived finally on the street level to find her, sitting in the open door. The worm was in the apple but I did not know. I pulled her to her feet but she shrugged me violently away. She dropped a Kodak envelope. I picked it up. She said: 'He said, Are you Marlene Leibovitz?'

Just as I had once thought we were being evicted because of Evan Guthrie's metacarpal, I now imagined this crisis was something to do with the Kodak envelope. Opening it, I discovered photographs of Dominique's painting, the one I had sanded to make the Golem. I was thinking, We've been caught. She's been caught.

'No, no, not that.' She snatched the photographs away from me and thrust a quite different sheaf of papers at my chest, but I could not concentrate on this because I had a whole different story running like a train, steel rails all the way from here to gaol.

'How did he get it?'

'Who?'

'Amberstreet.'

'No! No!' she cried, and she was in a fury, with me, with the world. 'Read it!'

We were still at the open doorway, half in Mercer Street, and it was here I finally understood the sheaf of papers. A writ. Some bastard in a London Fog had served a writ on her, an action for divorce issued by Olivier Leibovitz (plaintiff) against Marlene Leibovitz (defendant).

'This is what upset you?'

'Well, what do you think?'

But why would she be upset? She didn't love him. He had no money. Her reaction was a complete surprise to me. Also: we did not talk to each other like this, were never abrasive, sarcastic, hostile. Suddenly I was an enemy? A fool? These were not roles I liked to play. They turned me nasty.

'Then what about the photographs?'

'The photographs don't matter. They're not the point.' Her voice was trembling and I embraced her, trying to wring out all the anger from us both, but she would not be held and I felt a great wave of annoyance as she rejected me.

'I am the authenticator,' she said. 'It is me.'

Oh fuck, I thought. Who gives a fuck?

As I ascended the stairs, two steps behind, I could actually feel her heat. When we arrived in the loft where my painting stood waiting, her cheeks were pink, her eyes narrowed. She glanced at the painting briefly, and nodded.

'Now listen,' she said. 'This is what we're going to do.'

So what about my bloody painting? No doubt she saw the Golem but there was no—Well done, Butcher, who else could have ever made such a thing?

Rather she was busy hurling the writ across the room then laying out the Kodak prints like a hand of patience. There was the original Broussard in all its glutinous vanity. The photographs were extremely unsettling in other ways, suggesting an interest Marlene had managed to hide from me completely.

'You took these?'

'You didn't understand I knew what you were doing?'

'But why?'

She was completely without humour, all hot and closed down. 'You said I had to establish the provenance. Well this is how we're going to do it. You're going to paint the Broussard back on top.'

I laughed. 'Perhaps you'd like to look at it before I cover it!'

'Of course I've looked at it. What do you think I've been thinking about, baby?'

'You peeked.'

'Of course I peeked. What did you expect?'

'You like it?'

'It's brilliant, OK? Now you're going to paint this back over your Golem.' She slid the photographs around like a pea-and-thimble man on lower Broadway. 'Not exactly as it was, but close. Trust me. You're going to use the same pigments, exactly.'

'I threw them out.'

'You *what*?'

'Hey, calm down baby.'

'You *what*? Where did you throw them?'

'In a skip.'

'Skip where?'

'Leroy.'

'Leroy and what?' But she already had one foot in a running shoe.

'Leroy and Greenwich.'

She tied up the second shoe and she was gone. I watched her from the fire escape. Although I had often seen her set off for exercise, I had never actually seen her run. On another occasion it would have made my fond heart beat faster, for she ran over those cold grey cobbles as across the surface of a hamburger grill, so straight that she might have had a string attached to that little springy tuft of hair on her straw-coloured head. Seeing her then, my lover, my supporter, my tender funny angel, I was frightened by my own complacency.

Re: sexual intercourse. They say you DO NOT LOOK AT THE MANTELPIECE when you are poking the fire so I poked her, bless me, what blazing logs, she squealed and HOLLERED as if consumed by BUSHFIRE, crimson edges on the floating leaves, by crikey it was a long time between drinks.

It is true the BARONESS was not TOP HOLE. No kids at Sydney Grammar, etc., if Olivier did not have a job I would not have visited the Rousseau Houses at all. Olivier went to work, taking his bottles of LORAZEPAM and ADDERALL, but no SUBSTANCE could make him happy and he was continually saying bad things about Marlene. When he began to cry at breakfast I knew I had chosen the losing side, forgive me, bless me, I wish I was a nicer man.

I tried to return to Butcher but he would not answer the bell.

I had made UNSUITABLE friends, whose fault was that? They were often artists from the movies and the stage i.e. Vinnie and the Baron. I went to see them with my chair and they encouraged me to put my sausage in the baroness. Too many dead pigs cooked in that apartment. No LILAC and ROSEMARY as in *A TOUCH OF CLASS* when Butcher would sit out in the car reading *ART NEWS* wishing he could find his long-lost name.

The Baron said he respect me man but he took the money from my back pocket and also Olivier's VALIUM. But I was ON THE JOB, just on the foothills as they say, the tide just turning, seaweed floating, little fishes, bless me. Then Vinnie and the Baron took RABBIT EARS off the TV and used them to jab my bum. Then they went too far. The room was dark and small with six lava lamps and I knocked Vinnie on his bright red little SNOUT so he left a SNAIL TRAIL of black boot polish across the wallpaper as he descended. I should have done the Baron with a BELAYING PIN but not being a character in *The Magic Pudding* I was forced to use my chair instead. The Baroness, so-called, was screaming like a STUCK PIG in the backyard of a house in STARKVILLE MISSISSIPPI from where she came hoping to be a dancer although only five foot tall. I never hit a woman. I picked up my clothes and it was WALTZING MATILDA TA-TA BYE-BYE.

I had already given the Baroness twenty dollars, enough for all of them to have another Twenty-fourth Street BLOCK PARTY bless me but I had to walk down twenty flights of stairs because what the Americans call the ELEVATOR had jammed with people trapped inside shouting and screaming. I had been happy. Now I was not. I wished I was in the Marsh where there were not one single elevator, not even a LIFT, hardly any stairs more than ten steps I refer to the

Presbyterian Church, always trouble with the coffins it was called the WATERSLIDE.

On the fifth floor I passed Vinnie's apartment the sign on the door reading FILM MUSICIAN *CHELSEA DINER*. He was what is called a PACK RAT in VIOLATION of the fire regulations with his FANZINES and *BIG BUTT MAGAZINE* stacked up along the wall.

On the second floor I had time to dress but my head was sparking and my muscles very bad indeed and I kept on going, still pulling on my new CALVIN KLEIN socks as I hopped out on to Tenth Avenue. I started running with the evening traffic then realized that was wrong. I fitted my shoe and then ran back down Tenth Avenue all the way to the West Side Highway where I took a rest. Blumey, do me sideways as my father would have said.

I could have walked to the Bicker Club I wish I were braver but I'm not. I wanted a holiday from Olivier. He was going through a DIFFICULT PATCH grinding up his ADD medicine and sniffing it up a drinking straw and so his snot was red and clotted and the colour of his eyelids was the purple of a bruise, wild orchid to be polite, skin so weary from the effort to refuse admittance to the light of day. He swam in a sea of ghosts, stung by jellyfish, red welts rising on his hands and neck.

There was also the cassette recorder every night the same song. FLIES BLOWING ROUND THE DITCH. BLOOD ON YOUR SADDLE. He had been always so kind to me, had cared for me, paid for my room, had bought me clothes, sat with me, introduced me to so many laundries, and interesting people, Princes and Paupers old chum, but now I was afraid.

My socks were not smooth inside my shoes but I would not stop to fix them and by the time I finally found myself at Mercer Street my feet were bleeding in the dark.

I rang the buzzer.

It replied.

Thank God, thank Jesus, bless us all. I would not have cared if Blue Bones was waiting for me with the flex or razor strop I entered the dark stairs as a wombat returning to the smell of earth and roots.

49

Marlene rescued my five jars of paint from the skip on Leroy Street and when she came back into the loft her legs were shining, her eyes dulled with anger or distress, how was I to know?

My Golem remained in full view, angled to catch her eye as she walked in the door and I do not doubt that she already understood the impossible achievement, not just the 1944 canvas, the veracity of the handwriting, the daring composition, but that this work already existed in the writings of Leo Stein and John Richardson. But she did not say a word. Fuck you, I thought. First time ever.

I was to paint over the Golem, she said, bury it like an archaeological hoax.

Fuck you. Second.

We drank whisky. I explained, often calmly, I could not paint over the Golem which would not only be ruined, but never found.

She disagreed, on the basis of what she did not say. I had never encountered the hard sparkling granite wall of her stubbornness. But neither had she seen Blue Bones with his spinnaker up, flying in the full storm of a rage.

Then the buzzer sounded, always a horrid noise, but this time I thought Thank Christ. I threw a cloth across the painting, laid it against the wall, and sprang the door for my unknown visitor who soon revealed himself, with puffing and farting and a loud 'oh dear', to be my brother Hugh.

He hadn't taken his first sip of milky tea before Marlene was attempting, none too fucking subtly, to have him return to the Bicker Club.

'It's such a shame,' she said, 'there's not a bed for you.' At the time I thought she was just being bloody-minded, but of course this was all about the writ—she thought Hugh had become her husband's spy.

Hugh, by now, was terrified of Olivier and—in desperation I suppose—he produced a wet untidy wad of cash and announced he would buy a mattress and he knew just where to go. This independence was unprecedented. He headed out into the dark and left us alone with our violently clinking Lagavulin on the rocks.

An hour later we had been through War and Peace and back again. Hugh returned, having carried his mattress all the way from Canal Street. He slid his damp burden beneath the kitchen island countertop and this was the territory from which he watched our puzzling activity. Far from being a spy, however, he was an old and needy dog, sleeping, reading comic books, demanding I cook him sausages four times a day.

And of course he finally saw the Leibovitz. 'Who did that?' he asked, a question that alarmed Marlene who became suddenly and violently affectionate toward him, luring him out on an expedition to Katz's Deli, just to take him away from the sight of me burying the Golem.

But of course I wouldn't bury the Golem as she wished. That is the thing with artists. We are like small shopkeepers, accustomed to ruling our domain. If you don't like how I do it, get out of my shop, my cab, my life. I was in charge and I had no plans to bury anything.

Marlene was the woman who had climbed the power pole and cut the wires and now she was impatient, angry, anxious, I had no idea to what degree. She managed to endure my resistance for three long days, at the end of which time I returned—an exciting afternoon with Hugh's tartar problem—and saw she had laid a coat of Dammar varnish on the *Golem électrique*.

'Put that brush down,' I said.

She considered me, her eye slitted, her cheeks burning, defiant and afraid at once.

Finally, to my immense relief, she dropped the brush into the varnish pot, like a ladle in a bowl of soup.

'And don't you ever fucking touch a work of mine again.'

She burst into tears, and of course I held her, and kissed her wet cheeks and hungry lips, and once I had cooked Hugh his sausages she and I went out for a walk, squeezed tight together, lovingly, argumentatively, through the decaying cabbages of Chinatown, down into the shadows of the Manhattan Bridge.

I never suggested that her idea was not brilliant. Only that science made it impossible to do it as she insisted. I was right. She was as wrong as anyone who would drop a brush into a varnish pot. No one would trust a layer of Dammar varnish as a safe separation between a valuable work and the crap that must go on top.

Besides if we were to bury it, we would have to plan how it would be discovered, and we required the people with the Yale degrees to unearth the missing Leibovitz themselves. We wanted them—didn't we?—to feel it was their own genius which had led them to the gold beneath the pile of dung. We would take the Broussard canvas to a top conservator for cleaning—that was Jane Threadwell—and we would, with careful chemistry, let this Threadwell discover the mystery beneath.

She was Milt's lover, so they said. Meaning: Milt claimed it. Never mind, it's not the point. Here's the thing: conservators—even those reckless enough to shtup Milt Hesse—are as cautious as hamsters. Even in a simple cleaning of an undistinguished work by Dominique Broussard, Jane Threadwell would begin by cleaning a tiny spot—⅛″ diameter—not from the centre of the canvas either, not even from the corner, but on that peripheral area normally hidden by the rabbet of the frame.

This very clever trembling animal was the one we had to trap. And much as we might wish her to recklessly scrub away at the Broussard until the gorgeous Golem was revealed, forget it. The merest touch of colour on its swab . . . she's out of there.

So how could we lead her to the Golem in spite of all her caution?

'Tear the canvas,' Marlene said. 'She'll see the layers.'

'She's being asked to fix the canvas of a shitty painting. It's a drag, a nuisance. She might not even notice. And if she does, why would she think there was a masterpiece beneath?'

'Then how?'

'I don't know.'

Frankly I thought there must be a simpler way to establish a provenance for the Golem. It was a good painting, for Christ's sake, not some second-rate pastiche by Van Meegeren. Why take the risk of screwing it up when, surely, she could take it to Japan, for instance, or have it turn up in a deceased estate?

Oh no no, she couldn't.

For Chrissakes, why?

It was complicated, but no.

Why?

Not now.

She was distracted, irritated and sometimes I was irritated too. Just the same I tried to please her—who wouldn't? I really believed that if we could bring this off, we could get the hell out away from Olivier and—thank God—the fucked-up drama of his mother. Sometimes I began to imagine buying Jean-Paul's place in Bellingen—a ridiculous idea, please don't point it out.

Money had not been part of it at first but as I began to imagine our escape from the *droit moral*, a million dollars was clearly no small thing. I bought a copy of Mayer's *Artist's Handbook of Materials and Techniques* in whose eight hundred pages I attempted to find the answer to a crossword puzzle built on chemistry and chronology, believable paints, a likely solvent which would safely dissolve the veil. I slept badly in a merry-go-round of chemicals, ripolin, gouache, white spirits, turpentine, everything ending in disaster, myself in a foreign prison, the Golem washed away. I became the victim of sudden starts, cries, violent awakenings. Marlene was not much better.

'Are you awake?'

Of course. She was, on her back, her eyes glistening in the dark.

'Look,' she said. 'Listen to me. He was licensing his father's work for bloody coffee mugs. Can't you understand? He was a complete philistine ignoramus.'

'Shoosh. Go to sleep. It doesn't matter.'

'He was lazy and disorganized. The only reason he kept the advertising job was that he would fly to Texas to see his client who would take him to dinner and fuck him up the arse.'

'No! Really?'

'No, not really, but I saved the weasel from his nightmare. I looked after him. I really, really took care of him. I made sure he could ride his horses and drive in car rallies. And I would have kept on doing that, fuck him.'

'Let him be. He can't hurt us.'

'He has already, the prick.'

And yet she snuggled into me, my sweet baby, fitting her lovely head in against my neck and shoulder and her warm little pussy against my thigh and I could feel her as she sniffed my clavicle, inhaling my skin, and her whole lithe body fitted my lumpen Butcher mass.

'Don't stop loving me,' she said.

I blew out the altar candles and stroked her neck until she went to sleep. Her breath smelt of toothpaste and the air was smoky, waxy, like after evensong, once upon a summertime.

50

New York Central Supplies on Third Avenue had a great back room, a sort of junkyard of artists' paint and brushes, and it was there that I stumbled on to a museum piece, that is, twenty-three sample boxes of thirty-five-year-old Magna paint. If you've heard of Magna it's because Morris Louis used it, Frankenthaler used it, Kenneth Noland too I think.

Magna was invented by Sam Golden, a great chemist, the partner of Leonard Bocour, a great proselytizer. From 1946, when Magna went into production, Bocour had sent these sample boxes out all over the world. Here, try it, Morris Louis. Here try it, Picasso. Here try it, Leibovitz, Sidney Nolan. He threw in handfuls of greens or yellows, such an odd assortment of colours in each box. He didn't make it easy for me, but when I finally picked myself off the dusty floor at

New York Central Supplies, I had chosen thirteen boxes which contained, in sum, the quantity and palette I required.

If you're a painter, you're already ahead of the story. You know Magna was a breakthrough, an acrylic you could mix with oil. The finished result looked like oil, not Dulux.

If I used Magna on the Broussard the conservator, examining the finish, seeing the date, would confidently assume it was an oil. She would therefore use a solvent like white spirit, completely safe for oil. Ha-ha. Imagine. There is the little hamster—sniff, sniff, gently, gently—little Q-tip, smidgen of solvent, and lo and fucking behold: the pigments are coming off in floods.

A Red Flag, as they say.

This is not oil paint. Sniff, sniff.

Jesus Christ, Eloise, it's Magna! Another Red Flag. Magna not made till four years after the title.

By now we would have her attention. She knows Broussard is married to Leibovitz. If she thinks for just a second the title will not match the Broussard mud pie.

None of this is enough, but it's almost enough. If we can draw the creature a little closer, if I could just keep her applying that white spirit, she could remove all the Magna and reveal the gorgeous oil beneath. But she's a conservator. She won't do that.

Just the same, I returned to Mercer Street filled with optimism, my thirteen vintage packs of Magna in two huge plastic bags. On the work table I revealed them to my lover. I was such a fucking genius, such a big bad criminal. I needed pliers to remove the caps, but the contents of every single tube was fresh as the day it was packed.

You would think this would be enough to make Marlene calm down about the *droit moral*, but no. Just the same: I have been divorced, it isn't easy. I thought, Her divorce would come and go as divorces finally do. When it was over she would probably still continue to vent about the *droit moral*. Likewise I would rage about alimony whores. But we would, meanwhile, have achieved a very satisfactory private victory in New York. No one would know. We did not need them to.

It took exactly four hours to paint the Broussard, and even then I think I took more care than Dominique had done. Being Magna, it dried fast and I was soon able to spray it with a solution of sugar and water. I left it on the roof to pick up New York grime.

Did anyone say, Oh you clever bugger?

No, but it didn't matter. I had put the canvas on the rack above Hugh's spattering sausages and when they had added their contribution of grease I 'cleaned' the surface roughly with a filthy sponge.

Hugh watched all this, of course, but he was mostly absorbed with a copy of *The Magic Pudding* Marlene had unburied in the Strand.

At night I propped the filthy canvas near the bed and lit four altar candles before it, happily observing the carbon deposits build above the grease. This would really need a damn good clean.

Lying on my side, with Marlene against my back, I sometimes thought of money. It was very sweet.

'Here's the Broussard, toots,' Milton Hesse would say to Jane Threadwell. 'I know it's crap, baby, but it has some historical value, and anyway, the family wants it cleaned.' Something like that. 'Don't go nuts about it,' the mule would say. 'This is not brain surgery they're asking for.'

Jane Threadwell would not get to the canvas immediately, and then she would be too busy saving a cracking Mondrian or some Kiefer which had aged like a pig farm in a drought. She would give the Broussard to someone in her studio, a little chore, a sentimental favour for Milt Hesse. But then the lowliest assistant would start to clean it and then, dear Jesus, Marlene would get *the call* from Milt.

It was not just the anachronistic paint. When they removed the frame they had discovered, under the rabbet, that the frame had rubbed away a deal of the paint and there—how did that happen?—was what appeared to be an earlier oil painting. Given the marital history of the artist concerned, what did Marlene want to do?

Then Marlene would be duly hesitant and then Milt would call Threadwell and Threadwell would call her buddy Jacob at the Met and then they would go for the raking light, the infrared, the X-ray, and finally they would all have themselves in a huge bloody state. *Le Golem électrique.*

'Mrs Leibovitz, we really think you should give Jane permission to go ahead.'

Now it would be gently Bentley as they removed the Magna, sniff, sniff, sniff. Little white spirit. Oh, it would come away in floods.

Call the *Times*, call the *Times*. Milton would have his moment. 'I cried,' he would say. 'I cried like a baby when Jacques died.'

And I suppose there's something nasty in my satisfaction, the vengeance of the hick, the man from Iron Bark against the city barber, a perfect, provincial rather Bacchus Marsh affair, not loud, not public, but deeply fucking satisfying to those who knew. Oh how lovely, Mr Bones, how bloody lovely. Congratulations to you and yours.

51

WHO WOULD STEAL MY CHAIR?

I asked and Marlene said I must have lost it on the stairs so I took a flashlight and peered in amongst all the dust and filth there was a dead mouse bless the poor dried heart who would steal my chair?

I must have done something that SLIPPED MY MIND. Once when I was a boy I went walking in my sleep only waking when my bare feet touched the wet path to the dunny. Another time I drew with a biro across the sheets. Bless me, I could not explain it. Perhaps I stole my chair myself. There was a secret in the room like bad meat, a nasty odour, so FAMILIAR, from my very sad and disappointing birth, the long afternoons, sun through the flywire, the buzz of flies outside HOWLING FOR BLOOD, Mum's breath like roses, like communion wine.

WHO WILL SAVE ME NOW?

Butcher painted in DEATHLY SILENCE the strange opposite of his normal practice which is to EAR BASH to the point of madness SKITING and BOASTING he would TALK THE BACK LEG OFF A DONKEY. Look at this Hugh, this will be a bloody beauty. This will knock their bloody socks off. This will be a bull ant in their pants. In previous times he had rolled the canvas out across the floor and then he would need me to perform my ACT OF GRACE but now he had a tricky little nest of sticks like a surveyor out on the Darley Road. He had become, forgive him, AN EASEL PAINTER so he could put me on the wrong side of the canvas as if I was the floor.

All my life I lived amongst the perfumes of secrets, blood, roses, altar wine, who can say what happened to us all in Main Street, Bacchus Marsh, not me. We might have all continued as butchers, drawing the red line, all death arriving kindly. How I might have loved those beasts, me better than any man before. Never mind. They would not give me the knife and so I went to live with the so-called butcher and the darling boy, peaches in the grass, the sweet rotten aroma of his marriage, I knew it but could not name it as I circled round the boy, trying to keep him safe and then it was me that hurt him. Everything always wrong, badness at the centre, the sound of flies excited in the sun, the thin squeak and fat slap of the swinging door as one person entered and another left. This was the Marsh, voices in another room. I was not born slow, I know it.

In New York I sat on my CANAL STREET MATTRESS my mind was puzzling back and forth why my brother was now painting like a MEDIOCRITY. He did not say I did not ask. This was the worst feeling that there is.

In the Marsh I poked into the big drawer beneath Mum's wardrobe, when alone I was a STICKY BEAK, forgive me. They said I was born Slow Bones and broke my mother's heart. But something was taken from me. Something happened, never found, just the smell of camphor in a drawer. We walked around it then, as we now walked around my missing chair, as if circling some strange and dirty thing for why else would he paint a MEDIOCRITY? It made my head ache. I could not hold it still, as slippery as an earthworm before the dreaded hook.

My brother had come to New York and no one at a restaurant knew his name and he was angry they did not bow down to the great EX-MICHAEL BOONE and therefore he became small and shrivelled, dark as coal from the Madingley open cut. He bought ink sticks from Pearl Paint and off he went, rubbing and rubbing, as if he could erase himself, rub himself away to dust.

Whatever happened we can never know.

Walk around, walk around.

Marlene Cook from Benalla. Michael Boone from Bacchus Marsh. Kings and Queens on Mercer Street. He climbed up to the roof of the building and there lay his painting to the eye of night. Egg white, black grit, burnt souls falling.

WHO WILL SAVE ME NOW?

52

Hugh never changed from the morning I picked him up to take him down to Melbourne. He had attempted to drown his daddy, also vice versa, but still he glared at me as though I was the author of his misery. It was in my mother's low-ceilinged kitchen that I found him that day, blocking the light from the Gisborne Road window, like a giant Jehovah's Witness with his black church shoes, Fletcher Jones trousers, a short-sleeved white shirt and a tie. Brylcreem had turned his hair a wet burnt umber and his little seashell ears were burning red. And the eyes, they were the same, little baleful eyes which he now cast upon Marlene.

In Mercer Street I asked him, 'What the fuck is wrong with you?'

No answer.

'Have you been taking your pills?'

He stared at me belligerently, then retreated into the deep unhappy tangle of his bed, where, in company of toast crumbs, beneath the cowl of his quilt, he now watched my beloved read the *New York Times*, bestowing on her a special quality of attention you might think more suited to a dangerous snake.

Marlene was dressed for running, in baggy daggy shorts and a soiled white T-shirt. Until now she had ignored my brother's close attention, but when she stood Hugh cocked his head and raised an interrogative eyebrow.

'What?' she asked.

The buzzer sounded.

Hugh started, and went back under cover.

He was a silly bugger, but my own relation with that

buzzer was not much better. I certainly did not want to have Detective Dickhead enquiring about the painting I had wrapped so carefully with newspaper the night before. It lay now exactly where it had lain in its freshly sanded state, leaning against the wall.

Thinking to move it, I stood, but not before Milt Hesse walked in. It was the first time I was ever pleased to see the old cunt-hound, for he had come to take our treasure to be cleaned. As he entered my brother glared at him so fiercely I feared that he might charge.

'Whoa,' I said. 'Whoa Dobbin.'

Before Milt had a chance to properly understand his situation, he advanced on the huge swaddled creature, his arm outstretched. 'I haven't met you sir. Are you another Aussie genius?'

But Hugh would not touch him and Milt, doubtless having a New Yorker's well-calibrated judgement of all forms of madmen, swerved sideways to the table where he kissed Marlene.

'Doll-face.'

His left arm, having been injured in a fall, was supported by a sling and he now allowed Marlene to tuck the parcel beneath the right.

Hugh meanwhile was all hunched over, knees to his chest, rocking sideways. If you did not know him you would think he was ignoring the guest but I was not at all surprised when, as Milt was leaving, my brother suddenly lurched to his feet.

'I'll see you out,' Marlene said suddenly.

Hugh dropped back to his knees, burrowing in the tangle of bedclothes where he finally found his coat and separated it from quilt and sheet and then, with Marlene and Milt not too far ahead of him, he was heading towards the door.

'No, mate, you don't want to do that.'

I blocked his way, but he shouldered me away.

'Please, mate. No trouble.'

He paused. 'Who is he?'

'He's going to clean the painting.'

'Oh.'

He drew back, puzzled at first, but finally displaying a stupid knowing smirk, as if he, of all people, was privy to some hidden truth.

'What is it that you're thinking mate?'

He tapped his head.

'You're thinking?'

'Roof,' he said.

The fucking smirk was physically unbearable. 'What roof, mate?'

He withdrew further, back towards the mattress, his mouth now impossibly small, his ears slowly suffusing with blood. As he settled back into his nest his dry hair, confused by static, rose slowly on his head. He was still like this, a dreadful grinning fright, when Marlene came back from her run.

She also was on edge, had been on edge in any case, and no matter how she ran or worked her weights, nothing would give her any peace.

Sitting at the table, she went straight back to the *Times*.

'You burnt down the high school,' my brother said.

Oh Hugh, I thought, Hugh, Hugh, Hugh.

Marlene's colour was already high, a lovely pink that revealed the tiniest palest freckles.

'What did you say to Marlene?'

Hugh hugged his big round knees and giggled. 'She burnt down Benalla High School,' he said.

Marlene smiled. 'Hugh, you are very strange.'

'You too,' my brother said, somehow seeming contented, as if some puzzle had been solved. 'I heard you burnt down Benalla High School.'

Marlene was staring at him now, and for a moment her

eyes narrowed and her mouth tightened, but then her face relaxed.

'Why Hugh,' she smiled, 'you are as full of tricks as a bag full of monkeys.'

'You too.'

'You too.'

'You too,' until the pair of them were laughing uproariously and I went to the dunny to get away.

At lunchtime, Milt called to say Jane had the painting which appeared, she said, to have been hung in someone's kitchen. That night I cooked sausages for Hugh and after Marlene had taken her evening run, she and I went to dinner at Fanelli's where we drank two bottles of fantastic burgundy.

I didn't feel drunk, but I fell into bed and passed out like a light. I woke to find Marlene crawling back into bed. I had a splitting headache. She was freezing cold. At first I thought her shivering but when I touched her face it was aflood with tears. As I held her, her body shook convulsively.

'Shush, baby. Shush, it's all right.'

But she could not stop.

'I'm sorry,' said Hugh, standing in the doorway.

'For fuck's sake, go back to fucking sleep. It's three o'clock.'

'I shouldn't have said it.'

'It's nothing to do with you, you idiot.'

I heard him sigh and Marlene was almost choking, a dreadful noise like someone drowning. I could see her by the light from the street, all her smooth lovely planes crushed and broken inside a fist. It was the dumb divorce, I thought, the bloody *droit moral*. Why she had to have it, I really, really could not see.

'Can you still love me?'

Headache or no, I loved her, as I had never loved in all my life, loved her wit, her courage, her beauty. I loved the woman who stole Dozy's painting, who read *The Magic Pudding*, who faked the catalogue, but even more the girl escaping the vile little room in Benalla and I could smell the red lead paint her mother brushed on the fireplace every Sunday, taste the shitty ersatz coffee made from chicory, the canned beetroot staining the boiled egg white in the deadly iceberg salad.

'Shush. I love you.'

'You don't know.'

'Shush.'

'You won't love me. You can't.'

'I do.'

'I did it,' she cried suddenly.

'What did you do?'

I looked into her face and saw an alarming terror, a dreadful cringing in the face of my tender enquiry. She gave a little moan and hid her head in my chest and began to sob again. Through all of this, I detected Hugh. He was now standing right over us.

'Go to bed, now.'

His bare feet brushed across the floor.

'I did it,' she said.

'She burnt down Benalla High School,' said Hugh mournfully. 'I'm sorry.'

I took her chin and tilted her face towards me, all the street light trapped in a tide around her pooling eyes.

'Did you, my baby?'

She nodded.

'Is that what you did?'

'I'm vile.'

I took her to me, and held her, the whole cage of mystery that was her life.

53

I was wrong, quite possibly, I had sinned, very likely, had borne FALSE WITNESS, become a COMMON GOSSIP. Have you heard? They say Marlene Cook burnt down the high school. Who is THEY? Why, it was only Olivier. So it was just SCUTTLEBUTT and HEARSAY, bless me, I would never have repeated it if I had not SMELLED A RAT, as the saying is. I was DISCOMBOBULATED—that's a good one—and so I foolishly repeated what a DRUG ADDICT had ALLEGED and caused Marlene to weep, deep in the middle of the night, a human lost in outer space or inside a plastic bag, gulping for air, their GOOD NAME vacuumed from them, the HOOVER sucking oxygen, roaring like the mills of God.

What right did I have? No right, only wrong. Forgive me Lord Jesus, it was agony to hear her suffer and I could not wait for the dawn so I could go back to the Bicker Club and PUT IT TO Olivier that he had invented the story because he hated her.

When it was grey light I stood above them. I wished I was an angel, but there never would be feathers on my hairy back. She was sleeping, her head as always against my brother's chest. He opened one eye and peered at his watch.

Out? he asked.

Walk, I said.

It was a clear morning, just after seven, pigeons already cooing on the rusty fire escape, not knowing one day from the other I presume, or only wet from dry, hot from cold, their hearts the size of a lump of gum, insufficient blood to fill a cup. Nothing like my agony for them, I thought, but then again who can imagine the constant torment from the lice, the pain of diseases unknown to any but the sufferer, their own secret horrors, no worse, no better. Walking up Mercer Street, head down. All around me black plastic bags, erupting, spewing, restaurant fish for instance. What knowledge might a fish have? Who would forewarn a red snapper of the afterlife, this purgatory on Mercer Street? These dreadful thoughts pursued me SMELLS IN HELL as I bolted up Broadway, was nearly killed. Then Union Square, Gramercy Park, but where was Jeavons now? It did not matter. I had my key. As I have confessed. As I have told the sequence of events. As the story has been recorded, reel to reel.

I PROCEEDED to the second floor and unlocked the door, bless me. I did not know what I had done.

Olivier in black pyjamas, his face hidden by the chair, the legs of the chair closed like scissors around bruised white throat, a great blue birthmark, an underground lake spilling beneath his skin. His eyes were open. He was still. What had SLIPPED MY MIND I could not tell. I touched him with my foot and he moved like a dead beast but no more.

I did not touch the body with my hands. I ran from the club with Jeavons calling to me STOP. I ran down Broadway howling DON'T WALK DON'T CARE. Save us from me, tell me what is done.

54

Slow Bones woke us. Like sheet metal falling, flailing, slamming on the bed. No time for socks or underwear, we travelled, all three together, to the Bicker Club, and there we found the so-called Jeavons in a state that was unpleasantly like a snit.

It was he who pointed out 'the wife' to the police and as a result Marlene had the privilege of being taken to the crime scene—the cops getting very bloody physical with me when I thought I had a right to come along—and it was she who then became 'the deponent' who swore 'the remains' of the deceased had once been Olivier Leibovitz.

I waited on the mansion steps, which was as close to Olivier as anyone permitted me to get. Hugh and I were side by side, numb and dumb. Marlene emerged, opened her mouth to speak, and vomited across the stoop.

Hugh accompanied the police into the Bicker Library. Marlene was retching on the sidewalk, but I was directed to accompany Hugh a certain distance. I observed his tape-recorded interrogation from the high-arched doorway while they sat him beneath a nasty poster for a production of *Hamlet* with John Wilkes Booth. I could not hear what was said, but it seems he confessed to murder. I believed it, totally. As they applied their rat traps to his wrists my brother looked at me, no longer crying, his little eyes so weirdly still and dark.

They got the big old fellow on his feet and spun him round and left him standing, facing the corner of the library.

Something then occurred, God knows what exactly—coming and going on the stairs. Then the youngest cop, a young crew-cut fellow in sneakers and jeans, released Hugh's cuffs and the old bull rushed towards me, head down.

'Hugh!'

He brushed past.

The cop was a trim brush-cut fellow, not like any cop I knew, more like the Lebanese guys selling hash at Johnny's Green Room in Melbourne.

'That's your brother?'

'Yes.'

'He's a little slow?'

'That's right.'

'Get him out of here.'

'What?'

'He's free to go.'

Hugh was hovering with his little blaming eyes. He permitted me to put my arm around him and escort him down the steps.

'Sit here a minute, mate.'

I took off my sweater and my T-shirt, pulled the prickly wool back over my ruined skin, used the T-shirt to clean Marlene who had propped herself between two parked cars and was still gulping and gasping, although now she was producing little more than bile. I had not seen what she had seen, and I did not want to. I wiped her mouth, and chin, leaving the shirt coloured by the bitter green and when I was done I threw it—fuck them—across the rail of Gramercy Park.

An ambulance came, but no one bothered to get out. It was grey, overcast, damp, sweaty. We were lifeless, all our marrow sucked into the maw of God knows what dimension.

Police arrived and departed. Taxis hooted at the ambulance, but no one was in a hurry to bring the famous artist's son downstairs.

Of course I could not yet know about the freshly broken metacarpal bone in Olivier's right hand. I wonder what I would have done. Would I have tried to turn in my brother? Report him? Dob him in? How the fuck would I know? The real mystery, however, was not my character, but the crime itself. The killer had either had a key—but all keys were accounted for—or he had entered an open window by scaling a sheer fifty-foot wall.

Hugh, who did have a key, was still asleep at Mercer Street at the time Jeavons brought in the tea and found the body. Had Jeavons done it? No one thought so. As Hugh ran away from the scene, by the time he had seen the body, the corpse was already five hours old.

So it was nothing to do with Hugh, and yet the body contained a message to anyone who knew Hugh's history.

The Office of Chief Medical Examiner did not know Hugh, did not know it was a message, although God knows they went digging. They took little bits of Olivier's Brain, Liver, Blood. There was Adderall and Celexa and Morphine in his brain, but these drugs had not killed him. The cause of death was asphyxiation. The autopsy reported the telltale signs: intensive heart congestion (enlarged heart; right-side ventricle), venous engorgement above the point of injury and cyanosis (blue discolouration of lips and fingertips). That had been achieved by the folding legs of Hugh's chair.

Enough you would imagine, but not for them. They cut him up like a pig at the Draybone Inn, opening his beautiful body with 'the usual incision'. The flies were buzzing. They weighed his poor sad brain. They found the vessels at the base of the brain to be 'smooth-walled and widely patent', whatever that means. They weighed his lungs, his heart, and liver. Will that be all Mrs Porter? They found the oesophagus unremarkable. They poked around his stomach and reported 'undigested foodstuff with recognizable fragments of meat and vegetable and a marked odour of alcohol'.

They cut up his dick. 'The calyces, pelves, ureters and urinary bladder are unremarkable. The capsule strips with ease revealing markedly pale and smooth cortical surfaces.' I did not even want to know what this meant, but what had he done to deserve it? Be born inside the castle walls of art? They cut him from colon to bowel and wrote down the contents of his shit. This was a life, a man, in part, in whole.

The tabloids were almost as thorough—they noted that his mother, Dominique Broussard, had died a similar death in Nice in 1967. They went right into it. So enlightening to read that strangulation is normally the fate of women and children. Only one detail escaped them, although it was plainly stated in the autopsy if anyone wished to think what it might mean—the killer had also broken the bone of Olivier Leibovitz's right metacarpal.

Hugh had not done this.

I had not done this.

In all New York, there was only one person who would understand that this injury, inflicted at the time of death, had a direct connection to my brother's history.

Of course I did not know this straightaway. It was a Saturday morning when Olivier died, and it was not until Wednesday—very fast for the Chief Medical Examiner, or so they told me at the precinct—that I picked up the coroner's report and brought it back to Mercer Street. I cooked Hugh sausages and mashed potatoes and then I began to read. It took a minute or two before I reached the metacarpal bone.

Marlene had been sitting very still and quiet reading Mayer's *Handbook of Artist's Materials*, but she looked up so sharply it was clear she had been waiting for me to respond.

'What is it, baby?'

I slid the page through the toast crumbs, underlining with my nail the 'metacarpal bone'.

There was a small flicker in her mouth. Not a smile, but a meaningful contraction. She held my eyes, as she slowly folded the report.

'You don't need this,' she said. I finally understood—she had the *droit moral* now. Olivier was dead.

Beside me Hugh continued chopping up his sausages, sawing them into careful sections one quarter inch in width.

'I know it looks bad,' she said. 'It isn't bad, baby. It's just careful.'

What she was saying was monstrous, but she was just sitting at the table, her hand resting on my hand, as tender as she always was.

'What looks bad?'

'That injury,' she said, casting her eyes in my brother's direction.

'The break?'

'Insurance,' she said. This was the second time she almost smiled.

She had the fucking *droit moral*. God save us. I crossed the room, opened the trunk where she had kept her running things, her burglary tools if you want to know the truth. There was nothing left but smelly sneakers and a pair of shorts.

'Where's your rope?'

What did I expect her to answer? Oh, I used the rope to climb into my fucked-up husband's room. When I had finished killing him I threw the thing away. Then I came home and snuggled into bed. What she actually said was: 'God is in the details.' And thence solemnly stretched out her hand towards me. 'Nothing bad will happen now, baby. It's just I can be confident that our secret is secure.'

'For God's sake,' I nodded at my eating brother, 'he was sound asleep. He was here.'

'From an evidentiary point of view, that's sort of tricky. Anyway, no one wants to open up that can of worms,' she said. 'Certainly not me.'

I made a breathy, incredulous, limp-dick laugh.

'Baby, it's not anything I'll ever need to use. You're acting as if I plan to. I don't.'

'And what did you imagine I would feel about this?'

'That maybe we could all go to the south of France. And be happy together. Hugh would love it. You know he would.'

Hugh sat slurping at his tea. Who knows what he heard or thought?

Marlene came round the table and stood directly before me, a good nine inches shorter even in her heels. 'Australia is still OK. I don't have to go to France.' I felt her gentle hand upon my arm and, looking down into her eyes, saw, in the flare of iris around her pupil, the rocks beneath the ocean, clouds of nebulae, a door to something completely fucking strange.

Then, at last, I was afraid.

'No?' she asked.

I could not even move.

'Butcher, I love you.'

I shivered.

She shook her head, her eyes swollen with big tears.

'Whatever you think, I'll prove it isn't true.'

'No.'

'You're a great painter.'

'I'll kill you.'

She flinched, but then she touched my frozen cheek. 'I'll look after you,' she said. 'I'll bring you breakfast in bed. I'll place your paintings anywhere you want them in the world. When you're old and sick, I'll care for you.'

'You're a liar.'

'Not about that, baby.' Then, standing on her toes, Marlene Leibovitz kissed me on the mouth.

'It was only technical,' she said. She waited for a moment as if I might miraculously change my mind then, sighing, she slid the autopsy into her purse.

'You'll never find anyone like me,' she said.

Again, she awaited my response while Hugh stared fiercely at his cup.

'No?' she asked.

'No,' I said.

She walked out the door without another word. Who knows where she went? Hugh and I flew out of JFK the following morning.

'Is Marlene coming?' he asked.

'No,' I said.

55

The pilot said, Ladies and Gentlemen, Boys and Girls—the voice of our father, a CHARACTER—he said it is DOWN-HILL all the way to Sydney. I asked my brother what would now be the fate of his ART he said it was lost for ever, property of a Japanese he hoped the bastard died. When we were airborne he drank many small bottles of red wine and would not stop until the PRISSY BASTARD would no longer CATCH HIS EYE.

Very long night bouncing above the earth.

Then followed a ROUGH PATCH at various addresses in Sydney—Tempe, Marrickville, St Peter's. Butcher was completely GUTTED, his life-work stolen by the PLAINTIFF and the JAPANESE.

I HAVE SEEN ALL THE DEEDS THAT ARE DONE HERE UNDER THE SUN; THEY ARE ALL EMPTINESS AND CHASING THE WIND. He never knew what he was painting.

For a month or two he MADE ART but then he heard on Sydney radio 2UE that the Plaintiff and Jean-Paul had sold all their holding of Michael Boone to the Japanese. My brother had been a King but now he was a Pig, eviscerated. Turn the beast on its side and start pulling out the intestines. Take great care not to break open the stomach or intestines. When you've got the stomach and intestines pulled out as much as you can, you will find it hanging up just below the liver. RIP. He threw fifteen yards of good canvas on the Tempe Tip.

The ONCE-FAMOUS Michael Boone then established a lawn-cutting enterprise. I was never happier with an occupation but my brother was his father's son, always in a rage with traffic jams on the Parramatta Road, cost of two-stroke fuel, lawns too wet for decent care. FOR IN SUCH WISDOM IS MUCH VEXATION, AND THE MORE A MAN KNOWS THE MORE HE HAS TO SUFFER.

My sleep was penetrated by his bare feet, shuffling around the flat, his mind in a muddle, heart at its ceaseless work, fat collecting around the kidneys. I did not forget that my own happiness had been purchased at dreadful expense to him. BUT . . . MY TURN NOW. I wish I were a nicer man. I liked to cut the grass, spring blades, the sweet smell, thrips flying in the hazy light, monarch butterflies, others whose names I did not know.

For five summers we had NORMAL LIFE.

Then the letter arrived from OUR FORMER ENEMIES in Germany and everything was changed. We had BOMBED THE SHIT OUT OF THEM but no mention was made of that when writing to inform Butcher of RECENT DEVELOP- MENTS. The letter was from the MUSEUM LUDWIG ha-ha no batteries needed. They invited my brother to see his pictures hung inside their VERY IMPORTANT MUSEUM as he told me more than once. At the same time he feared it was a very CRUEL TRICK.

He was a great fat old fellow now, his head burnt violently by the summer sun, mouth turned down, hands always in his pockets looking for small change he was always SKINT. But the night he opened the letter from the Museum Ludwig it was FUCK THE EXPENSE he would talk to them ON THE BLOWER man to man. Thus in the kitchen of our comfy flat in Tempe it was officially confirmed that he had been rescued from the SCRAP HEAP OF HISTORY. The Japanese had donated two of his paintings to the Museum Ludwig and these two canvases—last seen in Mercer Street, New York, NY 10013—were now being given PRIDE OF PLACE. Well fuck me dead.

One minute we were broke—no money for anything but

scrag end of lamb—but now we could afford air tickets to Germany, not just the two of us, but young Billy Bones as well, a great tall handsome bugger, no credit to the sire. Where did this money come from? MYOB.

My brother was then SAVED. You could also say REVERTED. We travelled directly from Köln railway station and discovered his two best paintings facing each other across their own crypt in the Museum Ludwig.

I, THE SPEAKER, Michael Boone (Australia) b. 1943– Gift of the Dai Ichi Corporation
IF YOU HAVE EVER SEEN A MAN DIE, Michael Boone (Australia) b. 1943– Gift of the Dai Ichi Corporation

Being more knowledgeable re LAWN MAINTENANCE I did not understand that this strike of lightning would now be repeated in other places, bless me, London, New York, Canberra, poor Mum, beyond her ken, her private prayers held up in public, a raging mystery for the world to see. The sad battered grass-cutter confronted his WORKS he had wild eyes and a wobbly smile.

'Jesus Christ,' he said when he had read the plaque and saw the name of Marlene's PARTNER IN CRIME.

You have no idea, he said to me.

But old Slow Bones understood exactly. This was a love letter from Marlene. It was what she promised him the day he threatened her a violent death.

There was a CURATOR DOCTOR present at our viewing and when Butcher had found a hanky and blown his nose this chap politely asked would we like to see the Leibovitzes.

Butcher's answer was definite to the point of rude. N-O.

Well, said the Doctor, I thought you might enjoy the personal connection. We purchased a new Leibovitz from Mr Mauri, your great collector.

Oh, said my brother. Oh, I see.

He stood staring at the Curator Doctor as if someone had sneaked up behind him and shoved a broomstick up his arse.

Lead on Macduff, he said.

Then we were off and galloping through the galleries, all of us large men, big feet, leather slapping the floors of the Museum Ludwig until we were arrived before a painting of a mechanical Charlie Chaplin which is said in French *LE CHAPLIN MÉCANIQUE*. I was concerned I was about to LET ONE OFF so stayed a certain distance but Butcher poked his sunburnt nose right into it.

He asked when it had been purchased from Mauri.

No, said the Curator Doctor. Not that one. This one. This is our new acquisition.

And there behind us, bless me, was the dreadful thing my brother had put up on the roof in SoHo. Since then it had become *LE GOLEM ÉLECTRIQUE*. I held my tongue, but you should have seen my brother's face, like Melbourne weather, rain, sunshine, hail, smile, frown, scowl, blow the schnozzle, bless me, what will happen next?

How much?

Three point two said the Doctor slash Curator.

Deutschmark?

Dollars.

There was a wooden bench before this painting and my brother now sat down. He was very still. And then finally he gave a laugh right through his shiny nose. He looked from one of us to the other as he could choose who would be worthy of what he might say next. Not one of us. He spoke to no one in particular: Best thing Leibovitz ever did.

And then he walked towards the bar, a great fat lumpy man one short arm in his pocket, the other hand rubbing at his speckled freckled sun-baked head.

56

I want to be liked, to be remembered fondly, and I would be an idiot to stand before you naked, but what else have I ever done?

MoMA, the Museum Ludwig, the Tate—I can't list all the museums to which Mauri has donated my works, nor imagine the skuzzy deals these gifts were tied to. Enough to know I soon rose like a phoenix from the ashes of my Butcher life.

My saviour? A murderer. Actually, it's worse than that, because even though I had once walked away from her, I was still a Bones, and all the blacks and whites, so clear that morning in New York, were destined to be wet on wet, slow-drying, ambiguous, a shifting tide between beauty and horror. It swelled beneath my skin, filled my mouth.

In those polluted summer suburbs when Hugh and I were chained behind our filthy Victa mowers, I was still— in spite of all the death and deception—a prisoner of this tangled past. While I trimmed the floral fucking borders in Bankstown, I was reliving those days before the fall, when my baby and I looked at light together, drank Lagavulin on the rocks, walked hand in hand in the Museum of Modern Art, all those nights she pressed her lovely head in against my neck and I breathed the jasmine air around her brow.

A better person may have run in horror, but I loved her and I will not stop. There, I've said it plain. She is gone, not gone, out there somewhere, sending messages to me via Sotheby's and the Art Institute of Chicago. Is she taunting me or missing me? How will I ever know? How do you know how much to pay if you don't know what it's worth?

Acknowledgements

Late in 2002, at a time when we were both living way too close to 'Ino on Bedford Street, I became friends with Stewart Waltzer. Many lunches later it had become clear to me that the New York art world, which Stewart knew in his own very particular and personal way, was colliding and arguing with the distinctly Australian worlds that were presently coalescing in my notebooks.

Stewart sometimes bought an extra bruschetta, although less often than he remembers. He certainly fed me a thousand scandalous, possibly reliable stories, and introduced me to the first of many expert individuals who, in their turn, would give me what I needed to make my creatures stand up and walk around.

The first of these (blameless) volunteers was the New York conservator Sandra Amman, who in turn led me to Tom Learner, a conservation scientist at the Tate in London. Dr Learner enthusiastically engaged with the technical problem that Butcher Bones was going to have to solve. Jay Krueger, Senior Conservator of Modern Paintings at the National Gallery in Washington, would prove to be equally helpful, and it was he who later alerted me to the sample boxes of Magna paint that Butcher would later find at New York Central Supplies.

The sculptor Michael Steiner—another friend of Stewart's—was wonderfully forthcoming, and I stole and reconstructed whole slabs of his opinions before giving them to Milt Hesse to pass on to Marlene Cook.

Writers are of course obsessive, so there was hardly a friend who did not contribute in some way—David and Kristen Williamson, David Rankin, Patrick McGrath, Maria Aitken, Paul Kane, Philip Govrevitch and Frances Coady, thank you. All deserve my gratitude.